Gutter Mouse

By: Alex Ceranich

"A ship is safe in harbor,
but that's not what ships are made for."
-Anonymous

Phil 4:13

CHAPTER 1

"It's just a stain," Jason muttered.

He sat lingering in the driver's seat of his car as torrential rain poured down out of the night sky. The thick clouds hid the moon and shrouded everything in the kind of deep, rural darkness that's only possible far away from any city. The trees that encircled his new home swayed violently in the strong winds. The sound of the rain pelting the car's roof filled Jason's ears, and there was a strong smell of mud coming from what was normally Jason's winding dirt driveway.

But all the commotion from the storm couldn't disrupt Jason's distress. He was parked in front of his house and was staring through the large bay window into his living room. With each pass of the windshield wipers, he got a glimpse of the large black mark on the back wall.

The stain was just over a meter and a half in diameter and was located dead center on the wall. There weren't any leaks in that area that Jason had been able to find, nor any other obvious cause for the stain. And it didn't look like the rest of the grime that covered the old house. It was strange. Even though the room was only partially lit with a sliver of light from the kitchen, somehow Jason could still see the blemish clearly in the dark room. Something about it made it distinct, different, and it stood out amidst the aged grime and dirt on the wall.

Simply looking at the stain made Jason feel unsettled, anxious, and on edge. Those feelings were almost suffocating when he was in the room with it. Even more troubling, the other night he'd woken up and gone down to the kitchen for some water and could have sworn he'd heard hissing coming from the living room. But when he'd peeked in, there was nothing.

Lightning flashed in the distance behind him and was reflected in his rearview mirror. It drew his attention and he looked at himself in the glass. He was twenty-four years old, but even he thought he looked younger. He had pale skin and brown hair, but it was his green eyes that told the story; he was green.

Jason's eyes returned to the stain once more.

"It's nothing," he muttered, shaking his head. "Old houses make strange noises all the time."

Anyway, he didn't have time to worry about imaginary monsters in the dark. The lights were on in the kitchen, and that meant Lily had waited up for him.

Jason checked his watch: it was almost midnight. He'd been working late to earn extra money for the expenses they had from the move, and he'd hoped his wife would be asleep, but no such luck.

How to Save Your Marriage TODAY! was the title of the book he had found hidden under a pile of Lily's things the other day.

Remembering that moment, Jason dropped his head into his hand, rubbing his temples with his thumb and middle finger. He still hadn't fully recovered from the shock. Despite trying his best to act like everything was normal, deep down it had shaken him to his core. But he also felt like he should have known it was coming. They had been fighting a lot recently. A lot. And it wasn't just the move; it was something deeper. Jason could feel it. Lily wanted something from him, needed something from him. She wanted him to *be* something. But, for the life of him, Jason couldn't see what it was. He doubted if even Lily could put her unspoken longing into words, but he knew she felt it, and each time Jason failed to solve the riddle, he saw the light dim a little more in Lily's eyes.

Lily was the most wonderful woman he'd ever met, full of warmth, compassion, kindness, love . . . and Jason was blowing it. He was ruining everything.

Jason's hand gripped down hard on the arm rest and his whole body tensed. *What is it*? he wondered. *What am I not seeing*? But no matter how hard he thought, the answer eluded him. It seemed the riddle would remain unsolved, and all he could do was hang his head in defeat and stare blankly at the steering wheel in front of him. He felt so blind.

After a few more moments of listening to the rain, Jason sighed. He opened the car door and stepped out into the storm. The cool water soaked into his thin summer shirt and slacks as he slid around in the mud and darkness. He trudged up the creaking steps up to his front door, careful to avoid the holes and splintered sections, and quickly let himself in.

The house was dark except for the slice of light shining from the kitchen. There was the sound of water dripping into pots scattered throughout the rooms. There was a faint smell of dust and rot, and bits of each floated in the air, dancing in the light cutting into the entryway. Jason carefully removed his muddy shoes on the mat. His eyes involuntarily glanced at the stain in the living room off to his right, but he quickly turned to his left and headed into the kitchen.

As Jason entered, Lily sat up at the table, looking at him with her beautiful blue eyes. They both smiled weakly.

"Hey," Jason said softly.

"Hey," Lily replied.

She was a few months younger than Jason, with brunette hair, pale skin, and soft features. Every time Jason looked at her, it felt just like the first time he saw her in elementary school.

Dinner was on the table, covered and cold. There were two clean plates with two clean sets of utensils, and a thick baking dish that was in the middle of the table. Jason tossed his keys on the counter, then walked over and sat down.

"You're still up? You didn't have to wait for me," Jason said as he removed the covering off the top of the baking dish to reveal his favorite casserole.

"I tried adding some of those peppers you like and wanted to see what you thought," Lily said.

Jason could tell that was just an excuse, then was hit with a sudden realization. *She hasn't slept well a single night in this new house*, Jason thought. *She must be having trouble adjusting to being so far out here*. He silently vowed to make sure he would be home earlier tomorrow night so she wouldn't have to try and go to sleep alone again.

Jason served himself a generous portion from the baking dish, then started in on the casserole. Even cold it was delicious. "Mmmm. It's really good, thank you," he said. He looked up at Lily with a smile, and Lily smiled back. Balancing as much as he could on his fork, Jason began devouring mouthful after mouthful. "How was your day?" he asked between bites.

Lily's hands clenched. Her lips pressed together tightly, and her eyes glanced at the darkness in the living room across the entryway, then darted back to looking down at her lap. "It — it was fine," she said.

"That's good," Jason replied, preoccupied by the food. "This stuff is delicious."

The sounds of the storm filled the silence between the couple as Jason ate. Lily's smile faded. She moved her hands into her lap and played with the hem of her shirt as her eyes wandered around the room. Several times she shifted in her chair. Then, after glancing at Jason, she quietly inhaled.

"So," she began in her sweetest voice, "have you thought about that new job?"

Jason swallowed hard and looked away. Seconds ticked by as the question hung in the air unanswered.

When Jason finally spoke, his voice was firm. "Can we please stop talking about that?" he said.

"Why? Why won't you even think about it?" Lily pressed. She scooted her chair around the edge of the table until she was beside her husband, then reached out and touched his arm. "So what if it's a little new, a little different? You could figure it out. Everyone does."

Jason pulled away and stood up. "I don't want to talk about it anymore."

"But it would be so good for us," Lily said. "It's so much more money, and I wouldn't have to worry anymore."

Jason couldn't bear it. He turned and fled, walking briskly out of the kitchen and into the entryway.

"Wait! Stop!" Lily cried. She pushed her chair back, the legs scraping on the hardwood floor, then rose and pursued Jason. She caught up to him in the living room. "I *hate* it when you do that," she said, tears already beginning to form in the corners of her eyes.

Jason turned back, but stood askew, unable to fully face her. "I can't take that job, okay? I can't. I wish I could, but I can't!"

"Yes, you can," Lily said. "And I'm sure you'd be great."

"You don't know that," he said, turning away. "And besides, the job I have now is fine. It's safe, it's comfortable, and we have everything we need. I mean, it got us this house, didn't it?" But as the words left his mouth, Jason immediately realized his mistake.

Lily scoffed and her tears broke free. “This house?” she cried. “This terrible house?” The tears streamed down her cheeks as her face changed into a bitter scowl. But the sudden swell of emotion confounded her tongue and stifled her words. Mutely, she crossed her arms and pulled into herself, staring fiercely off to the side.

In his thoughts, Jason cursed. He shouldn’t have brought up the house. He knew Lily wasn’t happy with it, and if he were honest with himself, he wasn’t either. The house was an old, decrepit dump. Everything in it was worn and discolored, the doors hung crooked, the sinks didn’t drain, the floors were warped, and what wasn’t outright broken was offensively ugly. Jason had only gotten Lily to go along with it by promising grand and sweeping renovations. They’d transform this dump into a beautiful, secluded, cozy villa hidden in the forest. But now that they were here, that dream seemed increasingly unlikely.

To make matters worse, they were all alone out here. The house was so far out in the country that there wasn’t another soul for kilometers. It was only accessible by a winding dirt road through the trees, and it was over an hour’s drive back to the city, where both he and Lily had lived all their lives. They were separated from their friends and families. There was also nothing around, not even a hospital which Lily had been especially concerned with, though Jason didn’t understand why.

But at this point there was nothing that could be done. This was the only place Jason could afford, and the paperwork was settled. There was no going back; they had to make the best of it.

"I know it's bad right now," Jason said, "but we've only been here ten days. It'll get better. We'll fix it up. It'll be beautiful, just like I promised."

"No!" Lily snapped, her voice trembling with emotion. "We can't fix this house, there's something wrong here . . . ."

Jason's eyes involuntarily glanced at the large black stain on the wall next to him, but he quickly caught himself and returned to looking at Lily. Feigning ignorance, he shook his head dismissively. "There's nothing wrong, it's just an old house."

"I hear things, Jason. Whispers and hissing noises."

Jason flinched.

"When you're gone, it feels like something is watching me! And that!" She pointed directly at the black stain. "It's atrocious. Every time I look at it, I feel sick. I feel like something terrible is going to happen. And it keeps getting bigger! And it's not the only one; there's another one in the basement."

"It's nothing. It's just a stain," Jason replied. Lily was right though, it *was* growing.

Lily started to cry even harder. "Well, what about my things?" she sobbed. "My things keep disappearing — my phone, my water bottle, other things — they're not where I left them. And I keep finding them down in the basement . . . by the stain down there. It's even bigger than the one up here." She stared at Jason, her shoulders shaking.

"Maybe you're just tired from the move and you're forgetting things down there," Jason said.

"I *never* go down there," Lily cried. "Why won't you believe me? Why won't you listen? It's like you don't even care about me. Like you don't even care about *us*."

Jason's eyes softened and he reached for her. "I care about you more than anything," he said. "I just think you're letting your imagination get the best of you. There's nothing strange going on here."

Lily turned and withdrew from Jason. She sat down on the couch with her back to him, wiping away her still flowing tears. "There is something wrong with this house," Lily said. "And whatever it is, it's getting worse."

Jason sat down on the couch next to the woman he loved, feeling completely at a loss. She was really upset, and he didn't know what to do or what to think. Was there really something unnatural going on? He didn't believe in ghosts, but hearing Lily talk about the hissing and describing the same things he felt about the stain was extremely unnerving. He couldn't help but look at the deep shadows in the adjacent rooms, and then once more at the black stain on the wall. There was an eerie feeling about it all, he had to admit. The rain continued crashing down on the roof, and the wind screamed as it broke against the outer walls. Lightning flashed, and the sudden boom of thunder made Jason jump.

He took a deep breath and tried to think. *There's nothing to be afraid of*, he told himself. *It's just an old house, and she's tired from moving. We both are. There's nothing going on, it's just our minds playing tricks on us.* With that settled, Jason set to thinking what he could do to make her feel better.

Then Jason remembered he already had the perfect solution. Because he and Lily had been fighting so much recently, he had come up with a plan. That morning, he had left early in order to pick up some chocolates from a local confectionery-bakery in the city. It was Lily's favorite, and Jason's go-to move whenever they were fighting. He'd been so distracted that he'd forgotten it in his car. But remembering it now, he was almost giddy.

"Bee," he said, using his pet name for her, which he only brought out in the most desperate of circumstances. "I have something for you — I forgot it in the car — I'll go grab it."

This news went over as well as Jason had hoped. Lily still refused to face him, but she sat up straight and attentive at the very least. It seemed not even a supposed haunted house could get in the way of his wife's love for little surprises. It was perfect. They'd eat the chocolates together, and Jason would try and think up something to say to smooth this whole thing over.

Jason practically bounced up from the couch. He rushed back to the kitchen to grab his keys, but when he got there, there was nothing on the counter. "Hey, did you grab my keys?" he called to Lily.

"No," she said, following him to the kitchen.

"They were right here. I walked in, set them on the counter, and then sat down." Jason scratched his head, then turned to Lily, confused.

Lily gasped and covered her mouth with her hands. She looked down the hall at the basement door, her eyes wide with terror.

A jolt of alarm shot up Jason's spine, and his mind scrambled for a reasonable explanation. He was certain that he had had his keys when he arrived home, and since he had only been to the kitchen and living room, there was no way they could be anywhere else. Right? Jason shook his head. "It's . . . it's nothing," he whispered. "They're not in the basement, I'll show you."

Jason crept over and joined his wife in the entryway. Lily grabbed hold of his arm. Jason looked down the hall toward the basement door and a loud creak emanated from the house. They both froze in place.

The creak subsided, and Jason scanned the darkness ahead of him. Despite his firm belief that this was all in their heads, the lost keys, combined with his wife's story and the lateness of the hour, caused him to hesitate.

This is ridiculous, he thought. *There is nothing weird going on.* With that, Jason began walking slowly toward the basement door, Lily clinging to his back the whole way.

At the door, Jason's hand trembled slightly as it closed around the knob. He opened the door, revealing the darkness leading down to the basement. His body tensed as he reached for the switch. He flipped on the basement light, and his heart sank when he saw, lying at the bottom of the stairs, his keys.

Something is in the house. Something is in here with us. There's no other explanation. Jason cowered low and looked around. Now, every shadow hid a nightmare, around every corner was a monster, and nowhere was safe. He felt his wife shivering behind him, clutching his shirt. They had to get out of this house immediately.

Jason's mind raced. They had to leave, but where would they go? They were in the middle of nowhere. They couldn't go walking around in the forest at night. They needed to drive out of here . . . they needed those keys.

Jason had to think of something quick. As his mind worked, the light from the basement bulb glinted off a small silver mouse key chain and caught his eye. He stood up a little straighter. "I'll just go down and grab them," he whispered.

But as soon as he said it, a horrifying thought filled his mind: *Whatever took my keys wants me to go down there*. Jason shrank back, pressing against Lily behind him. More thoughts flooded into his mind and his breathing became ragged. He squirmed and pushed back farther.

As Jason wavered, an unearthly howl erupted from every direction. It was brutal, savage, and animalistic, inducing a primal panic in Jason. He fled, running for the front door and abandoning his wife in the process.

Jason covered the few meters to the front door in a heartbeat. He grabbed the doorknob, twisted, and pulled with all his strength. But to his shock, the door only opened an inch before slamming into something and coming to a complete halt. Jason tried again to rip the door open, but it wouldn't move. He looked and there was nothing in the way. Why wasn't it opening?

As Lily caught up to him, Jason gave up on the door and devised a new plan. He ran to the living room and picked up a folding chair. Another ghostly howl echoed through the house, and in a terrified panic Jason hurled the chair at the bay window with all his might.

But in defiance of all logic, the metal chair bounced off the fragile, single-pane glass without leaving a trace on the window. Unable to believe what he had just seen, Jason tried again. He picked up the chair and slammed it into the window, but once again the glass held strong.

Something was keeping them in on purpose. Some terrible force gave strength to the glass, just as it had held the door closed. It wouldn't let them leave.

Confused, terrified, and out of ideas, Jason cowered and fell to his knees. His wife joined him, huddling close. They were powerless; there was nothing they could do. All that was left was to wait for death.

And so they did, until half a minute later, when light came shining through the bay window. Nervously, Jason peeked out the window. The light was from headlights. There was a truck driving up toward their house.

CHAPTER 2

Jason watched as the small two-door truck drove up the muddy road and pulled in front of the house.

Lily sat up next to Jason, and they both stared at the vehicle. The truck came to a stop, and a man stepped out into the rain, then started walking toward the front door of the house.

"Who is that?" Lily asked.

"I don't know," Jason said, "but maybe he can help us get out of here."

Jason rose and hurried to the front door, with Lily following. He tried the door again, but once more it refused to open more than an inch. Jason shouted through the cracked door. "Help us! Help! Get us out of here!"

The stranger was walking up the stairs to the front door, and responded with a good-natured, jovial laugh. "Guess I found the right house," he shouted over the pouring rain and thunder. "You guys are really out here. I barely found the place."

Jason was taken aback. He tried to peer out through the slit between the door and the door frame, but it was so dark, and the slit was so thin, he had trouble making out anything. "Please," Jason shouted, "you have to help us! We're trapped in the house, and there's something in here with us. We have to get out!"

"Relax," the man said. "If you're still this lively, you're fine. You're not in any danger. Hang tight while I grab something from my truck. I'll be back in a sec."

Jason and Lily stared at each other in astonishment as they listened to the sloshing of the man's footsteps walking back toward his truck. What in the world was going on? And did this person outside have something to do with it? Jason wasn't sure what to think. With furrowed brow, he stepped back from the door and resigned himself to wait and see what would happen. If nothing else, it was a relief to hear someone say they weren't in any danger, even if it just seemed like empty words.

They soon heard the sound of scraping metal, then a loud splashing thud, followed by more scraping and dragging sounds. The man made it to the steps and dragged something up them. *Thump*, *thump*, *thump*, *thump*, and then he was at the front door.

"All right, stand back," the man called through the open crack.

The couple stepped back and waited to see what would happen next. As they watched, a large knife pushed through the crack at the top of the door. Lily squeezed Jason's arm hard at the sight, and Jason stared at the knife as it was pulled down along the doorframe. As the knife slid down, strange runes drawn on the flat metal of the knife illuminated with a bluish glow. Once the knife reached the floor, the door swung open, revealing a soaking-wet man standing in front of a very large metal box.

The stranger was dressed in military-style clothing. He wore strong-looking boots, long pants, and a thick long-sleeve shirt. The knife he had used to open the door had now been returned to a sheath on his belt. He was slightly taller than Jason, with a muscular, athletic build that was evident even through his clothes. He had blond hair and blue eyes. His face was worn and weathered, but still possessed the spark of youth, and he likely wasn't more than a few years older than Jason. His eyes were kind, but also fierce and determined. But his most noticeable feature was his genuine and disarming smile.

The stranger dragged the waist-high metal box into the entryway, but as he passed through, he let go of the door and it swung shut.

"No!" Jason shouted. He dashed past the stranger to the door and tried to reopen it. But the door was blocked again and refused to open.

The man watched as Jason fought with the door. "Huh, those grew back fast," he said.

"How did you open it?" Jason asked. "How? We need to get out of here right now. There's something in this house! It's howling and it won't let us leave."

"Easy, easy, calm down," the man said, lifting his hands as if to show them they were empty. "I promise there's nothing in the house except us. We're in no immediate danger."

Jason squinted hard at the man. "What do you mean? How do you know that?" he demanded. "Who are you and what's going on?"

The man smiled back pleasantly. "My name is Parch, and I'm here to help. I assume you two are the owners of this house . . ."

Jason walked back around the strange man and returned to Lily's side. Parch's calm and affable demeanor was comforting, and they both started to calm down.

"Yes, we live here," Jason replied. "My name is Jason, and this is my wife, Lily."

"Nice to meet you both," Parch said. "Now, it sounds like you two are getting quite the show. Lots of strange, inexplicable things happening, right? Strange noises, slamming doors, things being moved when you're not in the room?"

Jason and Lily both nodded emphatically.

"I can see you're both pretty stressed out, but you'll be happy to know I'm here to fix the problem," Parch said. "Give me twenty minutes and I'll have everything sorted out. Soon this will all be a fading memory."

Both Jason and Lily breathed a sigh of relief. Never had Jason heard sweeter words than those. But he still had a lot of questions.

"That sounds great, but I still don't understand. What is going on?" Jason asked. "Why is this happening, and how did you know to be here?"

Parch shook his head and held his hand up. "Let's skip the details for the moment and get this whole issue solved first."

Lily nodded in agreement.

"Now what I'm looking for . . ." Parch said as he started to scan the adjacent rooms, ". . . is a large black stain on a wall, floor, or ceiling that can't be cleaned off." Parch leaned to the side, looking around Jason and into the living room. "That's what I'm here for!" Parch snapped his fingers and pointed into the living room. Without hesitation he moved toward it.

Still very confused, Jason tried to stop Parch. "Wait," Jason muttered, shaking his head. But Parch slipped by him and entered the living room.

Parch walked straight up to the stain and crossed his arms as he looked it up and down. "Yep, here's your problem," he said. "Let's see what we're dealing with." He leaned in and squinted at the stain, shifting around, and looking at it from different angles.

Jason and Lily stepped into the living room and stared at Parch as the man inspected the stain. Jason didn't know what to make of this stranger. What did he have to do with all that was happening? How did he know to be here? How did he know they were safe? Was he telling the truth about anything? Jason didn't get the feeling Parch was dangerous, but it was very suspicious how he avoided answering any questions.

Lily leaned close to Jason. "I *told* you there was something wrong," she whispered, her tone harsh and contemptuous.

Jason was taken aback. He looked at Lily, but his wife crossed her arms with a scowl on her face and refused to look at him.

In silence, the couple waited as Parch continued to inspect the stain. Parch looked almost like he was reading a book, or maybe like he was an archeologist reading hieroglyphics.

"How's it look?" Jason asked.

"This one looks a little peculiar," Parch called back over his shoulder while still staring intently at the stain. "I'm not quite sure what its deal is, but every stain has its own oddities. It's nothing I can't handle. The good news is that we caught it early. So early I'm a little surprised that door was blocked."

Jason's brow furrowed as he processed the answer. *Caught it early?* he thought, *I guess that's good news*.

"You deal with this stuff a lot, then?" Jason asked.

"Yeah, a lot," Parch said.

"Do you work for the government, or something?" Jason asked.

Parch turned his head slightly, revealing a smile. "Why? Are you worried you're going to have to pay me? Don't worry, this is all free of charge."

"What? No, that wasn't —" Jason began to say, but Parch cut him off.

"Sorry, just give me a second here," Parch said. "I'm almost done looking at this thing."

Jason's eyes narrowed as he stared at Parch's back. He leaned closer to Lily. "This guy seems a little shady, doesn't he?" Jason whispered. "Why won't he tell us who he's with or what's going on?"

Lily looked at Jason fiercely out of the corner of her eye. "I don't care *who* he is or *what's* going on, I just want it to *stop*," she snapped in a harsh whisper. "So just leave him alone and let him do whatever he came here to do." Her scowl worsened, and Jason could feel how tense and angry she was.

Jason's mouth opened slightly at Lily's intensity. His body involuntarily leaned away from her. Why was she so angry?

"But what if we can't trust him?" Jason asked, still confused by her reaction.

At this, Lily turned and looked directly at Jason. Her face was contorted with raw emotion, and tears broke free from her eyes. "*I* can't trust *you*!" she said.

Jason inhaled sharply and took a slight step back. There it was: the look in her eyes that Jason had grown to dread — disappointment mixed with anger and frustration. On top of it all was a fury Jason had never seen in his wife before.

"Wh-what?" Jason stammered.

Lily wiped at her tears, but more followed. "I am *so* mad at you right now! You ran away. At the basement door. Whatever it was howled at us, and you just took off. You're supposed to protect me, but you ran away — just like always."

Lily had been trying to whisper, but her emotions had gotten the better of her and she'd grown louder with each sentence. She ended up so loud that Parch glanced over his shoulder in concern. Lily went quiet, pulled into herself, and hid her face in her hand.

Jason's heart flooded with shame, embarrassment, regret, and anger at himself. She was right; he had run away. A husband is supposed to protect his wife, but he had abandoned her. Jason closed his eyes and dropped his head, his lips pressed tightly together.

Lily turned toward the couch. "I have to sit down," she murmured.

Jason reached out and gently placed his hand on her upper arm. He followed her to the couch and they both sat down together. Lily turned her body away from Jason, and he was left to stare solemnly at her back.

"Why did this have to happen now?" Lily whispered under her breath.

The sound of the storm outside continued as Jason sat mutely next to his wife. His eyes drifted down to the ground, and he sat slumped on the couch. He felt weak and useless.

"Is everything okay?" Parch asked gently as he turned around and faced Jason and Lily.

"Everything is fine," Lily replied flatly.

Parch looked back and forth between husband and wife. "It's not really my place to say," he began, "but what's happening here can be very unsettling, very stressful. It drives people to do all sorts of crazy things. I know it can be hard, but right now it's best to be patient and gracious with each other. Everything will be back to normal soon."

Neither Jason nor Lily said anything in response. Jason looked off into the kitchen, and Lily shifted uncomfortably.

After an awkward but brief silence, Parch spoke again. "Anyway, I've seen all I have to with the stain. I'll get to work, and in twenty minutes I'll have this all wrapped up."

Jason sat up and smiled at the good news. This night had been bad enough, and he wanted it to be over. Lily sat up as well and faced Parch.

"Are you going to fix the other one, too?" Lily asked.

Parch's head tilted slightly, and his eyes narrowed. "The other one? There are two stains in the house?"

"Yes?" Lily said, her eyes widening. "Is that bad?"

Parch shook his head dismissively. "No, not a problem at all," he said, "just rare to have multiple in the same area. Is it darker than this one?"

"Yes, a lot darker," Lily said, nodding. "And it makes me feel even worse than this one."

"Ahh, things are making sense now," Parch said, his head tilting back, which eventually turned into an exaggerated nod. He put his hands on his hips and shifted around on his feet. "This other one sounds like it's a lot further along. That would explain why the door was blocked. I'll start with that one, then. Where is it?"

"It's in the basement," Lily said. "But I am *not* going down there."

In that moment, something stirred in Jason's heart. It silenced his thoughts, and he moved without thinking. His hands clenched into fists, his jaw set, and he stood up from the couch. "I'll go down there with you," he said resolutely.

Parch began to shake his head, but before he could say anything, Lily spoke first.

"You said you'd go down there before, and we know how that turned out," Lily said with a harsh whisper. "Just let him do it."

Jason looked down and away in shame, but his heart would not be denied. "I have to get my keys," he muttered, offering the first excuse he could think up.

Lily crossed her arms and looked hard at him. Her eyes searched him, penetrating down to his soul. Jason felt naked under her scrutiny, and he immediately regretted making such a flimsy excuse. She knew him far too well for that. He had never been able to hide anything from her.

"Your keys?" she said, raising an eyebrow. "Yeah, right. Why do you really want to go down there?"

Jason opened his mouth to speak, but no words came out, and he was suddenly very confused. He knew he was desperate to go down into the basement, but why? Why did he stand up in the first place? His eyes searched the floor as his mind raced, looking for answers; but the more he thought, the more confused he became. Mutely, he struggled in himself, trying to understand his own feelings.

All the while, Lily continued to stare into him, searching him. As she watched, her eyes softened, her frown receded, and her posture opened. After only a few moments, she spoke again. “Fine,” she said. “But hurry back. Don’t leave me alone up here for long.”

Jason smiled and nodded. He then looked toward Parch.

Parch hesitated as he glanced between them both, then shrugged. “Okay,” he said. “Let’s do it, then.”

CHAPTER 3

Still in his socks, Jason walked to the entryway and threw on his old pair of hiking boots. The basement was unfinished and quite dusty, so they were the obvious choice.

Meanwhile, Parch walked to the big metal box in the entryway. He opened the lid, revealing a partially hollow interior section that held various military-looking gear and supplies, all meticulously organized. He pulled out a backpack, and a five-meter-long coiled steel chain. He put the backpack on and hung the chain with a carabiner on his belt off to his side. Finally, he pressed a button on the inside wall of the box, and then shut the lid.

Jason watched curiously. Once Parch had closed the lid of the box, Jason pointed at the chain.

"What's that for?" Jason asked.

"Good luck charm." Parch gave him a smile and a wink.

Jason didn't know what to make of that response, but he didn't press further. Instead, he led Parch to the basement door, then braced himself as his hand wrapped around the doorknob. He opened the door, and as he did the same awful howl erupted from the walls around them. Jason nearly jumped out of his skin.

Parch, in contrast, didn't even flinch. "Shut up!" he roared back in response. He then promptly slipped past Jason and trotted down the basement stairs like it was nothing.

Shocked by Parch's complete lack of fear or hesitation, Jason stood aghast. But after a moment to collect himself, and after seeing the other man be completely unaffected, Jason was spurred to match Parch's boldness. *I guess there really isn't anything to worry about*, Jason thought, and followed Parch down the stairs.

The two walked into a dirty, dusty, empty basement. The lightbulb in the stairwell, which was the basement's only source of light, was primarily for the stairs, and, consequently, left much of the basement shrouded in darkness. But even if there was more light, it wouldn't have mattered, because there wasn't much to see. The basement was little more than a large barren room. It had a dirt floor, with ancient stone walls upon which the house rested. There was a pillar midway to support the beam, there were cobwebs, and there were a few small piles of dirt and debris. Besides that, there was only one other thing of note: back in the farthest corner, almost completely hidden in shadow, there was a huge black stain on the wall.

Once he reached the bottom of the stairs, Parch saw the keys on the ground, and waited next to them for Jason. Jason caught up, retrieved his keys, put them in his pocket, then briefly recounted the story of how they came to be there. After responding with a good-natured laugh, Parch headed off, seemingly unconcerned, toward the corner with the stain.

Jason wasn't sure if he should feel embarrassed or not. He'd been so terrified, but the way Parch was acting made the whole situation seem trivial and mundane. After a moment's thought, Jason ultimately decided that, more than anything, he was just curious to see what Parch was going to do. He watched as Parch walked directly up to the stain.

Even as deep in the shadows as the stain was, Parch seemed to have no difficulty seeing it. He stood right in front of it and began inspecting just like he did the previous, leaning in and looking at it hard.

This stain was much darker and more opaque than the one in the living room. It was also much larger, over a meter and a half wide and tall, with jagged but well-defined edges. The stain wasn't any particular shape but was instead an odd, irregular figure that seemed to conform to some unseen boundaries. Despite the wall being made of stone and mortar, the stain seemed to have no difficulty discoloring it.

After a few seconds, Parch straightened up and stepped back from the wall. "This one looks a lot more normal than the one upstairs," he said. "But you guys weren't kidding; you do have two of them."

Jason scratched his arm nervously. "But you said that won't be a problem, right?" he asked.

"Not a problem at all," Parch responded, still looking at the stain, "just rare. Been doing this a while, and I've only seen it once before. Usually when it happens, it's actually the same source that's causing both stains. So, when you fix one, you fix both. That's probably what's going on here." He pointed at the stain for emphasis. "And this one is definitely further along than the one upstairs. This is the one giving you all the problems. It'll be best to start here."

Parch took off his backpack and set it down on the ground. He opened it up and began rummaging through it.

Jason watched Parch curiously. "So how do you fix these stains?" he asked.

Parch continued rummaging through his backpack for a moment, but then stopped and looked at Jason. "Would you like to see for yourself?" he asked. "Since you came down here with me, why not keep going? I wouldn't mind some company, if you'd like to help."

The question caught Jason off guard. He had come down to the basement but had expected to grab his keys and leave right after. Now that he was down here, however, he wasn't sure how he felt. Curiosity, fear, excitement, and anxiety all mixed together and clouded his thoughts.

"What about Lily?" Jason asked, which was the first clear thought that came to his mind.

"She's perfectly safe," Parch replied. "The howls and the moving objects are scary, but the thing that's doing it can't hurt her or interact with anything near her. Besides, we'll have this wrapped up so quick that we'll be back up there before she even notices. And when we get back, you can tell her all about it."

I could tell her . . ., Jason thought. His eyes drifted upward. Something about that sentence made his whole body feel light.

Without thinking, Jason took a slight step forward. "Well, what do we need to do?" he asked. "Is it dangerous?" There was still a slight trepidation inside Jason, but he was growing more interested.

"Dangerous?" Parch repeated. "No, no, hardly ever. It's easy. I do, like, three of these a week. It's a sure thing. But first I have to find the . . ." Parch trailed off and returned to rummaging through his backpack.

Hardly ever, Jason wondered as his chest tightened and he recoiled backward. *So, it's sometimes dangerous?* The hairs on the back of his neck raised up. But soon that concern turned back into curiosity, as he watched Parch triumphantly pull out what looked to be a road flare.

"Here it is," Parch said, holding up the flare. "Not sure how that got put in the wrong pocket."

Parch zipped up his backpack, put it back on, and stood up. He grasped the flare in both hands, one hand higher than the other, then he twisted his hands in opposite directions in a quick, sharp movement. The two sections of the flare twisted along a hidden seam. There was a loud crack, and green fire erupted out of the top. The flame was about six centimeters. It burned strong and unwavering. Despite burning so fiercely, the flame didn't produce any smoke. After the flare was lit, Parch turned his attention to his watch, and pressed a button.

Jason watched in silence, staring at the green flame of the flare. "What's that?" he asked. He leaned in, wondering how this would help them with the stain.

"The torch?" Parch clarified. "Well, it's . . ." He paused in thought for a moment, then shrugged. "Normally I don't bother explaining things, since you'll just forget anyway, but because you're coming along, I might as well. It's a special fire." He moved his free hand directly into the flame. The green flame touched his palm, spreading around his hand, but Parch didn't make a sound. He held his hand in the fire for several seconds, then pulled it out and showed Jason. Parch's hand was unburned.

Astonished, Jason couldn't take his eyes off the flame. He stared intensely, his mouth slightly agape. Parch held the flame out, offering Jason to try for himself. Jason swallowed hard and held out a single finger, slowly approaching the flame. He got close and didn't feel any heat. Emboldened, he pushed his finger into the flame, and then his whole hand. Parch was right, it didn't burn at all. Jason felt nothing beyond the gentle pressure of the flame pushing up into his hand.

"Wow," Jason said, still moving his hand through the fire. "What's it for?"

"All this," Parch said, gesturing around the room.

Jason looked up and gasped, nearly falling over. The light from the torch illuminated the formerly dark basement, and Jason now saw clearly that all the walls and the ceiling were covered in gnarled, grey tree roots which had burst into the basement through the stain, which was actually a hole in the basement wall.

In wide-eyed bewilderment, Jason looked around at the roots. The roots varied in size from thicker than a man's leg to thinner than a finger. They ran out of the hole in every direction, randomly snaking their way all over the walls and ceiling, practically covering them, before converging at the stairwell and going upstairs.

"What? How did . . . ?" Jason stuttered, completely confused by what he was seeing. The sight was overwhelming, and his mind struggled in vain to come up with a logical explanation. He stepped over to some nearby roots that were off to the side of the stain, or rather the hole, to inspect them more closely.

As Jason investigated the roots, Parch took the torch and placed it into a specially fitted pocket on his shoulder strap where the strap met with the pack. The torch sat halfway in the pocket, burning over his left shoulder. With the torch secured, he then drew his knife and began clearing the roots at the hole. The blade slid through the roots effortlessly, and the runes on the blade glowed blue as it did. Parch cut off large pieces and threw the chunks into the hole, quickly clearing the way.

Fascinated, Jason leaned in close to the roots, inspecting them intently. He didn't know much about plants, but somehow these roots looked *off* to him. They looked sickly, vile, and extremely dry. *What in the world kind of plant could these belong to?* he wondered to himself.

"Hey, Parch," Jason called back over his shoulder. "Do these roots have something to do with everything that's been happening?"

Parch didn't respond, but Jason hardly noticed because he was so captivated by the roots. He leaned in even closer, squinting, and felt a slight tiredness as he did. But he ignored it and continued examining the strange plant extremity. He looked along the root's length and noticed something odd. The root he was looking at ran sideways along the wall, but once it reached his shadow, which was cast from his body blocking the green light of the torch, the root completely vanished. Even stranger was that on the other side of his shadow, the root reappeared, seemingly out of nowhere, running along the same path. It was unsettling but fascinating. He held up his hand to cast another shadow, and watched the roots disappear underneath it, then dropped his hand and watched as they reappeared.

Incredible, Jason thought. But suddenly the green light vanished, and all the roots with it. Jason turned around, wondering what had happened, and when he looked, Parch was gone.

"Parch?" Jason called out.

"In here," Parch called back, his voice coming from inside the hole in the middle of the stain. The green light shone out from the center.

In an instant, Jason's fascination vanished and was replaced by fear. He instinctively stepped back farther away from the hole. He became acutely aware that he had no idea what was going on, what the roots were, or what was in that hole. It was all mysterious and unknowable. He didn't understand any of it, and this terrified him. Jason's teeth clenched hard, and his hands squeezed into fists.

"What are you doing?" Jason asked, forcing himself not to stammer. "What's in that hole?"

"Just the usual," Parch called back nonchalantly. "Come on in."

But Jason didn't move. He stayed where he was, off to the side of the hole. His breathing and heart rate increased. What was Parch doing? What was happening? Parch couldn't seriously expect him to follow into that strange black portal, could he?

After a moment, Parch called out again. "Now, when you climb in, make sure to keep a good grip on the roots. It's very important, okay? Hold on to the roots at all times."

"Are you sure?" Jason asked. "Are you sure it's one hundred percent safe?"

"I mean, nothing is a hundred percent safe," Parch answered. "Sometimes, you just have to throw caution to the wind."

This answer caused Jason's throat to tighten. He brought his hands up defensively and stepped even farther away from the hole. There was suddenly a gravity to the moment, like this was the point of no return, and it caused Jason's entire body to tense up.

Jason looked back toward the stairwell. He could leave right now. He *should* leave right now. Parch's evasive answers and non-responses to all his questions left Jason completely incognizant of whatever was happening. How was Jason supposed to help if he was going in completely blind? In his mind, Jason imagined himself leaving and walking back up the stairs. But some deep longing inside him kept his feet where they were.

Trapped in turmoil, Jason looked back and forth between the stairs and the hole, until he suddenly became aware of something poking into his thigh. He realized it was his keys in his pocket. He pulled them out and looked at them. His eyes were drawn to his mouse key chain. He held it between his fingers, turning it about and rubbing it. It was a small thing. A cheap, metal carving of a mouse that he'd gotten years ago.

"You coming?" Parch called out from the hole.

As Jason looked down at the mouse carving, he spoke without even realizing. "Yeah, I'm coming," Jason said.

Wait. I didn't mean to say that! Jason thought. *I meant to say I was leaving.* Jason's teeth clenched and he grimaced. *Why did I say that?* He closed his eyes and covered his face with his free hand. But as he continued to breathe, the initial shock of his own words wore off. Slowly he relaxed and made peace with it. The choice was made, and something deep inside him was inexplicably happy with it. Even though his resolve wavered slightly, Jason stood up a little straighter.

Jason's hand dropped from his face, and he stared at the black hole in his basement wall. The only roots left visible in the basement were those around the mouth of the hole, and they immediately disappeared outside of the green light. Jason stuffed his keys in his pocket, then slowly walked over to the hole, approaching from the side. Once he got to the edge, he peered in cautiously.

The green light from the torch revealed that the relatively modest hole in the wall opened up into a much larger cavity on the other side of the house's foundation. From what Jason could see, this cavity was filled with a massive number of roots which loosely tangled together chaotically. The strands of roots were all twisting, turning, and weaving together and apart. It created something like a thicket, with just enough space in between the roots that one could barely squeeze through. Parch had worked his way several meters into the thicket, and was silhouetted in green light, surrounded by tree roots and darkness. But, of all of it, what Jason noticed most was a strange dark mist or fog that filled the hole.

"Make sure you get a good hold on the roots," Parch repeated, "then just pull yourself up and in."

Jason oriented himself toward the hole and placed his hands on the roots. The roots were dry, and bits of bark rubbed off on his hands as he found grip. He felt a strange pulling sensation inside of him, like his blood was being pulled from his chest through his arms and hands, and into the roots. Briefly, there was a faint smell of rotten meat, but the smell was soon overpowered by the smell of dust and dirt from the basement. Jason looked at Parch, who gave him a reassuring nod, then Jason leaned forward, stepped up, and pulled himself into the hole.

He was hit with an immediate feeling of closeness and claustrophobia. It felt like something was pressing against him from all sides, but Jason attributed this feeling to simply being underground, and so ignored it and focused on maneuvering into the hole. Shifting, sliding, and squeezing, he was able to make it inside the tangle, working his way toward Parch.

Parch smiled and nodded in approval. "That's what I'm talking about!" He slapped Jason on the back. "I'm not actually supposed to bring people along," Parch said, "but you seem like a good guy, and I've got a good feeling about this. Anyway, I like having someone with me. Now let's get this done. Stay there and hold on to those roots for a sec, and we'll get started." Carefully but skillfully, Parch slipped past Jason and worked his way back to the hole they had entered from.

With Parch moving back toward the entrance, Jason was left to collect himself. He adjusted his grip on the roots, feeling the roughness on his palms. He shifted his weight and pulled up his right leg, sticking it through some higher roots to get a little more comfortable. *How did all this empty space form right next to the house?* he wondered. *Maybe there's a cave system underground here and that's how the tree broke into my basement.* Either way, this whole situation made him nervous. The torch, the roots — it was all very weird. He was glad he'd only have to deal with such things for twenty minutes. Under the anxiety and nervousness, however, was a spark of happiness and excitement that he couldn't explain.

While Jason reflected on the situation, Parch maneuvered through the roots and quickly returned to the hole leading into the basement. While still inside the thicket of roots inside the cavity, he pulled the torch off his shoulder strap, and held the flame up to the edge of the hole. The flame spread to the edge, and clung there, as if held by some force. Parch traced the circumference of the hole, the green flame spreading the entire way, until he had completed the ring. Once all the circumference was ignited, a curious thing happened: slowly, all the edges started to shrink toward each other, growing closer and closer. The hole was closing in on itself, and the stain outside was vanishing. Parch watched placidly as the opening into the basement shrunk. After several seconds, the hole, with its enflamed edges all converging, shrunk down to a single point, then disappeared, as did the flame that had caught on the edges with it. There wasn't a trace left on the basement wall that it had ever been there to begin with.

CHAPTER 4

As Jason waited for Parch, he started to inspect this underground cavity they had crawled into. Maybe it actually was a cave system. It seemed much larger than he realized when he'd looked in initially. Jason started to wonder how far back it went, but it was so dark that it was hard to tell. With his anxiety growing, the thought of a cave-in crossed his mind. Jason reached across the roots, trying to touch one of the cavity's walls, and hoping to find hard-packed clay. But as he leaned out into the darkness, all he felt was empty space. He searched in every direction, and couldn't find anything but the roots, and beyond them, nothing. Even beneath him, there wasn't dirt or ground. The roots he sat on were suspended in the air.

Confused, Jason shifted his focus to the roots, hoping they might reveal some clue to this new space. It was immediately apparent that the roots were incredibly sturdy and tough, and even though they hung in the air, they didn't bend when Jason shifted his weight. There were hundreds, if not thousands, of root strands, and they formed a chaotic mess. Each strand twisted and turned about, weaving together and separating from each other, seemingly at random. But despite the capriciousness of each strand, they all collectively flowed together in a generally straight line from the hole in the basement off toward something in the darkness.

"There's so much space," Jason said, reaching out again to find a wall.

Parch laughed behind him. "A lot of space!" he repeated with a chuckle.

Curious about the strange response, Jason turned to ask, but as he turned back, he looked and saw only darkness behind Parch. Eyes wide with panic, he shouted, "Where's the hole? The one we came through. Did it cave in?" Frantically, Jason started to shift on the roots, trying to turn back around.

"Easy, calm down," Parch said. "Keep holding on to those roots! You'll fall if you let go."

Jason clutched the roots involuntarily. "Fall? Fall where? We're underground! We're in some kind of cave," Jason responded.

Parch reattached the torch to his shoulder strap, then maneuvered back through the branches closer to Jason. The green light from the burning torch illuminated the area around him, but Jason noticed the light didn't go as far as he thought it should. Somehow the darkness seemed to overpower it quickly.

Parch crawled next to Jason on the branches and replied in a composed, measured voice. "Everything is fine," he said. "But we're not underground, and we're not in a cave. We're not in the human world anymore."

Jason's knuckles turned white as he squeezed hard on the roots. But then he realized the outrageous thing Parch had just said. Parch had to be messing with him. "Stop kidding around," Jason said, his voice noticeably wavering. "I've had a rough enough night as it is."

But Parch didn't respond with laughter or apology as Jason was hoping. Instead, Parch responded with a look of seriousness; this clearly wasn't a joke. "This problem we're dealing with," Parch said, "doesn't originate from the human side of things, so to fix it we have to go where it is."

"Where it is?!" Jason swallowed hard. He closed his eyes and clutched at the roots even harder, wishing he hadn't done this, wishing he hadn't been so stupid, and wishing he hadn't climbed into the hole. He should have left when he had the chance. He couldn't do this! Why hadn't he just left?

As Jason's mind struggled to comprehend what was going on, small whisps of darkness started to reach for him from all sides. The whisps, which had the appearance of thin tendrils of pitch-black smoke, were a part of the darkness itself, melding in and out, making them nearly impossible to see until they were upon you. They stretched out toward Jason, slowly getting closer and closer. By the time Jason saw them, there were several touching him already.

"Parch!" Jason cried, while swatting at the whisps. "It's a monster! There's a monster in here! Help!"

"It's not a monster," Parch said. "They're just void fingers, they won't hurt you, I promise." But Jason wasn't convinced, and continued frantically swatting at the whisps, breaking them up only to watch them reform and reach for him again. Parch took a deep breath.

"Listen," Parch began, "I'll explain everything. Right now, we're in what's called the Great Chasm. Me and the guys call it the Abyss. We don't know much about it for sure, but we think it's like a transition place. Something like the separation between life . . . and the hereafter."

Jason balked in horrified confusion. "The separation between life and the hereafter?" The black whisps continue to swirl around him." What does that even mean?"

Parch scratched his cheek for a moment. "You've heard of near-death experiences, right?" he asked. "They're always the same. You know, dark tunnel, bright light, God. Well, we think this is the dark tunnel part."

"Death?" Jason asked, breathing quickly. "Are we going to die? Are we already dead?"

"We're not dead," Parch said. "To the living, the Abyss isn't a tunnel. It's an infinite empty void that goes on forever in all directions. Do you see a tunnel or an Abyss?"

Jason looked around and saw only darkness. It seemed, if Parch was right about all this, they were both still alive. Even so, the revelation about where they were was deeply unsettling.

"That's why I said you have to hang on to the roots, otherwise you'd fall, and there's no bottom in here. Anyway, the void fingers," Parch said, returning to the odd whisps, "we don't know much about them either, but they're harmless. They seem to like us, and they like the torch fire even more." Parch held up the torch in his hand, showing how the black whisps were drawn to it. The void fingers danced and swirled around the green flame, almost like moths, darting into the fire and consuming a spark or two before pulling back.

The magic of the moment, however, was lost on Jason. Upon learning the black whisps were not a danger, his mind turned to worrying about the lack of ground beneath him. *There's no bottom? I'd fall forever?!* He wrapped his arms around a particularly thick root and looked down.

Beneath the roots it was pure black, just like in every direction. There was comfort, however, in how dense and thick the roots were. Despite Parch's assertions, Jason saw one wouldn't be able to accidently fall through these roots from where they sat; both men were far too embedded. In the middle of the thicket as they were, they were practically enclosed by the roots. The strange feeling of closeness that was inherent to this place also helped alleviate Jason's fear of heights.

Completely bewildered by this bizarre place, Jason looked hard at Parch. "Why did you bring us in here?" he asked.

Parch smiled at him. "Straight to the point, then," he said. "I'll give you the quick version. The stains in your house are what we call bridges, which are like connections between places, like the human world and the Abyss, for example. These roots we're sitting on are what opened the bridges. The roots belong to a plant called the Mortem Cor plant, which is what's causing all the problems. The

Mortem Cor plant is what created this connection, and it's what we need to deal with to fix everything. But the plants don't live in the Abyss, they live in separate worlds, called the Ignotus, which we can only reach by passing through the Abyss. So, what happens is, the Mortem Cor plants in the Ignotus use their roots to find weak points, which are random, and open bridges from the Ignotus into the Abyss, and then from the Abyss into the human world."

Jason's brow furrowed and his mouth fell. "What?" he said. Whether it was the circumstances, fear, or the lateness of the hour, Jason's mind couldn't comprehend Parch's words. Jason shook his head as he clutched harder at the roots. "I don't understand anything you just said."

Parch chuckled. "This is why I try to avoid explaining things. Never mind, none of that matters. Here's what we have to do: we have to seal the bridges, and we have to destroy the Mortem Cor plant so it can't reopen them. I already sealed the bridge we came through. From here, we enter the Ignotus, follow these roots back to the plant, burn it down, then follow the other set of roots back out through your living room, all the while sealing every bridge we come across. That's the plan. Easy as that."

Things were starting to make sense to Jason. But the more he understood, the worse he felt. His initial surface-level shock was replaced with a deep-seated dread regarding this strange, unearthly place. It was truly unknowable and uncontrollable. Jason was contending with forces far beyond himself. He had to get out of here fast.

"I — I can't be here," Jason stuttered, staring back at Parch. "I can't do this. I know you think it's easy, but I can't do it. I should have stayed upstairs. I never should have come in here. Please, reopen that hole, or bridge, or whatever so I can leave."

"I know it's a lot to take in, but it's not as bad as it all sounds," Parch said.

"Please let me out!" Jason repeated, growing more anxious and agitated. "This isn't for me; I can't do this."

"I can't reopen the bridge," Parch replied. "I sealed it after entry, which is standard procedure, and I don't have a way to reopen it. Only the plants can open bridges, so unless you want to wait here until the plant reopens it, if it even does, there's no going back that way. We're committed."

Trapped? No way out? Jason's mind flooded with anxiety and fear. Going along with Parch into some horrible, unknown danger was terrifying, but so was staying here perched precariously in a dark infinity. Jason wrung his hands on the tree root, and he looked around futilely for some other answer, some way out of this situation, but there was none. Why had he come in here? He never did things like this, so why had he now?

After a moment, Parch reached out and placed his hand on Jason's shoulder. "Playing it safe isn't going to solve anything," he said. "Right now, we must dare boldly."

Despite all the fears swarming his mind, a small spark lit in Jason's heart, and suddenly he remembered his keys. As he continued to struggle inside himself, his hand dropped to his side and his fingers found the mouse key chain in his pocket. With a squeeze of the key chain his heart swelled.

Jason took a deep breath, then looked at Parch. "You're sure we can do this?" Jason asked. "Absolutely, one hundred percent sure we can do this without getting killed?"

Parch smiled. "Absolutely, we can. It's a sure thing. And it'll be fun, too. Nine times out of ten these are just little hikes through the Ignotus to the plant, torch it, then leave. It's really not as dangerous as you think it's going to be."

While he was still disturbed by everything, Jason was slowly starting to ease into the situation. It helped that, at least according to Parch, he didn't have much of a choice. "Okay," he said.

Nodding, Parch slapped Jason's shoulder. "Awesome. Then let's head in! We need to continue climbing through these roots until we reach the bridge into the Ignotus. It's usually not far; I think I can already see something ahead."

Significantly less excited, Jason nodded. He looked farther along the roots and noticed a concerning red glow ten meters away. "What is the Ignotus like, anyway?" Jason asked.

"They're not empty like the Abyss," Parch answered. "They are worlds sort of like the human world, although not everything works the same. Things don't always follow the same rules as the human world. What's really cool about the Ignotus is they're always different. You never see the same one twice."

That last comment caught Jason's attention. "Wait," he said. "So you don't know for sure what we're getting into?"

"That's what makes it fun," Parch responded with a wink. "Just follow me, and we'll get this done."

Having already resigned to his fate, Jason nodded. For now, he'd put his trust in Parch.

CHAPTER 5

Parch maneuvered past Jason, skillfully weaving himself through the dense roots. Once he was past, he pressed on and continued working his way toward the red glow several meters away.

Hesitating a moment, Jason looked down through the roots into the bottomless Abyss below him. He clutched at the roots, but as the green light of the torch grew dimmer, he knew he had to move. With extreme caution, he followed Parch through the roots toward the red light.

As Jason neared the source of the red glow, he saw that the mass of tangled roots curved upward sharply, changing from running horizontally to running vertically. But after rising several meters the roots then ceased, reaching a certain point then vanishing completely. But after rising several meters, the roots then ceased, once they reached a certain point, before vanishing completely. Looking intently, Jason realized the roots ran into another portal, or "bridge" as Parch called it.

The bridge was like a window into another world, floating in the oppressive darkness. It was several meters above them and oriented horizontally in the Abyss. It made

Jason feel like he was looking up from a pitch-black sewer at an open manhole cover above. The bridge was several meters wide, roughly circular but with ragged edges, and a dull red light shone out of it. The tangle of roots all condensed down and flowed through the bridge, out of the Abyss and into the Ignotus. The areas of the bridge not filled with roots revealed a glimpse into the Ignotus. It was hard to tell exactly, but it looked to Jason like he was seeing something like a night sky, filled with a strange, shimmering red light.

Jason caught up with Parch, joining him directly under the bridge. Captivated by the sight, Jason stared up into the strange new world, bathed in the red light.

"I'll crawl up there first," Parch said quietly, "to make sure the coast is clear. Wait here, and I'll let you know when to come up."

Jason remained nestled in the roots as he watched Parch climb up and into the Ignotus, disappearing beyond the opening. Left to wait and wonder, Jason stared up. As he sat in the quietness of the Abyss, suspended in infinity, and illuminated by the red light, he felt an unexpected peace. He relished the last few moments of calm before he embarked into whatever madness he was caught up in.

A moment later, Parch reappeared in the hole. He looked down at Jason with a stern face and held his finger to his lips, then motioned for Jason to come up. Jason's peace shattered. What had made Parch so serious all of a sudden?

Jason gripped the roots and pulled himself upward, the top layer of bark flaking off on his hands as he did. The dispersed tangle of roots condensed and compacted as it rose toward the bridge, turning from a thicket into more of a column. It made the climb easier because anywhere Jason wanted there was a foot or hand hold. He hauled himself upward, and slowly poked his head up into this new world.

Looking around, Jason saw the bridge opened into the bottom of a gorge. The gorge was five meters wide, and its walls rose over ten meters. The walls were made of smooth, bone-white stone, as was the floor. Dust and sand covered everything. Jason couldn't see far down the gorge because the walls curved capriciously, blocking the view in both the directions the gorge ran.

The roots ran out of the bridge, then coiled into a single, chaotic, tightly packed cord. With so many strands spinning together, the resulting tangled line of roots was well over a meter and a half in diameter. It ran linearly along the ground, down one direction of the gorge and disappeared behind a turn. But besides these, there were no other roots around.

Looking up, Jason realized the source of the red light he had seen from the bridge was a red aurora borealis that glimmered and danced far above, filling the entire night sky. A dull red light shone down from it and illuminated everything. There were no stars above, only the aroura borealis, and beyond that, darkness.

Jason paused, split between the two worlds. The contrast between the Abyss and Ignotus was stark. One was an empty void; the other was physical and solid. Jason looked along the separation, the bridge where one world became the other. It was a fine line, and an immediate transition. The one stopped and the next began.

With his shoulders still in the Abyss, Jason reached one of his arms out beyond the edge of the perimeter of the bridge, then bent at his elbow upward. His hand and forearm now rose in the Abyss above the level of the bridge, but as he waved it around, he felt nothing but open space. Neither could he see his hand. He wondered what would happen if he pulled it toward him and through the transition of the bridge but decided against trying it. Instead, he carefully maneuvered his arm back to himself, avoiding interfering with the bridge, then climbed the rest of the way up and into the Ignotus.

Parch, crouching down on the sandy floor, motioned for Jason to join him. As Jason climbed out of the bridge, his foot got caught on a root, and he stumbled. He would have fallen over, but Parch caught him, firmly holding him still. The noise from the stumble echoed through the gorge and Parch looked around vigilantly as it died off. Silence settled in once again, and, after waiting several moments, Parch breathed a sigh of relief and released Jason.

Parch's tense behavior set Jason on edge. He got free of the roots and bridge, then crouched down next to Parch on the gorge floor. "What's happening?" he whispered hoarsely.

"We've run into a bit of a wrinkle in the plan," Parch whispered back, his lighthearted tone incongruent with his darting eyes. He pointed at the ground; the sandy gorge floor was covered in strange, large footprints.

"What made these?" Jason whispered back, staring at the huge number of tracks. He looked over the prints, and his entire body tensed up.

The footprints were all similar in shape but varied in size from fifteen centimeters in length to nearly twice that long. Each print was composed of three thick, front-facing toes, and a single rear-facing one. There were hundreds of prints across the gorge floor, all mixed together chaotically, so it was impossible to tell how many creatures made them. But one thing was clear, they were all heading in the same direction the roots ran.

"It's pretty rare, but there are sometimes creatures in the Ignotus," Parch replied. "We call them the Malus."

Jason stared at Jeff wide-eyed.

"Won't be a problem," Parch said. "They're not around right now. Plus, these could be old, and the things who made them far away. Either way, it'll be best to be quiet from here on out. We'll slip through this place secretly, do what we need to do, get out, and nothing will even know we were here. Even if the worst should happen, we always have the torch, so we'll be fine. And on top of it all"—Parch pulled off his backpack and started rummaging through it—"I always come prepared."

As Parch dug through the backpack, Jason felt more and more ill. "I don't feel very good," Jason said.

Parch nodded. "Yeah," he agreed, "that's this place trying to kill you. Humans aren't supposed to be here. If you stayed here long enough, it eventually would kill you, but it takes about a month. We won't be here long enough for it to do any damage. After a little while, you'll get used to it."

A shiver ran up Jason's spine. "Parch, I still don't understand any of this," he said.

"No one does," Parch said, continuing to rummage through his pack. "The Abyss kind of makes sense to me, but the Ignotus doesn't. No one truly understands them. But as usual, the old guys have their thoughts and theories. They always talk about how they think the Ignotus worlds are like a low point, where the sins of our world drip down into and collect, like a gutter. This place isn't hell, but it's probably on the way there." Parch paused and shrugged. "Or so they say, but I try not to think about it while I'm in here."

"Old guys?" Jason replied. "So, there are more people like you? How do you know all this stuff? Who do you work for?"

Parch responded with nothing but a smile and a wink. He then pulled out several items from his pack: a chest harness, a sheathed knife, and a pair of holstered handguns, and set them down on the ground. He picked up the chest harness and offered it to Jason. "Put this on," he said.

The harness was designed to wrap around the chest, back, and shoulders. Jason put it on and Parch helped straighten the harness and tighten everything down until Jason felt quite comfortable with it on. With the rigging properly fitted, Parch pulled down a protective covering on the left shoulder strap, revealing a built-in flashlight. The flashlight was flat and square, and integrated into the strap. Parch uncovered a similar light on his own gear, then demonstrated how to use it: pressing it in and clicking it on and off. It was situated perfectly for shining light in front, hands free.

Next, Parch grabbed a sheathed knife similar to the one he had on his belt. "The Mortem Cor plant's roots are extremely tough, and it's hard to cut them," he said as he drew the knife. "But these knives are special." Parch demonstrated the knife on the nearby roots running out of the bridge, showing how effortlessly it cut through them. The runes on the blade glowed a bright blue as it glided through the wood. Ending the brief demonstration, Parch sheathed the knife, then affixed it to a holder built into Jason's right shoulder strap. "These knives have a habit of saving your butt in here," Parch said. "Keep it close; it's priceless."

When lastly Parch picked up the pair of handguns, Jason's eyes widened, darting back and forth between Parch and the pistols. He shifted about uncomfortably but didn't retreat. After a moment he settled and stared intently at the weapons.

The two guns were strange; they looked like pistols from decades past that had been heavily modified. The most obvious modifications were the additions of several odd wooden attachments that had been integrated into the metal, especially around the barrel. There were runes carved into the wood similar to the ones on the knives, except these runes glowed a constant, and much brighter, blue.

"You ever shot a gun before?" Parch asked.

"No," Jason said, shaking his head. "Never even held one. Why do we need them? Are we going to have to use them on those Malus things?"

"We won't run into any Malus, and we won't need to use the guns, probably. This is just a precaution. Everything is fine, just better safe than sorry." Parch watched as Jason stared down at the guns, fascinated. He unholstered one and handed it over to Jason, who took it cautiously.

Staring at the pistol in his hands, Jason held it loosely. Not overly nervous, but unsure, he turned it over several times in his hand, unable to look away.

Parch smiled as he watched how captivated Jason was with the gun. He briefly demonstrated how to hold and aim the pistol, but then commanded Jason not to use it unless specifically told. "Once we finish what we need to do in here," Parch said, "we can fire off a few rounds before we leave — just for fun, if you'd like."

"Yeah," Jason said. "I've always wanted to try."

"Deal," Parch said. "But for now"— Parch took the gun from Jason, holstered it, then attached it to Jason's rigging under his left arm so that it hung secure and ready to be drawn —"just leave it holstered. And don't lose it!" Parch then attached his own gun to his gear, likewise.

"One last thing," Parch said. He pulled out another watch from his pack, held it up to his own, and synchronized both together. Once he was done, he gave the new one to Jason.

Jason put the watch on. Strangely, it didn't tell the time, but instead was counting down, and was currently at five hours, fifty-five minutes. "What's this counting down to?" Jason asked.

"It's for the torch," Parch said. "But speaking of time, we've spent enough of it chitchatting. Let's get going." Parch stood up from where he and Jason were crouching down on the gorge floor and reordered himself and his gear, then turned back toward the roots.

Jason was still full of questions, but it seemed Parch was done answering them for now. Following Parch's lead, Jason stood up and adjusted his gear to get ready to move.

Despite all they had talked about, Jason was having trouble understanding everything. It was all too much. He couldn't fit it all together in his mind. The only thing he could do was trust in Parch, and that made him even more nervous.

Parch walked over to the roots running out of the bridge and placed his hand on them. "This is a root line," he whispered back to Jason. "They run above ground, and this one will lead us back to the plant. All we have to do is follow it, ideally as quietly as possible."

But as Jason listened, an awful thought suddenly crossed his mind. "Wait!" he whispered urgently. "Lily!"

Parch returned a questioning look.

"The hole!" Jason exclaimed. "The hole we came through, to the Abyss or whatever. If there were Malus on this side,"— Jason pointed down to the tracks in the sand —"then what if one of them crawled through the way we came? What if it's in the house right now?"

Shaking his head, Parch put up his hands to calm Jason down. "No, no," he said, "Malus can't cross through the Abyss; they can't get to the human world, even with a bridge."

"Why not?" Jason pressed.

Parch frowned in thought. But after several seconds, he shrugged. "I forget," he said. "They told me once, but I can't remember."

"What?" Jason replied. "You don't know? Well, what if it happened *this* time? What if Lily is in danger?"

"Lily is safe," Parch said. "No Malus has ever gone through into the human world, and it's not going to happen this time either. They just can't. Now, the sooner we get going, the sooner you'll get back to your wife. All right?"

Jason withdrew slightly but nodded his assent.

Seeing this, Parch broke from the conversation and headed over to the bridge. After quickly clearing away the roots with his knife, he took the torch off his shoulder and, repeating the same steps from before, dragged the green fire around the edges of the bridge opening, with the fire catching all around. Once all the edges were lit, the bridge slowly started to close in on itself until there was nothing left but dusty gorge floor.

"All right," Parch said, standing up. "Let's get this done."

With Parch leading the way, the two set off down the winding curves of the gorge, following the roots. The red light from the aurora above illuminated everything, making it easy to navigate. A slight, cool breeze blew down the gorge as they walked. Everything was silent as the grave, with the only sound coming from the occasional, and regrettable, scrape of one of the men's boots on the stone floor.

At first, Jason was scared of every shadow. In this dangerous and unfamiliar place, it was impossible to know what kind of terrible creatures lurked about, or what kind of horrific fate he could meet. Jason's mind was quick to fill in the blanks with all manner of nightmarish creatures. But as they continued on, without sight or sound of anything besides themselves, Jason started to relax. Plus, it was hard to proceed cautiously while still keeping up with Parch's relentlessly swift pace.

They passed through turn after turn without much change to the landscape: the smooth gorge walls, the sand, and the red light pouring down on them. Occasionally, the walls would pinch in, and at one point the men had to climb onto the roots to get through a particularly narrow section. Even so, it was a minor hazard, and they passed through quickly.

The first real obstacle they came across was a section where the wall had collapsed on one side. Loose rock and debris covered the gorge floor, blocking their way forward. They had to maneuver over it. Parch went first. After plotting the most efficient path, he scrambled quickly and carefully over the broken rock, all the while making only minor sounds.

Jason tried to copy Parch's traversal but had far more difficulty. After only just starting, he slipped and lost his footing, falling to his hands and knees, and kicking up rocks as he did. The cracks of the disturbed rocks echoed through the gorge, and Jason froze in terror. The pain from the sharp rocks he'd landed on shot up his arms and legs, but he dared not move. The sound of his fall quickly died down and all returned to stillness and silence. After several seconds, he completed the crossing on hands and knees.

As they continued on through the gorge, Jason started to feel more comfortable. Parch had been right, this was just a little hike, albeit through an incredible locale. And, if Parch's other prediction held true as well, any moment they would find this "Mortem Cor plant" and be on their way back home soon afterward.

Jason was glad he'd come along. He felt courageous and proud. He felt like he'd made progress. He couldn't wait to brag to Lily about this adventure he had gone on, and how he had helped defeat this strange, supernatural plant causing all the problems. She'd be so proud. It had all been strange at first, but it was ultimately, and thankfully, uneventful — not that he'd tell Lily that. Anyway, while Jason was enjoying the brisk pace of this little undertaking, he still felt that the sooner they left the better. While the disgusting feeling of this Ignotus had lessened, it hadn't completely gone away. It wasn't one he would soon forget, and he'd had quite enough of it.

As the two men approached another turn, one that appeared to be the same as all the others before it, the chain coiled on Parch's belt began to quietly rattle, all by itself. Seeing the ordinary object come to life made Jason nearly jump out of his skin in shock, but Parch had a different reaction.

Instinctively, Parch jumped back from the impending turn, then threw Jason and himself up against the rock wall. He snatched his pistol out of the holster and scanned the area in every direction, especially back the way they'd come. Not seeing anything, Parch let out a big, quiet breath. He looked at Jason and held a finger to his lips, then turned his attention to the corner ahead. With his pistol ready, Parch crept toward the edge of the turn and slowly, cautiously peered around it.

Stunned, Jason stood pressed up against the wall, afraid to speak and completely at a loss to what was happening. What was going on? Why was Parch on full alert? How did that chain move all by itself? Questions filled Jason's mind, but all he could do now was wait for Parch.

Parch pulled back from the corner and turned to Jason with a smile. He reholstered his pistol and motioned for Jason to join him at the edge.

Reassured by Parch's smile, Jason couldn't hold back the questions filling his mind. "What's going on?" he whispered. "Is it the plant? How did that chain move on its own?"

Parch looked down at the chain. "My good luck charm?" Parch whispered back. "The chain keeps me safe in here." As if on cue, one of the ends of the chain rose up like a snake head and coiled around Parch's arm. Jason stared in amazement, but Parch was nonchalant. "It sensed something up ahead, and let me know before we stumbled into it," Parch continued. "Take a look."

Dumbstruck, Jason stared at the chain as Parch moved further back from the corner to make room. The chain continued to move on its own, slithering like a snake up Parch's arm and around his back while Parch barely registered the movement. But as fascinating as the chain was, the prompting to look around the corner was even more enticing. Parch had relaxed considerably after seeing whatever was up ahead of them, so Jason guessed it wouldn't be too dangerous. He hoped they had found the plant they were looking for, but something told him that wasn't the case. Jason moved to the edge of the rock and slowly peered around the corner.

Ahead, the gorge temporarily widened, creating a large, oval-shaped open area. It was nearly twenty meters wide at its widest and ran maybe sixty meters before the gorge shrunk back down to its previous narrow width on the other side. The root line ran down the middle, but about halfway into the area was a strange irregularity in the roots. Interrupting the normal, chaotic but otherwise linear run, there formed a grotesque and tumorous growth in the roots. The individual strands of roots all bulged and balled into a large pile. They twisted together until this heap of roots was several times taller than the normal root line. But then, on the other side, the roots all somehow shrunk back down to normal size and found their way out of the mess, continuing their run just as they had before.

But the roots weren't what caught Jason's attention. Sitting next to the root tumor was a terrifying creature. It was human in shape, but larger and significantly more menacing. Standing up straight, it would have reached three meters tall. Its sharp teeth jutted out from its mouth in all directions. Every bit of the creature was thick and sturdy, fierce and muscular. Pitch-black from head to toe, it had a disgusting, shiny ooze that dripped from its eyes and mouth. It was a wretched, hideous thing that made Jason's stomach turn to even look at.

Jason cowered at the sight of this creature. He felt helpless and weak. All he could think about was it turning and charging at him, and how defenseless he would be. He wouldn't be able to do anything against such a terrible creature. His only thought was to run immediately, but he was frozen in fear and couldn't take his eyes off it.

Fortunately for Jason, the creature didn't turn on them or notice them at all. It sat hunched over and motionless in front of the root tumor, almost as if in a trance. Its head was hung low, and its jaws were slack. Its bulging eyes were unfocused and glazed over. The monster seemed completely oblivious to everything around it.

Parch, who had moved behind Jason, peered out at the creature as well. "It's your lucky day," he whispered. "You get to see a Malus."

"That's a Malus?" Jason asked as he stared.

"Yup. The sludge of humanity's sins given flesh," Parch whispered back, "or something like that. All I know is they are mindless, violent monsters, and if you stab them, shoot them, or light them on fire with the torch, they're not a problem anymore." The two men continued to stare. "Look at its hand," Parch said.

Jason shifted his focus to the creature's outstretched hand. It was difficult to tell from so far away, but it looked like the Malus had one of its hands stuck into the root tumor. Jason squinted to try and make out what was going on, and he saw an aberration in the roots. Half a meter off the ground, on the root tumor's exterior, there was a strange, exposed black surface that stood out from the rest of the wood. The oddity was roughly circular, maybe thirty centimeters across. Pitch-black liquid dripped out of it like an open wound. The Malus sat in front of this wound in the roots, and had its hand stuck directly into it.

Jason shivered in disgust. "Is that the plant we're looking for?" he asked, venturing a hopeful guess.

"No," Parch responded. "The Mortem Cor plant will be smaller than that, under a meter tall. They look like little shrubs. The huge roots are deceptive; the plant itself is tiny in comparison. That tumor-looking thing happens in the root lines sometimes; it's how the Malus interact with our world. They use those openings in the roots to sort of see into the human world, and, if they're strong enough, can even"— Parch smiled —"move some keys around."

Almost as if on cue, the mesmerized Malus let out a loud, familiar howl that echoed through the gorge. As Jason recoiled in shock, Parch instinctively pulled them both back behind the rock. They huddled low, and Parch drew his pistol once more. Both men nervously scanned in every direction, worried an army of Malus would be swarming down on them any second. But as silence settled back in, and it was clear nothing was coming, both men relaxed. Their hopes were confirmed when they looked out and saw the Malus right where it had been, back in its mesmerized state.

"Must have been howling all night," Parch whispered. "If there are more around, they're probably ignoring it."

This speculation was of little comfort to Jason, however, who was so afraid he was close to hyperventilating. "What do we do?" he said, trying and failing to keep his voice steady.

Parch looked down at his drawn pistol. "This will be too loud." He reholstered the pistol then drew his knife instead. "Maybe I can sneak up on it."

Jason gasped. "No, no, no!" Jason's mind was filled with thoughts of Parch being torn to pieces by the Malus, and then being left alone in what was quickly becoming a nightmare. "There has to be another way. You can't go near that thing. It'll kill you!"

"I'm open to suggestions," Parch said. He shook the chain so that it moved completely onto his arm that wasn't holding the knife. Its end coiled around his hand and fingers. Parch and the chain moved together so naturally that it was obvious this wasn't their first fight together. "I don't like our chances climbing up these walls, and there weren't any turns. So I think our only way forward is through that Malus."

Jason looked around. He knew Parch was right, but he didn't want to face it. Instead, he simply said nothing and went quiet.

With a deep breath and a nod, Parch set off and moved to the edge of the rock face. He muttered something under his breath, then clenched down on his knife and the chain. The chain responded by raising one of its ends. It moved weightlessly in the air and poised itself like a snake ready to strike. After one last slow exhale, Parch moved out from cover, and silently crept into the open area.

The Malus was still sitting in front of the root tumor, completely transfixed and oblivious. Parch's eyes stayed trained on the creature as he moved swiftly but quietly toward it. As he got closer, he slowed down and clutched his knife. The way the Malus was sitting, it was completely vulnerable. Parch would have no problem delivering the decisive attack if he could only get into position. The knife would cut through the Malus just as easily as it did the roots, so a quick stab straight to the back of the head would be the Malus's silent end. The plan was simple enough; Parch just had to get there.

Jason peaked out from behind the edge of the rock and watched as Parch stalked closer toward the Malus. Powerless, Jason could only look on with his breath held in desperate anticipation. Thankfully, things seemed to be going well. Parch was getting closer, and the Malus hadn't moved at all. But despite the optimistic signs, fear still crept into Jason's heart.

Instinctively, he looked back the way they'd come — his escape route. What would he do if Parch was killed? Where would he go if he had to flee? The hole they had come through was closed, so going back that way would be pointless. He would be stuck in this terrible place, without knowing how to get home.

Now, only meters away from the Malus, Parch slowed even more. Sweat was forming between his hand and the knife. The chain on his other arm was poised to strike. He crept closer. Almost there.

When Parch was only a few meters away, a light gust of wind blew down the gorge. The wind hit Parch's back, and gently blew past him toward the Malus.

In a sudden explosion of movement, the Malus jerked its head up and snorted twice, sniffing the air. It snapped its head toward Parch, staring directly at him. Its formerly glazed-over eyes were now clear and full of rage and violence. Parch was caught by surprise, but only for a moment. He processed the situation in a flash, and as the creature rose up to attack him, Parch threw the chain at it.

The chain hit the Malus as it stood up. One end wrapped around the Malus's throat, while the other cinched down onto a massive root in the root line. Now tethered, the Malus tried to charge Parch, but was violently yanked back by the chain. Parch took the opportunity and charged the Malus himself, plunging his knife deep into the creature's stomach. The Malus roared and swung its massive hands wildly, one of which slammed into Parch and sent him flying several meters. Crashing hard onto the stone floor, Parch tumbled and rolled on the slick sand-covered ground.

Back behind the rock, Jason watched in sheer panic. His eyes darted to his escape path, and every cell in his body screamed for him to flee. He went to run but slipped on the sandy stone floor and fell over. Awkwardly crashing to the ground, he fell sprawled out and disordered. He tried to stand up, but his feet slipped again. At a loss and driven by primal instinct, he crawled into a nearby small recess in the stone wall to hide.

Like an animal caught in a trap, the Malus pulled with all its might against the chain, trying to break free. The roots were first to give, and a large section of wood broke off under the tremendous force. As it was ripped off the root line, the wood was sent flying in roughly the same direction Parch had landed. Fortunately, Parch, who was still staggered from the blow he'd received, was alert enough to see the impromptu projectile coming. He dove out of the way as the wood crashed into the rocks nearby.

The Malus had broken the wood the chain had been attached to, but the chain wasn't done yet. Its now-free end immediately snapped toward the beast, coiling and cinching around it, binding it completely. The ensnared beast roared in rage again, once more struggling and fighting against the chain. Its strong arms strained in animalistic frenzy, flexing against the binding, and with its impressive brawn, it prevailed. The chain snapped in several places and shattered, bits and pieces flying all over the gorge floor.

This, however, was a hollow victory. Because while the Malus struggled with the chain, Parch had had time to recover. Just as the Malus freed itself, Parch charged, lunging forward and stabbing the beast underneath its jaws, up into its head. The runes on the blade glowed bright blue as the knife slid effortlessly through flesh and bone, piercing the monster's skull. Its black blood gushed all over Parch's hands and forearms. Parch pulled away with his knife, and the great beast fell on its back, then moved no more.

Jason had watched the fight from his hiding spot. He could hardly believe it, but somehow Parch had won. Jason crawled out from the recess and made his way toward Parch. "Are you okay?" he whispered as he got closer.

Parch nodded.

Looking over the huge beast's dead body, Jason marveled. "You killed this thing with just a knife? That's incredible!"

Parch groaned as he tried to move around. He clutched his side where the monster had hit him, but he eventually stood up straight and breathed normally. "You get the next one," he said with a smirk.

Jason shook his head emphatically. "No way," he said. "I could never fight something like that."

Parch looked like he wanted to say something in response, but suddenly the crack of a falling rock echoed through the gorge. Both men snapped to high alert, their eyes darting in every direction. The fight had been loud (much louder than Parch had wanted) — loud enough to be heard by anything nearby. Parch clutched at his holstered pistol, and the two men watched and waited in silent trepidation.

But as the seconds stretched on and the silence remained, nothing came. Everything in the gorge was still, and they didn't see anything but stone and sand.

"Maybe it was nothing," Parch whispered. "But let's not wait around to find out."

Jason completely agreed.

Before they left the area, however, Parch ran over to the closest length of broken chain, and reached his hand down toward it. The fractured segment immediately jumped up to his outstretched hand and coiled around his wrist. At once, all the other broken bits of chain scattered around the space began to vibrate and reach toward the one around Parch's wrist. Parch ran to the next closest piece, and it too jumped up to him. This new fragment met up with the one coiled around Parch's wrist, and the two instantaneously reformed, combining to make a single, longer segment. Sprinting a quick lap around the area, Parch set off reclaiming every piece of the chain in a similar manner.

Jason watched the whole process, marveling as the chain reformed. It didn't seem to have suffered any permanent damage, nor did it appear to be affected in any way from being torn apart. *What an amazing thing*, Jason thought. He observed how it moved on its own to reach down to reclaim pieces of itself. In some way it seemed the chain needed a person to function, but at the same time it also appeared to have some degree of complete autonomy.

In less than a minute, Parch had retrieved every piece of the formerly broken chain. It was now whole and wrapped around his back and arms. He motioned to Jason and, without a word, they both took off down the gorge, once more silently following the root line.

They ran at a faster pace than before and started to make significant progress. But despite the distance they covered, the gorge continued on with turn after turn.

Seeing the Malus had deeply disturbed Jason. Despite Parch winning the fight, the illusion this would be a simple hike was now shattered. This was a dangerous place filled with unknown horrors, and Jason realized the mistake he'd made in coming. He couldn't survive in here; things could spin out of control rapidly, and he could be killed at any moment. He needed to leave as soon as possible.

Finally, they came to the last turn in the gorge. The gorge walls abruptly stopped, and the two men stepped out from between them onto flat, open ground. Before them the land sloped gently downward for a way, then turned into a vast landscape of sand dunes that stretched as far as the eye could see. Drenched in the red light from the shimmering silk of the aurora borealis above, the landscape was beautiful in a desolate, barren kind of way. But neither man appreciated the beauty, because their attention was drawn to something else.

Approximately a mile away, rising several hundred meters up out of the sand dunes, stood an enormous pale white tree. Its leafless branches reached out in every direction, and dozens of thick root lines ran out from it, extending out over the waves of sand.

Puzzled, Jason turned to Parch. "Is that it?" he asked. "Wasn't it supposed to be small?"

But Parch said nothing. He only stared, eyes not blinking, mouth slightly agape. When he finally spoke, his words cut into Jason's heart. "I've never seen anything like this before."

CHAPTER 6

The dramatic change in Parch's demeanor sent Jason into a silent panic. Parch's previous self-assured and relaxed attitude had been diminishing since they entered the Ignotus; and now, seeing this enormous Mortem Cor plant, it had shattered completely. A tense silence had settled in as Parch stared at the tree, and Jason stared at Parch.

"What does it mean?" Jason asked, almost afraid of the answer.

But Parch didn't respond. Instead, he drew in a deep breath and exhaled. Then, without a word, he started making his way down the slope toward the sea of sand dunes and the massive tree.

The red light from above poured down on the landscape, illuminating everything like a full moon. From where they were, they could see for miles. The wind was less contained out here, blowing with gentle, mild gusts that were barely strong enough to kick up sand. Besides the wind, and the two men, nothing out here stirred.

Nearby, the root line continued on its course, running out of the crack in the rock face that formed the gorge, down into the sand dunes. Now superfluous on account of how visible their destination was, neither man paid much attention to it. But as Jason glanced around from their high vantage point, he saw that the root line meandered through the dunes, capriciously carving through, around, and up the large piles of sand. The bundle of roots was anything but a straight line to the tree.

Jason ran down the slope after Parch, careful not to slip on the sand-covered stone. "Parch!" he called. "Parch! Why is the plant so big? What does it mean?"

"I don't know," Parch called over his shoulder without breaking his stride.

Anxiety and uncertainty rushed into Jason's mind, provoking a thousand terrible questions. "What do we do, then?" Jason said. "Do we call for help? Do we leave?"

"The solution is the same: burn it down," Parch responded.

How could that possibly be the answer? Jason thought. *How could we even destroy something that big in the first place?* It felt like the ground had been pulled out from beneath Jason's feet. What did it mean, the plant being this big? How bad was this? Jason was left in the agonizing tension of uncertainty. All he wanted right now was to go home.

Leading the way toward the Mortem Cor plant, Parch increased his pace forward. Jason could hardly keep up, much less continue asking the myriad of questions on his mind, and he wondered if that was intentional.

The stone beneath them ended, and they stepped into fine, powdery sand as they moved into the dunes. The sand was deep and difficult to navigate through. Their feet sank in and turned their walking into trudging, slowing their pace considerably.

The dunes around them rose over fifteen meters high from bottom to top. They were well defined, with moderately steep slopes, separated by valleys running between them. They reminded Jason of mountain ranges, only much smaller.

The root line turned sharply, heading up a dune and disappearing behind it, but the two men paid no attention. With the Mortem Cor plant towering in front of them, the obvious choice was to head right for it. This had the added benefit of keeping them hidden in the valleys. It was impossible to know what lurked around, and it would be foolish to expose themselves by walking along the dune ridges.

As they walked, Jason noticed something that raised the hair on the back of his neck. "Parch," he said. "Look. More tracks!"

Parch looked back and saw there was indeed a line of solitary tracks, similar to the ones they had seen before in the gorge, running up the sand dune to their left. It appeared the tracks were heading in roughly the direction of the tree, but because they disappeared over the crest, it was impossible to tell for sure. After looking at the tracks for a moment, Parch nodded gravely, then turned and headed toward the tree once more.

Jason cursed. His concerns about the ominous Mortem Cor plant looming ahead were growing by the second. It stood there in the night sky like a giant, pale symbol of death. And the closer they got, the more Jason felt that something was terribly wrong about all of this. They shouldn't be here. They shouldn't be doing this. They needed to leave immediately. But Parch was intent on heading toward it, and Jason was left with no choice but to follow.

More and more tracks started to appear as they progressed toward the tree. With every new track he saw, Jason's heart sank, and his nerves frayed. He expected at any minute a mob of nightmarish creatures to attack them from every side. His only hope was that Parch would come to his senses and realize they needed to abandon this crazy plan, and instead find the nearest exit, wherever that was.

Besides the tracks, the two men made another discovery as they walked. They could hear a faint noise, but it was difficult to make out because it was so muffled or perhaps distant. Both of them stopped and traded questioning looks. They stood still and listened. It only took a few seconds for them to realize what they were hearing: howling.

Once they recognized it, the sound became unmistakable. Howling, akin to the previous Malus, was coming from the direction of the Mortem Cor plant. And it wasn't just a single Malus, it was clear there were many Malus not only howling, but yelping, growling, and making all sorts of other animalistic noises.

Alarmed at this new development, Jason looked at Parch apprehensively. The howling was indisputable proof they needed to flee; Parch had to see that now. But to his profound disappointment, Jason watched Parch's eyes light up with determination, and realized his companion had come to a different conclusion. Rather than abandoning this foolishness, Parch instead drew his gun and set off once again toward the tree. Bewildered by Parch's decision, Jason reached out and grabbed Parch by the shoulder. He had to talk him out of this!

"Parch!" Jason cried. "What are you doing? We have to get out of here right now!"

Parch turned back with his disarming smile. "What?" he replied innocently. "We can't leave yet. We have to destroy the plant first, and we're so close."

"We can't go over there," Jason protested, growing more frantic. "Something terrible is going on, and we have to get out of here before we get caught up in whatever it is!"

"It might not be that bad. Let's just take a look and see what we're up against," Parch said.

"Can't you hear all the Malus? What if they see us? They'll tear us to bits!" Jason said. "This isn't how things were supposed to go. The plan is ruined, and it's not a sure thing anymore. We have to leave while we still can. How do we get out of here?"

Parch smiled. "The plan was always to figure it out as we go. And the sure thing is us winning in the end," he said with a wink.

Confounded by Parch's brazen response, Jason was left speechless. But it wasn't just the flippant statement, it was also the glib way Parch had said it that made Jason think not even Parch believed what he was saying. And yet the man was still dead set on heading into danger. Why? The obvious course of action was to escape!

Jason watched Parch turn and head for the Mortem Cor plant again. He didn't want to follow, but what choice did he have? If he went off on his own, where would he go? Parch had said before that they would follow another root line back out of this horrible place, but where was it? Jason didn't have the slightest idea how to find it. Everything had sounded so simple in the Abyss, but now that they were in the middle of it, Jason felt completely helpless. He felt trapped with no choice but to follow, despite his misgivings.

The howls got louder and the tracks more numerous as they marched on. They were getting close now. They arrived at a large sand dune that was much taller than the others.

"That will be a good vantage point," Parch whispered, looking up toward the top of the large sand dune. "We can survey the situation from up there."

Jason, in contrast, was much more concerned with how exposed they would be so high up. If there was anything behind them, they would be easily seen.

Parch started to cautiously make his way up the backside of the dune, and Jason followed suit, fretting every step. The Mortem Cor's crown loomed ahead, filling the sky in front of them beyond the crest of the dune.

They climbed higher, rising above the surrounding sand dunes. Jason couldn't help but feel vulnerable. He looked around, expecting to see some Malus they had missed come charging at them, but there was nothing. They reached the crest of the dune and peered over the top.

Before them, in the middle of the endless sand dunes, was a flat basin. This deviation in the landscape was sunk lower than its surroundings. It was roughly circular in shape, over a kilometer in diameter, and surrounded by dunes on all sides. Inside, the ground was flat and made of hard-packed dirt, with surprisingly little sand. The geographical feature was like a gigantic flat-bottomed bowl, of which the sand dunes formed the sloping sides, and the two men were on the lip looking down into it.

And in the middle of the basin stood the mighty Mortem Cor plant. The Mortem Cor plant was a bleak and terrible sight. Unlike a normal, natural tree, this was a grotesque abomination that turned Jason's stomach to look at. It was an insult to nature, as well as all things good and pure. He wasn't immediately sure why, but it made Jason feel like he was looking at a desiccated corpse, like a mummy, with the dry, rotten skin shrunken and stuck to the dead bones. Then he realized that it was the smell. Even from as far away as he was, Jason could smell that the tree reeked of the dull stench of rotten meat.

The topmost branches of the massive pale-white tree rose almost three hundred meters into the air. These branches were leafless and barren, devoid of life, like the rest of the tree. Its imposing trunk looked twenty meters wide but strangely didn't run all the way down to the dirt. Instead, at the base where the plant met the ground, all the dozens of root lines feeding into the plant combined and twisted around each other. The roots created a large, messy, loose, shadowy, tangled ball that the entire tree stood on. It was even wider than the trunk, over ten meters tall, and was hideous to look at.

But for Jason, the most terrifying sight wasn't the plant, but instead the large mob of Malus clustered in the basin. There were hundreds of them, of the same kind that Parch had fought earlier, all meandering about, predominately situated between the two men and the tree. There was no organization or structure to the group; the monsters all roamed around aimlessly. Some lay in the dirt, some fought each other, and some howled in the air. They were like wild animals, and it wasn't clear why they'd gathered together around the tree.

Jason cowered at the sight. "Get down! They'll see you!" he whispered, hiding behind the sand dune. All it would take was a single stray glance from a Malus, and their fates would be sealed.

But Parch ignored Jason's pleas, and instead glared at the massive tree. "There you are," Parch said, like a hunter eyeing prey. "That tree is the real problem. The Mortem Cor plants come into being in here, same as the Malus, and they're just as wretched. But the plants can do something the Malus can't: break out of the Ignotus. They use their roots to get into the Abyss pretty easily, but getting into the human world is a lot harder. They can't just open bridges anywhere.

"Between the human world and the Abyss, sometimes transient weak points will randomly appear. The weak points are natural and temporary, and would resolve themselves over time, but not if the Mortem Cor plants get to them first. The Mortem Cor plants use their roots to seek out these weak points, and when they find one, they bind it by creating a bridge into our world. The roots infest whatever place the bridge opened up into, and then they"— Parch paused and stared at the tree, his eyes filled with burning hatred —"the roots start killing anyone nearby. They draw out the life energy from people. It's a painless process — most people don't even realize it's happening. They just get weaker and weaker, until they finally collapse, and never wake up. Not everyone gets the fireworks show you two got. Sometimes when we show up, we just find bodies."

Hiding behind the dune, Jason was barely following anything Parch was saying. His mind was consumed with thoughts of a Malus looking up and seeing Parch peaking over the crest, then alerting the others. But with what little he did understand, a single question came to mind. "Does that mean . . . are the roots doing that to Lily right now?" he asked, looking gravely at Parch.

But Parch didn't respond, and instead focused on scanning all the root lines feeding into the tangle at the base of the plant. He glanced over most of them, only stopping on a few before quickly moving on, until he came to the last root line. He stared at it, puzzled, and looked over all the others again. When he returned to that last root line once more, he stared at it hard. "Looks strange," he muttered to himself. "But everything about this one has been strange. It has to be that one; but we'll go out that way to make sure."

After one final look at the root line, followed by a resolute nod, Parch looked back over at Jason, who was still waiting for an answer, looking at him with increasing expectancy and alarm. "Oh, Lily? No, she's fine," Parch said finally. "Those roots in the Abyss will keep that weak point in your basement bound; but without the bridge open, there's not a true connection into the human world. The plant will have to use those roots to reopen the bridge before it can draw any life energy, and that takes a little time. And that bridge in the living room — it's open, but the root connection isn't fully formed yet, so the plant can't draw from her that way either." He reached out and gave Jason a good-natured jab. "Don't worry, man. I told you she's safe. I know what I'm doing."

But despite Parch's cavalier attitude, Jason was already starting to doubt him. Nothing had gone the way Parch said it would, and now they were here, flirting with certain death, for reasons Jason couldn't understand. He sunk his fingers into the sand and squeezed, letting it slip between his fingers. His teeth clenched hard, Jason looked off anywhere but at Parch or the tree. The waves of fear crashing against his mind and heart were overwhelming. He wished desperately to be back with Lily, safe at home.

"I have to go down there," Parch said.

"What?" Jason was hysteric." You're going to leave me here?"

"I'm not going to leave you in here," Parch responded. "But one of us needs to go down there to torch the plant, and unless you want to do it, I have to do it."

"That's crazy!" Jason replied. "Do you not see how many Malus there are? You barely fought off one, and now you're going to go down there with hundreds? We need to get out of here. You said there was a way out; where is it?"

Suddenly, the two men were interrupted by a strange noise coming from the basin that sent them both ducking for cover. It was like the rattle of a rattlesnake, except higher in pitch, faster, and combined with a hiss. It was so loud that it echoed through the basin. But just as quickly as it started, it subsided, and both men listened intently for what was to come next. What followed was an eerie silence. Even the raucous, animalistic noises from the horde of Malus had ceased. Something was clearly happening. Eventually, curiosity overcame fear, and both Jason and Parch peeked back over and looked down into the basin.

Below, all the Malus scattered around the basin had begun moving toward the tangled base of the Mortem Cor plant. It was as if they had been called and were obediently answering.

"What's going on?" Jason asked. "What are they doing? Did they see us?"

"Doesn't seem like it," Parch answered. "But I don't know what they're doing. I've never seen Malus act like this. They don't form groups or gather together. They're stupid, savage creatures that attack anything, even each other. They shouldn't be doing this."

"*We* shouldn't be doing this!" Jason shot back. This strange behavior of the Malus was another unknown, another uncertainty; he could hardly take anymore.

The hissing rattle sounded again, and they realized it was coming from the tangle of roots. Both men looked closer and saw that when the massive roots coiled about chaotically at the base of the tree, they created large, empty spaces between them. The result was that the tangle was porous, and it reminded Jason of a gigantic funnel cake. The exterior roots blocked nearly all the light from above from reaching the hollow spaces between, so the interior spaces of the tangle were shrouded in shadow. And it was from one of these dark hollows that the noise was emanating from.

As the two men watched, a large, insect-like arm extended out from a hollow spot in the tangle. The arm was several meters long and had a pincer so large it could easily cut a man in half. The creature it belonged to, however, remained hidden in the shadows.

Jason shuddered, wondering what new horror had arrived. The Malus in the basin, on the other hand, watched the arm attentively, crowding and pressing closer. A second arm emerged from the darkness — similar to the first, but with one exception: this one held in its pincer a fair, pure white flower. The flower looked like a lily and appeared delicate and soft. Jason thought it was the most beautiful flower he'd ever seen; a jewel shining in this foul place. And to see it being held by some horrible monster caused a swell of indignation in his heart.

Parch gasped when he saw the flower, then cursed and clenched his teeth. "When the Mortem Cor plants kill someone," he whispered in a quiet, cold fury, "they make those flowers. That flower used to be someone. Someone with family and friends who loved them. Someone with hopes and dreams. The Mortem Cor plant killed that person. And from the looks of all these root lines, it's killed many others too."

The huge insect arm held up the flower for all to see, and a violent chaos erupted among the Malus. The Malus, especially those closest to the flower, all attacked each other. The fighting was savage and vicious, and the smaller Malus quickly fled, escaping the melee, leaving the largest and fiercest Malus to contend with each other. More and more Malus were ripped to shreds and brutalized, and quickly only the greatest few remained. They tore, bit, and struck at each other, until there was only one left. A single massive Malus stood over a dozen bodies, while the rest of the crowd shrank back in fear.

Appalled by the savage violence, Jason ducked lower behind the sand dune. He was terrified but couldn't look away.

With the contest decided, the triumphant beast lumbered up to the tangle, snatched the flower from the pincer, and irreverently devoured it in a single bite. After eating it, the creature started to move erratically. It stumbled around for a few seconds, then abruptly swelled in size, growing a foot taller and even more muscular. Its arms, claws, and teeth elongated. Once its transformation was complete, it roared into the air as if relishing its new size and strength.

Parch had seen enough. He pulled back from the crest of the dune and looked at Jason. "That plant dies tonight," he said, his voice ice. He pulled out his pistol and motioned for Jason to do the same. "Looks like we might need to use these after all."

Jason's heart sank. "No!" he cried. "Are you crazy?" Jason pulled back away from the dune crest, hiding behind the sand.

But Parch ignored Jason's protests. "We don't have time for a full class on how to shoot, so I'll just touch on the basics," Parch said sitting back, hiding behind the crest of the dune and holding up his pistol. "First rule is don't point it anywhere near me, only at the Malus. The guns themselves are pretty easy to use. The trigger is here; I'm sure you know what that does. There's no safety, and you won't have to reload it. I can guarantee that. The only two things to keep in mind are: they have some recoil so be ready for it, and —"

"Wait, stop, please. There has to be another way," Jason begged.

But once more, Parch pushed through Jason's objections. "The other thing is the guns have to recharge between shots. The runes along the barrel tell you when the gun is ready. They'll go dark after a shot, then the glow will gradually start to come back. Once they're fully lit up, the gun can shoot again. It takes several seconds, though; they're not machine guns."

"Stop!" Jason demanded. He grabbed Parch firmly by the arm. "I'm not going to just let you go down there to get ripped to pieces, and then I get ripped to pieces right after. There's nothing we can do. There's too many of them. We need to leave before they find us. How do we get out of here?!"

With eyes full of fire, Parch looked hard at Jason. "Listen! This is about more than just you and me right now. You see all those root lines? Those could lead back to other people's houses. This plant could be about to kill them just like it was about to kill you and Lily. Dozens of people could be in danger right now! Dozens! And they need our help. They're counting on us. We can stop this plant right now before it hurts anyone else, but I need your help! To protect them and protect Lily!"

Amidst all the fear and confusion, something stirred in Jason's heart. He let go of Parch and instinctively reached into his pocket. He pulled out his mouse key chain and clutched it. At first, his hands shook terribly, and he stared down into the sand beneath him, but slowly his breathing became steadier and more deliberate. He raised his downcast eyes and looked squarely at Parch. With a solemn exhale, he nodded.

Parch smiled and nodded back. He then returned to looking into the basin. "Besides, I think we can pull this off without much trouble. Now, I have to light the main body of the plant. Just lighting the roots won't work, so I have to go down there. But even so, I think we can do this in a way that the Malus won't know what's happening until it's done, and we're halfway to the bridge."

"How?" Jason asked, stuffing the mouse key chain back in his pocket.

Parch surveyed the situation once more. He took a deep breath and exhaled.

"Okay, here it is," Parch began. "Imagine that basin down there as a clockface. We're at the six o'clock position. There's a root line running in from the four o'clock position. All the Malus are on the one side of it. So if I crawl along the other side, I can nearly make it to the tree without being seen. While I do that, you'll stay up here. This dune is higher than the others, so you'll have a good vantage point in case I need help. Watch for me as I'm crawling, and when I'm nearly at the tree, I'll signal you. When I do, work your way down the back side of this dune and once you're at the bottom, use your gun to fire a shot in the air. Then you run as fast as you can around on the outside of the basin, out of sight behind the dunes to that root line over there at the nine o'clock position. That's the one that leads back to your living room. All the Malus in the basin are going to start rushing toward the noise of the gunshot, but if you run hard, you should have enough of a head start that you can get far enough away to where they won't see you. You'll be lost behind the dunes. While those Malus are off chasing the noise, I'll be able to get at that Mortem Cor plant, torch it, then run to meet you at that root line, and we'll both race out of here before the Malus know what hit them!"

Parch had finished in a flurry of excitement, but Jason was hardly convinced. “You want me to be bait?!” Jason asked incredulously, his heart already wavering.

“Only for a moment,” Parch said. “By the time those Malus reach halfway up this dune, I’ll have the tree lit, and we’ll be on our way out. If we do it fast, they’ll never see us.”

Jason stared back in a horrified silence. How could that be the plan?

Parch sighed. “Look, I hate it too,” Parch replied, “but we have to try.” He took a deep breath, then looked at Jason solemnly. “You’re my backup, okay? If they see me while I’m crawling down there, I’ll be counting on you. Do what you can from here; try and take out as many as you can.” Parch paused. His tone was turning increasingly somber. “But if things start to look hopeless, you’ll have to get out of here by yourself. Follow the root line back out to your living room. The connection is incomplete, but the bridge is open, so you should be able to squeeze through. Once you’re home, use that knife to get out of the house and get far away. Okay?”

Something about Parch’s tone was unsettling. “There are so many root lines down there. You’re sure that’s the right one?” Jason asked.

“It should be that one,” Parch said, pointing at a root line positioned counterclockwise to them running out from the Mortem Cor plant. “Nine o’clock position.”

“*Should* be?” Jason asked.

"It's that one," Parch said. "It's not any of the others, so it has to be that one."

Jason stared back, but Parch didn't give him time for any more questions. Instead, he reached over and unsnapped the strap that held Jason's pistol in its holster.

Jason's eyes looked down at his pistol then down at the sand beneath him. His hand wiped across his mouth as he struggled with the fear infesting his heart. But after a moment he once more looked back at Parch.

"You with me on this?" Parch asked.

Jason nodded and drew his own pistol.

Parch slapped Jason on the shoulder then crawled back from the crest and got to his feet. "This is going to work, I promise," Parch said with a smile. "And remember, wait for my signal before you move." With that, Parch turned and started making his way down the backside of the dune, moving toward the root line at the four o'clock position that he'd indicated.

Half-walking, half-sliding down the back side of the massive dune, Parch was at times up to his knees in the fine, powdered sand. The root line he was to crawl alongside ran into the basin over an adjacent sand dune along the lip of the basin. Despite being a part of the same basin perimeter as the massive one he and Jason had climbed, this adjacent sand dune was significantly lower, and the drop in elevation made his trek much easier. He descended the dune, heading toward the root line.

As he watched Parch leave, Jason suddenly felt even more vulnerable. He was now alone in this terrible place he didn't understand. Every last feeling of safety and confidence he had left vanished as he watched Parch move farther away. It was just him up here now, in this place.

His breathing became faster and more ragged. He instinctively looked behind him, back down the dune, his eyes darting around searching for threats. He clenched his teeth and cursed himself for his foolishness. Why had he been so stupid to come in here?

Closing his eyes, Jason tried to calm down. *Remember the plan. I just have to walk back down the dune, fire a shot in the air, then run to the root line that leads out.* The root line! Jason peaked over the crest and stared at the root line that Parch had said led home. That was the way out. No matter what happened, he could get out that way.

His eyes shifted to Parch, who was still descending the back side of the dune, then to the Malus, then Parch again. His heart felt tight in his chest and his resolve was hanging by a thread. He squeezed the pistol in his hand and wished for it all to be over.

Parch arrived at the crest of the new, smaller, adjacent sand dune. Like the larger dune Jason was still perched on, this dune too served in forming the perimeter of the basin, making up a section of the "side" of the "bowl." The new root line ran over the crest of this dune, then down the slope and into the basin before ultimately connecting to the tree. The root line was almost a meter tall and would make great cover for Parch as he crawled alongside it toward the Mortem Cor plant. He would remain hidden so long as the Malus remained clustered and preoccupied on the one side of the root line while he crawled on the other side. Parch peaked over the dune's crest and saw the Malus just as they were before — a good sign. He then stealthily climbed over to the far side of the root line and positioned himself in preparation to enter the basin.

Jason looked back at the Malus in the basin. Whatever creature was in the tangled roots was holding their attention. The same hissing rattle from before echoed from the tangle, and the situation reminded Jason of a speech, or maybe of a general giving orders. Whatever it was, it was gravely unnerving, but at least it kept the Malus' attention.

His eyes drifted once more to the root line at nine o'clock and lingered there. *This could all be over*, he thought. *I could go home right now.* The storm in his heart was turbulent and chaotic. His thoughts betrayed him, and he could only think of one thing. He grimaced as he struggled under the weight of his distress and shook his head, trying to clear his mind. But the singular thought remained.

His turmoil was interrupted when movement in the corner of his eye drew his attention. Parch was vehemently waving at him from the lower sand dune. Jason turned and looked at him. Parch looked annoyed, like he'd been waving for some time. Once he made eye contact, Parch stopped waving and held up a thumbs-up gesture and waited for it to be returned. But instead of responding in kind, Jason responded with an awkward mix of a nod combined with some kind of a strange head bob. Weird.

Parch's head tilted and his brow furrowed as he looked up at Jason's gesture, but he ultimately shrugged, returned a nod, and turned back toward the basin. Now that Jason was watching, Parch prepared to descend into the basin.

Jason sat up and watched nervously. Once Parch crossed over the top of the dune, he would be fully visible to the Malus in the basin until he made it to ground level. If any of the Malus turned around and looked Parch's way as he descended the slope of the dune, they would see him, and all would be lost. Jason looked over at the Malus and saw they were all still preoccupied. A good sign, but Jason still covered his face with his free hand, watching through spread fingers. Before Jason was mentally ready, Parch began.

Parch smoothly crawled over the crest of the dune in one motion. He hit the other side and stayed crawling on his stomach, letting his falling momentum carry him down the slope. It took only a few seconds before he reached the floor of the basin, and once he did, he laid still. But as he laid there, a cloud of dust that he'd kicked up during his descent drifted over him and into the basin.

Jason, who had watched the whole thing, breathless from the peak of the large sand dune, panicked at the oversight. The dust cloud was like a giant sign saying: "Here I am, Malus, come and kill me." Jason sunk lower behind the dune and watched the Malus. His mind and heart racked with apprehension, he waited for the seemingly inevitable moment when Parch would be discovered. Feeling utterly powerless, he cowered behind the sand and fretted. And all his fears were confirmed when he saw one of the Malus in the back of the group turn and look in Parch's direction, and stare at the dust cloud.

Jason froze in terror. He couldn't speak — he couldn't breathe — he could only watch. His mind screamed at him to run, to save himself. *It's over!* he thought.

But then the Malus in question finished scratching itself, and obliviously turned back toward the tangle, looking at the creature hidden in the roots, who was now building to a crescendo with its grotesque noises.

Jason exhaled in exasperation. Parch had nearly gotten caught, and it was only the start. Despite the relief of not being discovered, Jason couldn't calm down and remained at that extremely heightened stress level. His heart couldn't take another scare.

The dust cloud dissipated, and Parch was hidden behind the root line. Not even Jason could see him now. All that was left to do was wait and watch.

Seconds felt like hours as Jason laid there at the crest of the dune. He squirmed about nervously in the sand, adjusting his legs and arms, continually checking behind him for Malus. Despite the cool night air, his arm pits were soaked with sweat.

After a few torturous minutes without sight of Parch, Jason started to hear noises around him. It sounded like something small was moving around in the sand nearby. Even more unnerving, it wasn't just coming from one spot, there were several sources.

Panicked, Jason froze, hoping that if he didn't move, he wouldn't be noticed. But the gritty noises of the moving sand continued, and as his heart rate spiked he became more frantic and started to look around. He saw only sand, and everything appeared fine, when he suddenly felt a sharp pain in his ankle. He reflexively jerked his leg away, and when he did, he dragged from out of the sand a small creature that had bitten into his boot.

The small Malus was eight inches long. It had the body of a fish, and four froglike legs. Dull, mindless eyes occupied the space above its mouth, staring out at nothing and completely unfocused. Its body was gray and yellow and blended in with the sand. It reeked of the smell of rotten fish. Its mouth had several needlelike teeth sticking out that were each five centimeters long, and with these it had bitten into and attached itself to Jason's boot.

When Jason saw it stuck to his boot, he kicked his leg hysterically and the thing flew off into the sand nearby. It flopped about clumsily on the surface of the sand, making gurgling noises.

Horrified, Jason stared at the fishlike Malus, unsure of what to do. He recoiled from it, but as he backed up, he heard half a dozen more of the same type of Malus emerging from the sand around him.

Jason bolted to his feet and backed away from the dune crest. His sudden movement, however, provoked the Malus. The one that had bit him let out a loud ear-piercing scream. When the others heard it, they did the same.

Jason's fragile mind cracked. "Shut up! They'll hear you!" he whispered as he reached down and threw a handful of sand at one of the screaming fiends. But the sand did nothing to stop it, and the screams only grew louder.

Overcome by the terror of being discovered, Jason turned and ran. He initially meant to only run a few meters away, just to get a little distance between him and the fishlike Malus. But when he reached that distance, his legs refused to stop. The inertia and the fear pushed him on. Soon he was sprinting full speed down the back of the dune, running clockwise around the basin toward the root line that led home.

When Jason realized he wasn't stopping, something deep inside rebelled against him. He briefly thought of firing his gun into the air, fulfilling his part of the plan, but his hands refused to grab the pistol. Instead, he just kept running. Feelings of anger and disappointment flooded in, but just as quickly as they came those feelings were silenced by a few simple thoughts. *I can't be here. I can't fight those things. I can't do any of this,* he thought. *I'm sorry, Parch, I can't help you. I'm sorry.*

****

Parch was nearing halfway along his journey to the tree. He had been right, and the root line had provided excellent cover, but the crawling was hard work. His hands and knees were scuffed from the hard-packed dirt, and the stench from the root line stung his nostrils, but he crawled regardless.

He was getting close to the group of Malus now, and he could hear them just on the other side. Their mindless barks and grunts were confirmation that they hadn't moved, and the loud hissing rattle echoing through the basin from the creature in the tangle suggested they were still preoccupied.

But as he crawled, he heard something that almost sounded like screaming. It was faint and muffled by the distance. He couldn't be sure, but it seemed to be coming from the large sand dune that loomed behind him, the one where Jason was. Parch stopped crawling, turned to look over his shoulder, and leaned away from the root line so he could get a better angle to see the large sand dune. He squinted, but there wasn't much to see. He could only see the front side; he couldn't see the back side where Jason was, so if something was happening, he had no way of knowing. Soon the hiss rattle grew so loud that it drowned out every other sound, and Parch was left to wonder.

Parch lay silent, grinding his teeth as his eyes darted around. He looked again at the sand dune, then back the way he'd come, then forward toward the Mortem Cor plant, and then finally back again toward the large sand dune. He stared intently, but still saw nothing. After a few moments of thought, he turned and resumed his crawl toward the Mortem Cor plant.

****

With a loud hiss, the veiled monstrosity beneath the Mortem Cor plant concluded its ghastly oration then stuck its pincered appendage out of the tangle once more. This time, it pointed up toward the branches of the tree. All the Malus looked and saw what it was pointing at: high up on the outermost branches — the ones that reached out over the boundary between the basin and sand dunes — was another white flower.

After seeing the flower, the Malus all eagerly surged toward it; but the creature in the tangle let out a terrible hiss, and the Malus obediently stopped. With order now restored, the basin went silent. All the Malus were motionless, captivated by the flower above. Then, almost as if on cue, a gentle breeze blew through the tree branches, and the flower broke free and began to fall.

****

The feelings of anger and disappointment in himself only grew as Jason kept running. But despite the outrage flowing from his heart, his legs didn't stop. *Parch does this all the time,* he thought. *He'll be fine on his own. There's nothing I can do.* But all the excuses and justifications did nothing to alleviate the pain in his heart. He was abandoning Parch, and there was no mistaking it.

He had reached the bottom of the large sand dune and was now circling around the basin. Keeping to the back side of the sand dunes that made up the basin perimeter, Jason ran in the low points in the sea of sand dunes, keeping hidden and out of sight. He couldn't hear the screams of the fish Malus anymore, but whether that was because they stopped screaming or because he was too far away, he didn't know. His only objective now was to find the root line that led home, and he knew if he continued following the basin perimeter around, he would run into it eventually.

****

Parch hadn't crawled ten meters before he'd looked back three times at the large sand dune. Each time he did, everything looked the same; nothing was revealed about the strange noise he'd heard. And to add to it all, the creature in the tangle had sounded one last loud hiss rattle, then all the Malus had gone silent.

What is going on? Has something happened to Jason? Have they found him? Why did they all go quiet? Whatever was happening, it couldn't be good.

****

The crowd of Malus all watched in unison as the precious flower floated down from the high branches. It fell slowly and delicately, drifting down toward the ground. The impatient Malus stared at the flower with rapt attention and jostled for position at the front of the mob. But all were being held in check by the creature in the tangle. Like a master controlling a pack of dogs, the creature kept them from rushing forward while the flower was falling. It hissed aggressively whenever any Malus pressed ahead in front of the others. But when the flower touched the ground, the game would be on.

****

The silence was deafening and Parch couldn't take it anymore; he had to know what was happening. He stopped crawling and sat up slightly, rising to the very edge of the top of the root line. Then, after a breath to steady himself, he slowly and cautiously peered over the top of the roots. All the Malus had their backs to him. He relaxed and sat up a little higher, trying to see what was happening. The Malus seemed to be intently staring at something in the sky, off toward the other side of the basin.

Parch squinted hard, trying to determine what the Malus were all looking at, and then he saw it. There was a white flower floating down from the topmost branches, and it was going to fall between two small sand dunes on the border of the basin. It had already fallen most of the way down and was quickly approaching the ground.

****

Jason suspected he was nearing the root line that would lead him home. He had circled clockwise around the basin and, driven by his fear, had covered quite the distance in the short amount of time. But he soon arrived at a predicament. Up to this point, he had been hidden from the basin behind the dunes. But up ahead, Jason saw there was a section where this would no longer be possible.

In front of him, the next two consecutive sand dunes running along the boundary were incongruously smaller than the rest that encircled the basin. They were so small that Jason would likely have to duck down as he passed behind them to make sure he wouldn't be seen over the top. And to make matters worse, there was a gap between them — a stretch of open ground that was completely naked and visible to the basin interior. If Jason continued on his planned route, he would have to cross this short space where he would be completely exposed.

Overwrought, Jason glanced around, hoping to find another way. But there were no easy answers here. The only way to avoid this open stretch would be for him to backtrack and head farther into the sand dunes, costing precious time and possibly getting him lost for his trouble. Jason cursed. He felt like the walls were closing in on him. He didn't have a second to spare. He had to get out of here.

In a frenzied, split-second decision, Jason decided to just sprint through the section, hoping the Malus would be looking anywhere else. He lowered his head and surged into the fastest sprint he'd ever run. Jason passed by the first small sand dune and moved into the open ground, desperately hoping nothing was looking. He ran as hard as he could; but in the middle of the stretch, something light and delicate fell in front of him and brushed across his face. The sudden, unexpected touch caused him to trip and tumble to the ground. He flopped onto the soft sand, which cushioned his impact. An instant after the fall, he was up and looking back, questioning what he'd run into. He saw a meter behind him, lying in the sand, a white flower.

CHAPTER 7

Jason choked on his own breath as he stared in wide-eyed horror at the army of Malus looking right at him. His mind went blank and his entire body seized up, unable to move. Despite the ear-splitting howls that rang through the basin as the Malus surged in one body toward him, Jason's ears didn't even register the sound. All he could manage was to clumsily fall backward into the sand and watch as the beasts barreled down on him.

Running on all fours, the clumsy beasts fought each other as they jockeyed for position. They were all pulling, pushing, and grabbing in their bloodthirsty, headlong dash toward Jason. It would be only seconds before they were upon him. But then Jason saw a white flash erupt from behind the mob of Malus, followed by a white bolt blast through the mob of Malus with incredible speed and slam into a sand dune twenty meters to his side. It was all concluded by what sounded like a loud crack of thunder that echoed through the basin.

****

Parch lowered his pistol and looked over the carnage. He'd fired into the pack but had been careful not to hit Jason. The round had devastated nearly a dozen Malus, blasting an outsized hole in any that were in line with the shot. The Malus who had been hit and were still alive rolled on the ground and howled in pain, their entire bodies broken and bleeding.

The sudden, deafening thunderous crack from the pistol, as well as the blinding flash of light, sent even those Malus not hit by the round into a stumbling panic. Confused and disoriented, they tripped and fell over each other in animalistic fear, partially scattering. This confusion bought Jason the seconds he needed to rise and flee into the dunes.

Parch then returned his focus to the mighty Mortem Cor plant. But as he looked at the tangle, the creature inside let out a terrible hissing rattle. The disordered mob of Malus snapped to attention and, after more hideous sounds from the creature, split into two groups — one chasing Jason and one rushing toward Parch.

Shocked by this precise coordination, Parch hesitated. He looked toward the tree, his purpose and objective, then back toward the group of Malus now quickly advancing on him. It only took a split second for him to realize he couldn't make it to the tree. He wasn't close enough; the Malus would cut him off before he could reach it. Parch roared a curse, then ripped the torch off his shoulder and touched it to the root line — a last-ditch effort.

The extraordinary flame took to the root line like a blowtorch to a gasoline-soaked rag. The roots were instantly engulfed in the green fire, which spread swiftly, racing down both directions of the root line. But as the fire quickly approached the tree, the root line, as if alive, tore itself from the tangled base, and flung itself back and away. The massive weight of the root line's new end came crashing down onto the basin's floor several dozen meters away from the Mortem Cor plant. As the root line burned, the deadly tree stood strong and unaffected.

Parch's stomach dropped. There was nothing more he could do. The smallest and quickest Malus of the pack was nearly upon him; there was no hope of getting to the tree now. Parch uncoiled the living chain around his arm and lashed out at the nimble Malus barreling down on him. The living chain pulled itself through the air, adding its own strength to Parch's, and struck the Malus with tremendous force, shattering its face and sending it sprawling. After one last look at the tree, Parch turned and retreated, heading for the dunes.

****

Jason was running mindlessly. There was no plan or destination; he ran like a scared animal. Because of the adrenaline coursing through his veins, he didn't feel the exhaustion or notice the blankness of his mind. He ran faster than he had ever run before, but it wasn't enough. The group of Malus chasing him were still gaining on him.

Looking over his shoulder, he saw the pack. He could see the lust for violence in their eyes. He could see the all-consuming desire of a predator chasing its prey. It terrified Jason even more, if that were possible. He pushed on, running deeper and deeper into the dunes with the howls following closely behind.

Jason had stayed in the valleys so far because it was easier to run, but as he turned a corner, he saw that was no longer an option. The two dunes on either side merged, and the valley ended. He would be forced to climb. With the howls getting closer, he started up the closest dune. It was slow going, with the soft, fine sand giving with each step. The Malus were at the bottom of the hill before Jason was halfway up. With certain death so close, Jason pulled his pistol and fired haphazardly at the group.

There was an ear-shattering crack, and the gun jerked back hard. But this was no ordinary firearm. Once the bullet had travelled a meter and a half on its course, it exploded again. This secondary explosion was confined into a two-dimensional shockwave that expanded perpendicularly to the bullet's direction of travel, spreading in front of Jason like a bright white, ring of fire and cutting a fine line in the sand in front of him. It also boomed so loud that it rattled Jason's teeth. Thanks to this extra detonation, the bullet's speed more than quintupled and turned it into a streak of blinding white light.

The astonishing light show and accompanying thunderous boom startled both Jason and the Malus. But the shot missed badly and, after a second of bewilderment, the Malus resumed the chase. Jason cursed himself for missing as he pulled the trigger again several times, but nothing happened. He looked at the gun and saw that the formerly glowing runes along the barrel had gone completely dark, and remembered they needed to recharge. "Come on, come on!" he screamed as he resumed trudging up the dune, now nearing the crest. But as he got to the top, he looked down and saw that the clumsy Malus were having even more trouble than he had had at managing the slope. They were also their own worst enemies, selfishly pulling and grabbing at those ahead of them. Each time a Malus got out in front it was pulled back by several others. To his great relief, Jason realized he was gaining ground.

As he reached the top, Jason saw the runes on his gun were glowing brightly again. This time, he tried his best to aim, and fired. Again he missed. But it did startle the Malus and buy Jason a few more seconds. Instead of running down the other side of the sand dune, Jason decided to run along the crest, hoping the Malus would continue to struggle. And he was right. As Jason ran, they continually fell and tripped over themselves, grasping and clutching at the others. Jason was gaining even more distance. He breathed a sigh of relief and finally had a moment of clearheadedness.

On top of the dune, he could see for miles. The aurora waved and shimmered above him, sending down its blood-red light. A cool wind dried his sweat. He thought he could see mountains in the distance. But the beauty of his surroundings was lost on him as he scanned the area, looking for his way home as he ran. By some miracle, Jason saw that he'd been running in the same direction as the root line Parch had indicated. He saw parts of it peeking out several dunes over. He also saw he could follow the crest he was on to a place where it intersected with the roots' path. He ran carefully along the dune and started making his way there.

But as Jason ran, a nagging thought returned. He looked back the way he'd come, scanning for Parch. He saw the pack of Malus becoming increasingly more frustrated with the inability to manage the slope, but beyond that he just saw the peaceful waves of sand dunes, a few root lines burning in the distance, and the mighty Mortem Cor plant towering over all. He had no idea what had happened to Parch, no idea if Parch was still alive. And here he was, trying to save his own skin.

The Malus behind howled in rage as they saw their prey escaping. And, to Jason's horror, their howl was answered. Another howl sounded from the dunes in front of Jason. And then another from the dunes off to the right. Jason couldn't see the Malus that answered, but it was clear they were close. He was being surrounded. This fear drove him on faster, and he ran along the crest with less caution and more speed.

He quickly covered the distance to the root line, all the while scanning the areas in between the dunes, searching for more Malus attempting to join the chase. The howls continued to surround him, but he didn't see any yet. Thankfully, Jason had put about one hundred meters between him and the Malus behind him, and it was all thanks to his strategy with the dunes. But he'd have to leave the safety of the dune crest now to meet up with the root line.

The roots ran at the bottom of a valley, twisting and turning through the mountains of sand dunes. They left Jason no choice but to descend to join them. As Jason started running down the slope to meet the roots, he realized he had no way of knowing just how far it was to the bridge. One hundred feet? One thousand miles? He cursed, and his whole body clenched at the thought of his only exit being so far out of reach, but he had no choice except to continue running.

The soft, forgiving sand made his run downhill easy, and he was soon at the root line. Similar to the last one, this new root line was a linear tangled mass of roots at least a meter in diameter, all various sizes, twisted together and running off in a single direction. Jason was relieved to have found his path home.

Looking at the root line, Jason decided to climb on top of it to get out of the sand. The top of the root line was uneven and irregular, but at least it was solid, unlike the yielding sand. Jason found he could run on top of the root line faster and with less effort, so long as he was careful enough to maintain his balance.

Jason looked back over his shoulder to see where the Malus were and saw they had crested the last dune and were now flooding into the valley. They were still a hundred or so meters behind, but there were now many more than there had been originally. They were filling the valley behind him like a swarm of locusts. He couldn't outrun them forever. He needed to quickly find that bridge.

The root line curved around another dune and led into a straight valley a couple hundred meters long. This gave Jason a chance to speed up, and so he did. His heart thumped in his ears, almost drowning out the howls resounding around him. He was nearly a quarter of the way through the valley when disaster struck. Ahead of him, on his left side, a swarm of Malus emerged over the top of the sand dune and started charging down.

Even from a distance, Jason could see these new Malus' eyes were full of violence, and he could feel their bloodlust and their eagerness to tear him to pieces. Their jaws dripped with anticipation as they raced down toward the root line. They looked to be trying to intercept him and cut off his exit from the valley.

Despite the panic-inducing sight of the Malus, Jason saw that if he was fast, he might be able to beat the Malus to the point where their paths would intersect. He didn't see any more Malus beyond this new pack, so if he passed them before they made it down from the dune to the root line, he'd have a straight shot out of the valley, thereby escaping the trap. If not, he'd be encircled, with Malus in front and behind. It was going to be close, but it was his only chance.

Jason ran hard, but so did the Malus. The fastest Malus of the pack pulled ahead of the rest, and as Jason approached the intersection of their paths, he noticed this lone Malus would beat him there. It was then that he remembered his gun. Pointing in their general direction, Jason fired.

The gun put forth another amazing display. The rapid double explosion rattled through Jason's body, and the bright white ring that expanded out in front of him was beautiful. The sharp smell of burnt gun powder filled the air. Jason could feel the power as he held the pistol. But sadly, all that power was poorly aimed, and the white streaking projectile missed the Malus and hit nothing but sand. Fortunately for Jason, however, the resulting flash and deafening crack startled the Malus enough to buy Jason a few precious seconds.

Jason sprinted past the intercepting Malus with only centimeters between him and their reaching claws. But it was enough. He slipped by them and continued running along the root line toward the valley exit. He'd escaped being encircled, and now was running harder than he had ever run before, urged on by the howls and panting now behind him.

The group of Malus joined with the rest behind Jason and became one giant mass. And they weren't the only ones who joined. The host grew every second as Malus from all directions joined in the pursuit. The air was filled with howls and roars. But as more appeared, the more they all fought each other to be first. Each Malus clawed and bit at every other Malus in front of it. The fighting slowed them all considerably, and eventually turned into a great melee. Enraged, the Malus all fought savagely, forgetting about Jason entirely, and began tearing at each other with the violence they had intended for Jason.

All the while Jason kept running. He turned corner after corner, following the root line and working his way through the dunes, until eventually the sound of the Malus diminished. He was drenched in sweat, and not even the night air could cool him off. His heart was beating out of his chest and his breathing was ragged. Eventually, he slowed to a trot, but still continued on. He had to get out of here.

After turning another corner, the maze of sand dunes abruptly stopped. Jason found himself on the edge of a vast, flat area several miles across. The dunes resumed on the other side, as well as encircled the area along its edges. The ground was dark, pitch-black even, and the root ran straight ahead for a hundred yards, then dove underground. Jason was hopeful he'd found the end, so he pressed forward to get a closer look. But as he got closer, he heard a faint trickling sound. Water? He walked forward and, soon enough, felt his boots turn cold and damp as he walked ankle-deep into water. The revelation sent shivers down his spine and his hopes plummeted. This was indeed a vast, calm lake.

Staring down into the water, he couldn't see more than an inch below the surface. It was pitch-black and opaque; the red light from above barely penetrated the surface. Jason shivered at the thought of what secrets a lake in this horrible place might hold. The root line ran directly into the lake and disappeared. Jason began to realize the consequences of this. How deep was the lake? How deep did the root go? Was there anything in the lake? Was this even water? Jason's already frayed mind was tearing even more. This was an insurmountable obstacle. Jason threw his hands on his head and grimaced. Hadn't he been through enough? Standing on the shore, Jason cursed.

A familiar boom sounded from the dunes and broke Jason out of his stupor. A gunshot? Parch! Jason turned and saw Parch cresting a nearby sand dune. Jason jumped and waved, shouting at the top of his lungs in happiness, but his joy faded when the terrible howls came. Parch was being chased by his own host of Malus, and they were flooding over the sand dune in pursuit.

Parch was in a poor state as he sprinted toward Jason. He was breathing hard, and his clothes were ripped in several places from Malus attacks. His face told a story of pain and exhaustion. But none of this slowed him.

"Go!" Parch screamed. "The bridge is close!"

"The roots go into the water!" Jason screamed back. "It's too dark; I can't see where it goes!"

Hearing this, Parch ran nearer to the root line, then pulled the torch and dragged its flame along it as he ran. The green flame caught and spread just as quickly as before. Flying along the surface of the roots, the strange fire reached the water and continued on shooting down the root line, unhindered. The water had no effect on the flame at all, and it burned the roots underwater just the same as above. The fire also turned the root line into a blazing pathway to the bridge, its green light partially illuminating the dark lake.

As Jason watched the flame spread, he marveled at its apathy toward the water. He now saw that the root line ran only a moderate way into the lake, and that the bridge was on the bottom, about ten meters below the surface. But despite knowing the path, his fear at entering the water hadn't diminished. The green ·light, though evident, radiated only so far before being consumed by the oppressive darkness of the water. The vast lake remained mostly opaque except for the relatively small area around the burning roots.

While Jason stared into the water, Parch finally caught up to him. But Parch didn't stop; he charged past Jason, into the lake, and was soon pushing through waste-high water. Parch turned when he realized Jason hadn't followed him.

"Come on!" Parch screamed.

"I-I can't," Jason stuttered.

While Jason hesitated, three smaller Malus bounded toward him. These three were faster and nimbler than the rest, and they had raced ahead of the pack. They were nearly upon Jason, emitting a high-pitched screech as they prepared to lunge.

Hearing this, Jason screamed and stumbled into the water, but his movements were too slow to avoid the impending attack.

Parch, conversely, reacted with military precision and speed. In one fluid motion he drew his pistol and shot. The bullet fired and, with perfect spacing, the secondary explosion detonated in front of Jason, narrowly missing him due to its restricted nature. The bright white streak obliterated one of the Malus. With two Malus remaining, Parch charged forward to protect Jason.

As the two Malus lunged at Jason, Parch reached the other man and threw him out of the way. In that moment, the chain on Parch's arm leapt toward one of the Malus and intercepted it mid-lunge. The chain ensnared the Malus, binding it and dragging it down into the water, leaving only one remaining Malus to be dealt with.

The last Malus's full weight crashed into Parch. The two fell into the water, the Malus attacking Parch with tremendous ferocity. It bit and scratched and howled and screamed. Parch tried to defend, putting up his forearms to shield himself, as the Malus raked its claws over him. The Malus bit down hard into Parch's left arm. Parch grunted in pain, but then used the Malus's attack to his advantage. With the Malus distracted, Parch used his free arm to draw his knife. With his bound arm, Parch pulled the Malus in close, then stabbed his knife into the Malus's chest. The Malus let go of Parch's arm and howled in pain. But Parch wasn't finished. As the Malus tried to pull away, Parch grabbed it by the throat, then slammed his knife into the creature's skull.

Without a pause, Parch threw the now lifeless Malus away, then leapt on the last living Malus — the one still bound with the chain. He ruthlessly stabbed into the Malus's head, killing it instantly. Afterward, the chain uncoiled from its lifeless captive and returned to Parch's arm.

But there was no time to celebrate the triumph. The army of Malus was only seconds away. Parch pulled Jason up from where he lay stunned in the water, and they both started pushing deeper into the lake.

They followed the burning root and were soon swimming in chest-high water. Despite the distortion of the water, it was easy to see where the root line vanished, and thus where the bridge was. It wasn't far, but it was at the bottom. They'd have to swim down to it.

As the Malus host arrived at the shoreline, Parch dove underwater and started swimming down toward the bridge. He swam hard and without hesitation. They were almost to the safety of the Abyss. The green torch burning on his shoulder shone like a beacon for Jason to follow.

Jason hesitated at the surface, but only for a moment. There wasn't any other choice; the Malus were in the water advancing toward him — he had to follow Parch down. So, he gulped down as much air as he could, and dove under. The cold water stung his eyes as he swam down. His body immediately started calling for air, despite the deep breath he had taken. His fear and anxiety caused his body to quickly burn through the precious oxygen. But he swam for the bridge all the same.

Under the water was a mix of light and dark. The fire burned the root line and shone with green light that danced in the swirling, shifting waves. It all combined to make an incredible show, but one that made visibility suspect. Jason could hardly tell how far down the bridge was, or if the shadows around him were real or just the product of the shifting flame and fluid environment.

Parch showed no concern for the darkness or the shadows. He swam ahead of Jason straight for the bridge. Ahead of them both, the root line turned and vanished into a dark hole located at the bottom of the lake. That was their goal: the bridge.

The bridge was on the floor of the lake, amid the sand and mud. The green fire illuminated everything around it and burned right up to the bridge. But the flames didn't pass through into the Abyss. The void fingers, the black smoke tendrils that had scared Jason before, consumed the fire at the mouth of the bridge and stopped it from spreading along the roots into the Abyss.

The bridge itself was three meters in diameter, and thus much larger than the previous bridges the two men had passed through to get here. But despite being much wider, the entire bridge was filled completely with roots. The roots blocked up the bridge as if it were a clogged drain. There was no way through.

Undeterred, Parch swam down and grabbed the roots. He drew his knife and plunged it into the wood. The knife cut just as easily as ever, while Parch began hacking away. He focused on clearing away a single, small section. He didn't have to open up everything, just enough for the two of them to get through.

Above Parch, Jason was still struggling. He swam slowly toward the torch, awkwardly kicking and thrashing in his best attempt to move through the water. But he was starting to worry there was something down here besides Parch and himself. It was impossible to be sure, but Jason kept seeing shapes in the darkness. First on his left side, and then on his right. All he could do was tell himself it was nothing and continue swimming. But as he was nearing Parch, something brushed up against Jason's leg. He panicked, and all the air in his lungs escaped as he tried to scream. Then, in exponentially increasing terror, he tried to breathe again and inhaled water. He started to flail wildly.

To make matters worse, the shapes in the darkness grew larger and more defined. It was no trick; something was down here with him, and it was moving fast. Jason thrashed about involuntarily as his body screamed for oxygen, and his stupefied mind went blank. And in this helpless state, his eyes saw a giant, meter-wide mouth full of teeth swimming directly at him.

But just before Jason was devoured, he felt a hand grab his leg and yank him down. As the jaws snapped shut, Jason was dragged clear and pulled down through the bridge.

CHAPTER 8

Like a drain being unclogged, the weight of the water in the lake pushed clear the now weakened roots that had blocked up the bridge. The water rushed into the Abyss, dragging Jason down with it. Tumbling through the currents, Jason became disoriented and had no idea where he was or what was going on. The strength of the water slammed him into root after root, and he was dragged along violently for several meters until finally crashing onto a hard, flat surface. Now, as if under a large waterfall, torrents of cascading water smashed down on him, pressing him against the strange horizontal platform he'd fallen upon.

The oppressive weight of the water crashing down from above made it difficult to move. On top of that, Jason was still completely confused. He was seconds away from drowning, but his survival instincts kicked in. Fighting hard to crawl out from under the thousands of gallons of water pouring down on him, Jason pulled himself along the flat surface until he finally made it out of the path of the flow. He burst into the open and coughed up all the water he'd swallowed, then gasped for air.

Looking over, Jason saw Parch nearby, having also escaped from the waterfall. Finally out of danger, both men now collapsed onto the roots, coughing and gasping.

The bridge they had fallen through was ten meters above them. The roots ran downward into the Abyss from the bridge and spread into a loose tangle much like the one they had climbed through when they first entered from Jason's basement. The water from the lake above flooded in and down this loosely tangled column of roots. This was what Parch and Jason had been pulled through so violently. But once the roots, running downward in their course, reached the level where Jason and Parch currently lay, they all inexplicably ordered themselves together, forming a flat, level, horizontal platform. It was almost like a walkway several meters wide. The water cascaded down through the roots, and then, once it hit the platform, spilled off into oblivion. The root platform ran from this root column to another bridge thirty meters behind Parch and Jason. This would be their way out, and it would lead back to Jason's living room.

As the two men laid there recovering, a terrible, guttural cry sounded in the Abyss, audible even over the sound of the rushing water. They both looked up the waterfall, wondering what foul fate would befall them now. In the darkness of the Abyss, it was difficult to see the source of the noises. Parch eventually found it, then spotlighted it with his flashlight. There, caught in the roots, struggling and making all sorts of gurgling noises, was the sharklike Malus that had almost devoured Jason.

The monster had been caught in the same vortex that had pulled down both men. Unable to swim hard enough to escape the flow, it had been dragged into the Abyss and was too large to pass through some of the thicker sections of roots. Now as if in a net, it was caught halfway up the root column, squirming and fighting in vain to break free.

As the creature struggled, nearby void fingers started to drift toward it. The first wisp of darkness to reach it gently poked at the Malus. This seemingly harmless act sent the Malus into an extreme panic. It struggled and fought even harder, screeching and howling in pain. It tried to recoil from the void fingers, but there was nowhere for it to go.

The surrounding void fingers, having tasted their prey, began forcefully and eagerly stabbing into the Malus, attacking it from every angle and causing it to scream all the louder. The void fingers cut into the Malus's flesh, and every part they touched dissolved into nothingness. The Malus was quickly being cut to pieces. Soon the guttural cries vanished, and only large chunks of carcass remained. These chunks of flesh fell free from the roots but didn't travel far before they were caught and obliterated by more hungry void fingers waiting below.

Mesmerized, Parch and Jason watched. Once it was over, however, and the creature had been obliterated, Parch collapsed once more. Conversely, Jason had a different reaction. Seeing what the void fingers had just done set him on edge. He looked apprehensively at the wisps encircling him, worried they would do to him what they had just done to the Malus. But just as before, the playful wisps reached out, harmlessly touched him, then dispersed back into the darkness. After several more void fingers repeated the benign action, and after seeing Parch seem totally unconcerned, Jason fell back to recover as well, hoping that the terrible power of the void fingers was reserved for the Malus alone.

Both men lay there, soaking in the profound peace of the Abyss. In the midst of the infinite void, with the pleasant sound of the cascading water, there was a calming serenity. It was a much-needed safe haven from the terror they had just experienced.

After a few minutes of rest, Parch sat up and began inspecting his arms. Carefully, he took his knife and cut away the shredded bits of his sleeves that the Malus had destroyed. The discarded bits of the shirt revealed more about its makeup. On top was a sturdy canvas material, but underneath it had been reinforced with the same strong type of fibers used to make bulletproof vests. This protection provided by the shirt had served Parch well, taking the brunt of the bites and scratches. He had a few cuts that would need to be bandaged, but beyond that most of it was superficial. He took off his backpack and began taking out his medical supplies.

Jason watched Parch moving out of the corner of his eye, unable to fully look at the other man. Parch had received those injuries saving him from the Malus, and that fact caused a deep flood of shame in Jason's heart. Jason knew he was responsible for everything; it was all his fault. He felt disgraceful and humiliated, and for a time, he chose to pretend not to see Parch tending to his wounds. But as the silence dragged on, Jason couldn't stop himself from speaking.

"Are . . . are you all right?" Jason asked.

Parch ignored the question and continued bandaging his wounds.

"Did you get the plant?" Jason asked, even more timidly.

This time, Parch looked up at Jason and stared at him with cold eyes. "No," he said.

Jason wilted under Parch's gaze. He looked away, staring into the darkness of the Abyss.

"What happened back there?" Parch asked, his voice tense but restrained. "Why didn't you stick to the plan?"

Jason said nothing, and only turned further away.

"Everything was going great, then suddenly you disappeared from that dune," Parch continued, his voice growing more tense and less restrained. "Then the next time I see you, you're across the basin running for the root line. What's the idea? Abandon me and head for the exit?"

Jason's head drooped low. His entire body felt like it was contracting in on itself. His chest was tight, and his face was hot with shame.

"I was counting on you," Parch said quietly but no less angrily.

"I'm sorry," Jason replied, still unable to face the other man.

Parch shook his head contemptuously, then turned away from Jason and looked out into the darkness. "No, I didn't get the plant," he continued. "I burned several of the root lines, but they'll grow back, including the one leading to your basement. In a week, maybe longer, we'll be right back to square one. All of that was for nothing! The only difference will be that in that time, that tree will kill others. We had a chance to save people, and now that chance is gone."

Jason started to wonder if silence would have actually been the preferable option. Each word from Parch felt like a physical strike. He had no response. Deep down, Jason knew he deserved all the anger and frustration being hurled at him.

Closing his eyes, Parch drew in a deep breath then exhaled fully. "What's done is done," he said. "All we can do is go forward. I'll report all this up, and let the smart people figure out what to do. If we're lucky . . ." Parch stopped mid-sentence and stared at the roots.

Mouth agape in confusion and eyes darting around, Parch looked the whole tangled root column over, from where it first entered the bridge down to where the roots all oriented together to form the platform. His eyes squinted as he stared unblinkingly at where the roots all seemed to shift from running in their normal chaotic course to organizing, as if by design, and creating this unnatural shape. There were still a few errant branches sticking out from the platform, but contrasted with the messy tangle the roots were before, this change to uniformity and evenness was prominent and unmistakable.

"Something's wrong here," Parch said. "The roots shouldn't be like this; and there're too many." He pulled the torch off his shoulder and held it close to the roots, letting its light shine over them. He then leaned closer and looked intently at the wood.

Jason looked over nervously. “What now?” he asked, fearing the worst.

Parch shifted around, examining the wood from different angles. He fixed on a specific spot, then pulled back blinking rapidly and shaking his head, only to look again this time harder and more intently. “There are two sets of roots mixed together in here,” he said finally. “But . . . if there’s another set of roots in here,” he reasoned aloud, “then that must mean . . .” Without finishing his sentence, he turned and followed the roots with his eyes to the next bridge, the one further down the root platform.

The other bridge was located thirty meters away, and the roots led right to it. The void fingers obscured the view, but it looked like a light was shining through into the Abyss — much too bright of a light to be coming from a dimly lit living room.

Parch rose, looking suspiciously at the bridge. He glanced at Jason, who rose as well, and they both walked slowly toward the opening, unsure of what to expect. They approached the bridge, and it was clear whatever was on the other side wasn’t Jason’s living room. Instead, the two men saw grey rock and what appeared to be a skyline filled with white clouds.

“I don’t think that’s your living room,” Parch said.

Jason’s heart sank and he threw his hands on top of his head. He ground his teeth as he stared into the strange new environment. This was supposed to be over. They were supposed to be going home. "What's going on?" he asked frantically. "What is that?"

"Looks like another Ignotus," Parch responded, "with another Mortem Cor plant that these roots belong to."

That was the last thing Jason wanted to hear. He stepped back from the bridge. "Where's my living room?" he cried. "How do we get home?"

But Parch said nothing, and his only reply was the worried look on his face, which he tried to hide by continuing to peer through the bridge.

"You took us through the wrong one!" Jason said.

"This is the right one," Parch said. "I know how to read a root line!"

"Then why doesn't this go back to my living room?"

Parch stepped back from the bridge and furrowed his brow. He took a deep breath as he looked around. "That is a very good question," he said. "And it's not the only one." He looked down at the root platform. "Why are these roots so organized? And why was that plant so big? And why would two plants connect their roots like this at all? None of it makes sense!"

Brusquely, Parch started to walk around the root platform like a detective pacing around the scene of a crime. With his brow still furrowed, he looked over everything, scratching his chin and muttering to himself. He looked at the new bridge leading to the strange skyline. He knelt and looked at the root platform, then walked the full length back to the waterfall and root column they had fallen down. Staring up at the previous bridge they had entered from, he went still, absentmindedly watching the green fire from the root line he'd lit being continually devoured by the void fingers as it tried to spread into the Abyss.

Jason's patience for Parch's silence was wearing thin. He'd restrained himself as Parch went off to think, hoping he'd come to some brilliant moment of understanding and figure everything out. But as the seconds passed, and his anxiety grew, Jason couldn't contain himself any longer. "Well?" he asked.

"Okay," Parch began, "let's start with what we know. We came in here assuming it was just a single plant with two root lines into your house. Since the root line we followed out doesn't lead back to your living room, it's clear that's not the case. Which means there's a second plant connected to your house that we have to find."

"There's another one?" Jason cried.

"Has to be," Parch replied. "It might be this next one, whose roots are mixed in here, but it might not be."

Jason threw his hands up and cursed. His heart raced. He just wanted out of this madness.

Parch, however, continued on without reacting to Jason's distress. "It's impossible to say where that other plant is, or if it has anything to do with the strangeness we've seen so far." He knelt down and ran his hand along the wood. "But two bridges into a single house, and then we find two plants connected like this. It can't be a coincidence, can it? Maybe if I can take a look at the heart."

Looking up, Parch finally noticed Jason's emotional state. Jason had two handfuls of hair and was grinding his teeth as he frantically looked all around. "Easy," Parch comforted, "we're going to be all right."

"We're trapped in here!" Jason shouted, his emotions boiling over.

"Trapped?" Parch replied.

"Yes, trapped!" Jason wailed. "We can't go back the way we came, and this way only leads to another Ignotus. There's no way out!"

"We're not trapped," Parch rebutted calmly. "There's always another way out."

"And what if there's not?" Jason asked.

Parch stood up, unscrewed a cap on the bottom of the torch, and revealed a button. "If things get really bad, we always have this," Parch said. "As long as the torch is burning, we can hit this button, and it'll instantly pull us out, back to that box I dragged into your living room. In the blink of an eye, we'll be transported back to the human world. No matter where we are in the Abyss or Ignotus, no matter what's going on, if we have the torch, we have a way out. It only works once per torch, though, so its emergency use only. And if we do have to use it, make sure you grab on tight; because if you don't, you'll be left behind. It's a one-way trip, so I won't be able to come back for you."

Stunned, Jason looked at the torch, then back at Parch. "You had that the whole time?"

With a good-natured laugh, Parch shot Jason a wink. "I told you, man, we're good. We'll make it out of here just fine. But speaking of the torch, we have about four and a half hours of burn left, which means we have four and a half hours to find that second source. I think that's where we're going to find our answers, and where we can put a stop to all this. It might be this one here." Parch nodded toward the next bridge. "But even if it's not, this next one might be able to tell us more about what's happening, and it needs to be cleaned up either way."

Reinvigorated, Parch surged forward toward the next bridge. "No sense wasting time closing these bridges," he said, "since they just lead back to the Ignotus anyway. We'll get right to it and follow these roots back to the plant they belong to, assess the situation, then go from there. We've had a rough start, but we're going to finish strong. Come on!"

But despite the swell of bravado, Jason didn't move. He just stared at the torch on Parch's shoulder. "I don't think we should go any further," Jason said. "I think this is an emergency, and I think we should use that button on the torch."

Parch's eyes went cold again. He turned and faced Jason. "Cut and run, huh?" he replied.

Jason wilted under Parch's stare. Like a guilty man before an honest judge, Jason looked away, ashamed.

"Ten years ago," Parch began, "when I started this line of work, I thought it wasn't a big deal. My first two were nothing. The first root line got into an empty chicken coop on an abandoned farm. The second was in an unmanned weather observation shack in the mountains. But the third . . ." Parch turned away and stared out into the darkness of the Abyss. When he spoke again his voice was tense but controlled. "My third one, the root line got into the basement of a children's hospital. By the time I got there the Mortem Cor plant had . . ."

Jason thought Parch was going to continue the story; but Parch went silent and just stared out into infinity.

"Every time I look at a root line, I think about that," Parch said finally. "Every time I look at a root line, I think about all the silent houses I've pulled up to. All the bodies I've found. All the devastated family members and friends. All the sadness, all the pain. For ten years that's all I've been able to think about."

Parch turned toward Jason, his eyes filled with fire. "I hate the Mortem Cor plants. I hate the Malus. I hate the Ignotus and all the rest. I don't do this for fun. I don't do it for the pennies they pay me. I do it because people need me to do it. This is serious. People's lives are at stake. And that Mortem Cor plant back there, with all those root lines leading off to who knows where, gets to keep killing people all because you couldn't stop thinking about yourself."

Jason winced, and his head dropped. He stared at the ground in contrite resignation.

Seeing Jason's reaction, Parch stopped. When he spoke again his tone was softer and more reconciliatory. "I know this isn't going how I told you it would go," he said. "But something bad is happening here. Who knows how many others are in danger right now and they don't even know it. They're counting on us. We have to figure out what's going on — find that second source and stop it."

Jason continued to stare at the roots beneath his feet. Parch waited patiently for a response, but one never came. After several moments, Parch turned and headed off toward the next bridge, leaving Jason alone in the silence of the Abyss.

CHAPTER 9

The bright new world Parch and Jason stepped into was an expansive and unending sea of clouds. In every direction there was open sky, filled with puffy white clouds drifting endlessly. Churning in the sky were clouds of all types — from cumulus to cirrus to stratus. The men couldn't see a sun or light source; but based on how bright it was, it must have been hidden somewhere in the giant sky.

They stood on top of a gray stone pillar of unfathomable height. Its diameter was approximately twenty meters wide. It was impossible to know how tall it was because it rose so high that the clouds filled in the space below, obscuring any sight of ground. Jason wondered if there was any land at all, or if he would simply fall forever through the clouds if he fell. Jason walked to the edge and kicked a small stone off and watched it fall. It hurtled downward until it vanished into the mist.

But the stone pillar they stood on was not alone. The sky was littered in every direction with similar stone pillars that were scattered around irregularly and chaotically for as far as the eye could see. Some pillars were taller, others shorter, and a few were exceptionally tall.

Jason looked out, soaking in the sight. The clouds roiled gently all around. The breeze was crisp and cool and the air smelled fresher than he'd ever smelt before. The only noise was the wind. Everything felt so clear and pristine.

While Jason marveled, Parch was looking at something else. Behind them, balanced atop a pillar several kilometers away, stood a Mortem Cor plant even taller than the previous one. It was massive, almost twice as tall as the last, with a spread of its crown and branches to match. Even from as far away as they were, it was obvious this tree was much older — ancient, even. Signs of decay and age littered its mighty trunk. Bits of dry rot sloughed off with each breeze, large sections of the tree were discolored with yellow and green hues, and black ooze seeped out from various old, unhealed wounds along the tree. A large branch dangled on the backside, partially broken but still hanging. Other branches bent limply downward.

At the base of the terrible Mortem Cor plant was a tangle of roots much like the other. The tangle stabilized the tree atop the pillar, fixing it to the stone and keeping it from tipping over. From this tangle, hundreds of root lines ran out like cables. The root lines ran on top of the stone pillars and were suspended in the open air between them. When a root line ran over a stone pillar, part of the roots would weave themselves into and about the rock, anchoring themselves to the stone and using it for support. They ran for kilometers out from the Mortem Cor plant and created a massive web that supported the tree and gave it much more stability than it otherwise would have had. The web of roots was astonishing in its breadth and vastness.

A crisp, cool wind blew on the two men. Jason turned and joined Parch in staring at this new Mortem Cor plant.

Parch shook his head. "What madness have we stepped into?" he muttered. But he shook it off. "We've got lives to save," he said, then turned his attention to the roots.

The bridge the two men had exited was on the surface of a boulder that sat in the middle of the stone pillar. The roots ran out of this bridge, then, after entangling a large section of the stone pillar for support, ran suspended to another stone pillar fifty meters away. In this way, the root line zigzagged between stone pillars, all the way back until it reached the Mortem Cor plant.

Parch followed the roots back to the tree with his eyes. The path was long, and every crossing between stone pillars was different due to the capricious twists of the roots and the irregularities of the pillars. It would be difficult and dangerous, but they had no other choice.

He turned to Jason. "We'll have to crawl on the root line all the way to the Mortem Cor plant," Parch lamented. "If I can get a good look at the plant's base, it may tell me what's going on here, and why these Mortem Cor plants are growing so large. We need to find out what's happening, and it's our only lead."

Jason looked out at the section of root line suspended between the stone pillars. There was nothing but open sky underneath. Crawling out on it would be extremely dangerous; falling would be certain death. But Jason didn't voice any objections to the plan, he just stared out into the open air and nodded silently. He was dejected and melancholic. The argument in the bridge had taken all the fight out of him. He was resigned to follow Parch mutely.

Parch didn't react at all to Jason's behavior, and instead only focused on the mission. "But there's no way we can navigate those roots with a swarm of Malus chasing us," he said.

Parch unholstered his gun and positioned himself near the bridge mouth, then motioned for Jason to do the same. When they were both ready to jump back into the bridge at a second's notice, Parch pointed his pistol in the air and fired. As the crack of thunder echoed around them, the two men diligently scanned the skies, pillars, and roots for any sign of movement. But after several minutes of nothing except the sound of a gentle wind, the pair became convinced it was safe. Parch holstered his gun. "I guess we're good," he said.

The two men went to inspect the roots. The roots exited the bridge, then bunched up on top of the pillar into a large messy pile before spinning together into a single two-meter diameter cable and running suspended to the adjacent pillar fifty meters away.

It was also clear that these roots were nearly as old as the tree itself. They were decrepit, and bits of wood were falling off everywhere. The discoloration and dry rot evident on the trunk of the Mortem Cor plant was here on the roots as well. There were even holes in the roots like small insects had burrowed into the wood, though

Jason didn't see any insects themselves. It seemed sturdy, however, due to the sheer mass of wood which made up the root line. Perhaps their relatively small weight wouldn't disrupt it too much.

Parch pushed and pulled on the roots in the pile and the cable portions respectively, testing their strength and looking for weak points. The roots remained taut and immobile, and all Parch could do was flake off surface-level decay. It appeared the rot was only superficial and didn't go deep into the wood. Satisfied, Parch looked out toward the adjoining stone pillar. The roots ran horizontally over to it with only a slight sag in the middle. By all appearances, this looked to be a simple, straightforward crossing.

As Parch investigated the roots, Jason was growing more nervous by the second. Despite his silent demeanor, his mind was filled with thoughts of falling. Even though he was standing on solid ground, he felt unbalanced. He knelt down and tried to calm himself by taking several deep breaths, but it only slightly helped. When Jason looked up, Parch was climbing atop the root pile.

The roots audibly cracked and groaned as Parch pulled himself up, but nothing broke free. And once on top, Parch appeared quite stable. The roots were wide and broad, and there was plenty of room for him to move around. There were also plenty of places to grab on to if he slipped.

"This should be easy," Parch called out as he looked down at Jason.

Jason was silent. He was still kneeling, and his hands went down to feel the safety of the cool stone. He moved slowly and cautiously, even though he was in the middle of the pillar, far from any edge.

Seeing this, Parch shook his arm, causing his chain to loosen and come to a coil in his hand. "Here," Parch called out as he threw it.

Jason looked up and panicked as he saw the chain flying at him, uncoiling in the air. He held his arms up to protect himself, but the chain wrapped around him. Jason tried to fight it as the chain wove itself through his chest harness and around his hips. It sent a shiver up Jason's spine as it crawled around him. Once the chain had fully encircled him, one of the chain's ends shot out and fastened itself to a thick root at the base of the root pile. Startled, but also curious, Jason gave the chain a pull to test its strength and found the chain firmly secured him to the roots.

"It makes climbing a lot easier," Parch called out. "It'll move with you and won't let you fall."

While this was a great relief to Jason, all he could manage was a nod in response. He walked over to the root pile, and after a brief moment to brace himself, he grabbed the roots and started to climb. He was clumsy at first, his feet slipping as he tried to find purchase, but the chain kept him firmly attached. After a few failed attempts, Jason dragged himself up. As he neared the top, Parch pulled him the rest of the way.

After giving Jason a slap on the back, Parch looked off to the next platform. "I'll go first to make sure it's safe," Parch said. "Wait here." Without another word, Parch crouched, and started the crossing.

He walked carefully and slowly, maintaining a low center of gravity, and keeping his hands ready to grab at the roots should he slip. The roots creaked as he walked but showed no signs of breaking. The wind was gentle and pleasant.

With his steady pace, Parch made it across quickly and without incident. He jumped down onto the next stone pillar and looked back toward Jason. "It's safe!" Parch waved at Jason to cross.

Jason hesitated. His eyes drifted, and he looked out into the empty sky all around him which caused his breath to catch in his throat. He then looked back at Parch, but the other man just stared at him in patient expectation, with an encouraging smile. Left with no choice, Jason began the traversal.

Instead of crouching and walking, Jason chose to crawl on his hands and knees along the wide root line, clutching at any root that was available. He progressed slowly, taking extreme care. The chain was a great comfort to him. It moved with him, fastening itself to roots ahead, and anchoring him down in case of a fall.

As Jason neared the halfway point, his heart was beating fiercely, and his hands were soaked with sweat. He welcomed the breeze — it cooled him and dried his hands. Every movement felt physically and mentally exhausting. Jason wanted to take a break, but he was far too scared to spend any more time hanging in the air on these roots than he had to. His eyes and mind continually drifted toward the edge, on the endless clouds below. But he fought through it, refocusing on moving forward. After what seemed like hours, Jason finally made it across.

Parch waited patiently, watching Jason and nodding silently at each measure of progress. Once he reached the other side, Parch met the shaken man with a big smile and helped him down onto safe footing.

Breathing heavily, with his forearms aching, Jason fell onto the hard rock surface and laid himself out to catch his breath. Despite his best efforts to hide it, a smile spread across his face and an ounce of pride filled his heart. He'd done it. Now he rested and stared into the sky above.

The peaceful white clouds continued to churn overhead, combining and separating in the light wind. Magnificent cumulonimbus clouds rose high and mighty. Puffy little cumulus clouds floated by. Long strands of stratus clouds streaked through them all. It was very calming to watch. After only a short respite, Jason's strength returned. He stood up, ready for the next section.

Taking a section at a time, the two men made their way closer and closer to the foul Mortem Cor plant towering ahead. Each new section was slightly different and unique, depending on the placement and height of the next pillar as well as the peculiarities of the root line. They surveyed each new span of roots before crossing, with Parch offering tips and suggestions. Neither man spoke much; they were both focused solely on making progress. Jason's nerves held strong, and he moved faster with each new section. Parch continued to navigate the roots adeptly. Seemingly unfazed by the height and danger, he proved a skilled guide, keeping them both moving through the endless sky.

Nearly halfway to the Mortem Cor plant, Parch halted on one of the stone pillars so he could evaluate the next section. This next part would be the crux of the whole route. It was the most challenging crossing of all on their path to the Mortem Cor plant. The difficulty arose from where the Mortem Cor plant ultimately resided. It was almost a hundred meters higher in elevation than where the two men had started from. This next crossing was where the root line began to rise toward it. But this rise didn't start with a gradual incline or a slight slope. Instead, the next section of roots ran horizontal for twenty meters, then went completely vertical, rising fifty meters to where it attached to the next stone pillar. The two men would have to climb; there was no getting around it.

And how the root line attached to the next stone pillar was a difficulty in and of itself. The next pillar was much taller than any around it, so the root line couldn't run over top of it like it had all the previous ones. Instead, the root line had attached itself to the side of the stone pillar, a partial way up. The powerful roots had woven themselves into the rock like a vine on a brick wall, only on a much larger scale.

The situation meant not only would there be a climb involved with the next crossing, but also that, unless they wanted to spend extra time perilously sitting on the roots precariously attached to the side of a stone pillar, there would be no rest after the climb — they'd have to transition to the subsequent crossing immediately. Only after that would they reach the safety of another stone pillar they could rest on. Despite the second crossing looking easier and more horizontal, taken as a whole, this would be a challenging traversal. And worst of all, everything looked so tenuous and delicately balanced.

Parch stared intently at the problem ahead of them and scowled. He then looked back with concern at Jason who was still resting from the previous crossing. "This next one would be easy work for experienced climbers and mountaineers," Parch said. "Any chance you're one of those?"

Jason responded with a sarcastic laugh. But even the forced laughter ceased when Jason looked back at the path before them. His lips closed tightly, and his hands clenched as he looked at the roots climbing up the tall pillar before them.

"We'll go together," Parch said in an encouraging tone. "I'll show you how to climb. It's not as bad as it looks." The only response from Jason was a mute nod, which Parch took to be assent and began. Without wasting another moment, Parch mounted the roots and prepared to cross.

Reluctant, Jason lingered where he was for a moment. He looked up at the towering stone pillar in front of them. It rose so high; Jason couldn't even see the top — it was lost in the clouds. It was no wonder the roots had to attach themselves to the side. *At least I have the chain*, Jason thought, which was the only positive notion he felt regarding this terrible endeavor they were about to attempt. After giving the chain wrapped around him a quick squeeze, Jason joined Parch on the roots.

Crawling out into the open sky, they both started the crossing. The horizontal portion was easy work (or would have been if the fifty-meter vertical climb wasn't looming ahead of them). Jason tried not to think about it, to not look up and see it, but with each centimeter he moved forward, it grew larger and more real. He desperately wished there was another way, that Parch would turn around and say it was impossible. But Parch's pace never faltered, and soon they were at the foot of the climb.

The vertical section was even more intimidating up close. As the two men surveyed it, a rush of wind swept over them and caused the entire hanging root line to sway. The roots groaned, straining under their own massive weight. Jason panicked and clutched desperately at the roots. He wished he was anywhere else. Parch, conversely, was undaunted. Once the roots stopped swaying, he steadied himself, then grabbed the roots and began the climb. As usual, Parch had started before Jason was ready, forcing the issue. But Jason said nothing.

Parch only climbed a couple of meters before stopping. The tangled weave of countless roots made the root line easy to climb. There were sturdy places to grab anywhere you wanted, and footholds just as numerous. He looked down toward Jason, to help advise him on how to get started, but before he could say a word, a shower of small pebbles and dust rained down on him.

Eyes wide in alarm, Parch looked up the wall of roots. But the shower of dust had already stopped. The root line looked just as it had before, and all was as it should be. “Just a little dust shaken loose, nothing to worry about,” Parch muttered. He and Jason were both committed out here. If something was wrong, there was nothing they could do but hurry up and get through this section as quickly as possible.

Jason started the climb. He followed Parch’s example and used the same hand- and footholds. But where Parch’s movements were effortless and agile, Jason’s were slow and clumsy. His hands wrenched down on the roots, and his entire body was stiff. No matter how hard he tried not to, his eyes constantly drifted off to the side, gazing into the open sky all around him. And when he saw the height, the fear flooded in. Parch called down advice and encouragement, but often Jason barely registered it. Despite it all, however, Jason continued to make progress. With the help of the chain, Jason dragged himself up the roots.

The two progressed slowly. Parch continued to try and coax as much speed out of Jason as possible, but Jason could only go so fast.

As they neared the halfway mark, Jason had to take a break to let his burning forearms rest. He leaned into the roots, burying one arm deep in them while he shook out the other, letting the blood flow back into his aching muscles. The climb had been difficult, but Jason had gotten into a rhythm, and had managed it well so far. And with each meter he climbed, his spirits rose with him. *This isn't so bad*, he thought to himself.

"You ready to climb again?" Parch called down, failing to conceal the nervousness in his voice.

Jason looked up to answer, but before he could speak, he was met with a shower of pebbles and dust from above. He coughed and shielded his face with his hands until the pebbles stopped. "What . . . what was that?" Jason asked.

"Just some dust that shook loose," Parch responded, but much too quickly and emphatically. "Hurry."

Without another word, they both promptly resumed the climb. Each man doubled his efforts, racing for the top. Jason's arms were growing numb, but his frenzy pushed him on. He scrambled up the roots faster now, trading caution for speed. All he wanted was to get back on solid ground.

Parch was still able to stay comfortably ahead of Jason and seemed to never tire. Instead of focusing on the climb, his attention was divided between helping Jason below and trying to look ahead to the next section of roots after the climb. But both tasks were suddenly interrupted when the entire root line dropped a centimeter.

"Hurry!" Parch screamed, dropping all pretense of calm.

But it was too late. A thunderous crack sounded above them. Jason looked up in horror and saw the rock the roots were attached to splitting and breaking off. In slow motion, Jason watched the side of the stone pillar crumble apart, and then the roots and everything else began to fall.

"Hold on!" Parch roared, clenching his hands down hard on the roots.

But before Jason could react, he, and everything else, were in free fall. Wood, rock, and men all fell together. Jason screamed, but it couldn't be heard over the deafening cacophony of splintering wood, cracking rock, and rushing wind.

This free fall came to an abrupt halt only seconds later. The roots had been pulled off the one tall pillar, but they were still intact and still attached to the two adjacent stone pillars. Without warning, the roots caught hard and suddenly. The violent jolt ripped Jason off the roots, and he would have fallen and been lost forever, but the chain saved him. Despite the violence, it remained anchored deep in the tangle and stopped Jason's fall, but at the cost of biting into his chest, ribs, and hips. Jason was left dangling two meters below the roots, in pain and struggling to breathe.

Parch, conversely, had managed the fall better. As it all had started to go, he'd forced his arms into the roots as far as possible, then gripped the interior roots. The jolt at the end threw his legs off, but his arms held strong. And as the roots came to a relative stop, he quickly pulled himself back up, and was hanging on the underside of the roots.

The situation was getting worse by the second as Jason hung feebly at the end of the chain. It had saved his life, but now he struggled to breathe against it as it squeezed his chest and ribs. With eyes blurred by pain, Jason looked up at the root line. Despite catching for the moment, Jason saw the root line was tearing itself apart under its own weight. Strands of roots snapped and shattered, raining bits of broken wood down, causing the root line to sag more and more.

A massive chunk of rock that had been ripped out from the side of the pillar fell and struck the already overburdened root line. The whole root line shuddered from the impact and sunk lower. This was followed by more thunderous cracking as large sections of rock continued to break off from the now weakened and crumbling side of the stone pillar. Massive boulder-sized fragments plummeted into the clouds all around Jason as he spun helplessly in the air.

Jason tried to reach up, tried to grab the chain and pull, but his arms had no strength. "Help!" he gasped weakly.

Parch was already moving toward him. Upside down, Parch crawled along the underside of the roots toward his companion. "I'm here!" he shouted as he got as close as he could get to Jason, then lodged his legs into the tangle of roots so they held him up. Now with his hands free, he let his upper body hang down, and reached toward Jason. "Grab my hand!" he shouted.

Jason was close to passing out. The pain and the lack of oxygen were both taking a toll, and his vision and focus were fading. He reached weakly for Parch's hand but missed. Parch roared for him to try again. Jason, summoning all the strength he had left, threw his hand out one last time. It was just barely enough.

Parch grabbed Jason's hand and gripped hard. Using every ounce of strength he had, along with the chain's help, Parch heaved Jason up close enough to reach the tangled roots. "Grab on!" Parch growled through clenched teeth as his arms began to weaken. Jason grabbed onto the roots, and at the same time drew in a deep breath. With Jason now supporting his own weight, both Parch and the chain quickly adjusted. The chain anchored higher up on the root line, while Parch grabbed Jason by the belt. With another mighty heave, Parch, the chain, and this time Jason as well, all pulled together and hauled Jason up to where he was able to hook his legs into the roots and hang under his own strength.

Jason felt the relief immediately and breathed deeply. But there were no breaks here, and there was no time to waste. The two men scrambled to the top of the roots. As they mounted the root line, wood was breaking all around them, and rocks continued to rain down from the pillar. The next stone platform was almost one hundred meters away up a sharp incline. No longer crawling or crouching, each man took off running at full speed, desperate to get off this rapidly deteriorating span of roots.

Jason ran hard, following Parch along the roots. But suddenly the loudest crack yet resounded throughout the sky. It was so loud it sent a jolt through Jason's entire body, stopping him in his tracks. He looked back at the tall pillar, the obvious source. When the roots fell, they had ripped out a huge portion of rock with them and left a gaping concavity in the side of the pillar. The now-compromised stone tower was listing to one side and was beginning to buckle. And when it did, it would fall across (and onto) the roots.

Jason wanted to scream and curse, but that breath was better saved for running. Both he and Parch turned and sprinted up the inclined roots toward the next root platform, toward safety, glancing back at the leaning stone tower every few steps. With the sound of shattering stone as its symphony, the pillar finally fell.

The two men were only twenty meters away from the next pillar, but they were out of time. "Grab on!" Parch roared when it was clear they couldn't make it. Both men dropped down and clutched at the roots right as the pillar impacted.

Jason looked back and watched as the massive stone tower fell across the roots fifty meters behind them, about halfway along the span. The pillar ripped straight through the roots, severing them completely. Then the resulting newly formed ends swung down limp, each swinging back toward the respective pillars they were attached to.

Jason clutched the root line hard as it began to swing. It slammed into the stone pillar, nearly shaking both men off. The collision felt like a car crash. Pain pulsed through Jason's entire body.

Fortunately, the worst was over; they had survived. The roots came to a halt, and the pillar that held them remained sturdy. Slowly, they both climbed the last few remaining meters of roots to the top of the stone column. Once they both had reached the top, they collapsed onto the safety of solid ground.

CHAPTER 10

"I'm done," Jason said. "I can't do this. Just leave me behind because I'm not going any further."

Jason lay on his back on the cool stone, despondent and staring up into the cloud-filled sky above. This latest brush with death had broken him. His body was wracked with tension and stress, and his mind was completely preoccupied with his own suffering.

Why? Why couldn't they just use the torch to leave? Why did they have to stay trapped in this horrible place, and continue on in this agony? They just nearly died — again! And they would definitely die if they kept going! Why didn't Parch see that? Jason didn't understand, but he was too weak and defeated to fight with Parch anymore. Instead, if he was to die in here, Jason decided he would do it on his own terms, and lying on this peaceful stone pillar until this place killed him seemed as good a plan as any.

Parch rolled his eyes at Jason's outburst but didn't reply. Instead, he quietly sat down and leaned back against the root line. After quickly checking the time, Parch got comfortable and closed his eyes to relax, taking advantage of the tranquility and peacefulness of the moment.

The pair sat like this for a while. They were both too tired to move, or even speak. Silence settled in between them, and the only sound came from the soft, soothing breeze. All the world around them was still.

Jason watched the clouds floating above. He started to calm down, and the shock and fear from this latest catastrophe receded. As he lay there, his mind began to drift, and he thought about all that had happened so far. He thought about himself, and his life. Then, as always, his thoughts came back to Lily. Was she all right? They'd been gone a long time. Was she worried? What would she think if she saw him right now? Jason sighed. This last question stuck in his heart like a knife.

Agitated and filled with a wave of contempt for life, he got up and walked to the edge of the pillar with the devil-may-care attitude of a child throwing a tantrum. For the moment, his heart was numb to the fear of falling, but his hands still shook as he sat down and dangled his legs off into the clouds.

Before him, the endless sky continued in every direction. It was a sea of clouds, with the only deviation being the stone pillars rising up out of unfathomable depths. Jason marveled at it all. It was so pristine and resplendent, like a painting. But as he looked around, he eventually saw a stray root line, which drew his attention back to the hideous Mortem Cor plant.

Jason didn't know why, but when he looked at the Mortem Cor plant, a feeling of deep disgust and anger welled up inside him. Just seeing it made him scowl and recoil. It was a blight that seemed an insult even to this dangerous and unearthly place. It was also massive, standing much larger than even the last tree. The vast network of its roots was like a giant spider's web, spanning for kilometers, with root lines anchored on the stone pillars for support. Everything about this Mortem Cor plant was old and decrepit. It looked to Jason like the thing could fall over at any moment, and he would be happy if it did.

He sighed and slumped over, feeling beaten and discouraged. He hated being here, and not only because of the danger and terror. The Ignotus had exposed something in him: a deep-seated, unspoken fear he had tried to conceal and dismiss his entire life. But now all was laid bare. There was no hiding from it any longer, no excuse that could dismiss it. All that could be done now was to admit the obvious truth.

Jason reached into his pocket and pulled out his keys. He singled out the mouse key chain and held it between his fingers. It was painful to look at. He quickly opened the key ring and slid the key chain off, then returned the rest of the keys to his pocket. Now holding only the mouse key chain in his hand, he stared out into the distance.

It was time to get rid of it. It was time to admit what he always knew deep down: a stupid key chain wasn't going to change anything. Some things can't be fixed. This key chain was nothing but trouble, and this would be a fitting place to forsake it.

But just as Jason was about to throw the trinket off and lose it forever, he heard movement behind him. Parch was walking toward him. In a silent panic, Jason instinctually went to hide the key chain, but there wasn't enough time to stuff it back in his pocket. With no other choice, Jason awkwardly but stealthily hid the key chain by tucking it underneath his leg. He immediately felt the discomfort of the metal figure poking up into the bottom of his thigh, but his hands were empty, and the key chain was hidden from view.

"Quite a sight, isn't it?" Parch said as he sat down next to Jason on the edge. "The Ignotus aren't always pretty, but when they are, it's a real treat."

Jason continued to stare out into the clouds.

"I'm sorry I yelled at you back there." Parch sighed. "I've been doing this forever, so I'm used to it. But you're seeing this all for the first time, and it's been a pretty rough one at that. I've no right to be so hard on you. I'm sorry for what I said."

Jason felt suddenly overcome with relief, happiness, and sadness all at once. Deep down, Jason felt he'd deserved every word Parch had said back in the Abyss, but he was grateful for Parch's apology all the same.

"I'm sorry too," Jason replied, trying not to reveal just how profoundly Parch's apology had affected him. "I'm sorry for running away. I'm . . . I'm not like you. I wish I was, but I'm not."

Parch glanced at Jason with concern. "Just so you know, even though I wasn't supposed to, I don't regret bringing you along," Parch said with a pat on Jason's back. "I can't explain it, but I still think something good will come of all this."

Leaning back, Parch lounged, taking every advantage of their brief respite. "Don't worry about that last plant, either," he continued. "When we get back, I'll put the word out, and someone will come across it eventually. I think there's a good chance the guys can find it before it can . . . get to anyone else."

It seemed to Jason that Parch had intended his words to be comforting, but when Jason heard them, he felt much worse. It was obvious that Parch was just trying to be nice, and Jason could tell Parch was still deeply concerned about that last Mortem Cor plant, regardless of how much he stated otherwise. Jason's head dropped and his spirits fell even further. People would suffer, maybe even die, because of what he had done.

Silence took over between the two men. They sat idle, staring out into the sky. Minutes ticked by uncounted. The clouds continued in their endless dance, drifting aimlessly, combining and separating. The wind blew, light and pleasant. All continued on in this place as it always had, unchanging and steady.

After some time, Parch surreptitiously checked his watch, then spoke again, unhurried. "Hey, did you hit anything back there?" he asked. "Back when we were running from those Malus. I heard you shooting."

Jason shook his head. "No," he said flatly.

Parch quickly sat up and drew his gun. "Would you like me to show you how to shoot?" Parch asked with a beaming smile. "I'll actually show you this time instead of rushing through it like before, I promise."

Reluctant to end the tranquil silence, Jason tried to think of a polite way to refuse Parch's offer. But eventually, Parch's insistence, bolstered by Jason's own interest in guns, won out. Jason drew his pistol. Despite his initial hesitation, he was happy for an excuse to try shooting again.

Nearby, there was another root line running parallel to their own. This adjacent strand was just one more in the Mortem Cor plant's massive web and, in its run, had attached to a stone pillar that was only forty meters away from where Parch and Jason sat. Not only was it close by, but, as if by luck, it offered a tempting target for the two men's shooting practice: an oozing tumor, like the one they had seen before, sat atop the pillar.

The root tumor was about two meters wide. It was a chaotic mess of roots twisting and turning about, tying themselves into a dense ball of knots. On the surface of the tumor, facing Parch and Jason, there was a gooey, oozing black spot about thirty centimeters in diameter. It was situated like a bull's-eye, nearly dead center on the target.

"Try hitting that root tumor over there," Parch said, pointing out the mark.

Jason eyed the target, staring at the viscous spot at the very center of the mass of roots. It was relatively close, but because there was nothing but open sky between the tumor and himself, it somehow felt like it was much farther away than it was. Jason clumsily held up the pistol. Everything felt awkward, and he was sure he was doing it all wrong. The pistol swayed back and forth, and the target blurred in and out of vision. Jason tried to steady himself, but he wobbled even more. After a few seconds of trying, he lowered the pistol.

"I can't hit that thing," Jason said. "It's too far. I don't even know how I'm supposed to hold this gun. It feels like I'm doing it all wrong."

"Don't worry about anything right now," Parch said. "Just take a shot and see."

Resigning himself to failure, Jason raised the pistol again. It wobbled and swayed about as he tried to look down the sights. He closed one eye and then the other, trying to find the best view. Everything felt out of sync, like his whole body was fighting against itself. And to make matters worse, his mouse key chain was still poking up into his leg, distracting him with an uncomfortable twinge of pain. With little hope of hitting the target, Jason clenched down hard to brace himself, closed his eyes, then pulled the trigger.

The gun erupted in Jason's hands, firing the bullet, and violently jerking backward. The bullet flew for two meters, then exploded again, sending out a shockwave perpendicular to its direction of travel, and accelerating exponentially faster. With this new energy, the bullet screamed forward at incredible speed, far faster than any normal bullet, and turned into a bright white streak. But that white streak missed the tumor by several meters, and flew off into the sky, where Jason had erroneously pointed it.

Jason opened his eyes. "Did I hit it?" he asked.

Parch laughed. "That was terrible!"

"I told you!" Jason snapped, covering his face with one of his hands. But Parch was still laughing, and Jason couldn't help but crack a smile himself.

"Your grip is all wrong," Parch said. He aimed his own pistol at the root tumor. "Look at my hands and copy them."

Jason looked and saw how Parch's hands enveloped the gun, covering every bit of the pistol's grip. He held his own pistol up and tried to mimic the grip as best he could. Jason glanced back and forth, adjusting his hands, trying to get it perfect.

Parch shifted around, looking at Jason's hands from different angles. "Turn your hands over so I can see," he said.

While keeping the muzzle pointed at the target, Jason turned his hands over revealing his hand positioning.

"Stack your thumbs like this," Parch said, holding up his pistol and wiggling his thumbs. "And overlap your fingers on the bottom of the grip."

Jason followed Parch's instructions and shifted his thumbs and fingers around. After a few more pointers, he got to a place where the pistol felt very good in his hands. He felt like he had significantly more control, and it was here that Parch finally gave his approval.

Now with the correct hold, Jason took a moment to concentrate. He wanted to memorize how his hands felt around the gun, and where they were positioned. His grip felt good, and he wanted to be able to repeat it. After a few seconds, he was sure he could remember. The runes had long since recharged, so Jason, feeling slightly more hopeful, aimed at the root tumor and fired again.

It was another miss, but the white streak screamed through the air significantly closer to the target than his last shot, missing it by only a meter or so. Jason was silently pleased.

"A little better," Parch said. "Next, we'll have to work on your breathing. Try exhaling before each shot. Shoot at the bottom of your breath before breathing in again."

As he waited for the runes to recharge, Jason focused now on his breathing. He aimed the gun and exhaled, feeling how still he was in that short time before inhaling again. The gun wobbled around much less, and he felt a lot steadier. After several breaths, the runes recharged, and he fired. Another miss, but again there was improvement. He almost hit the root tumor.

Jason smiled. He turned to Parch again, looking for more instruction.

But Parch just nodded toward the target. "Keep shooting," he said. "Take some more shots."

Parch sat back as Jason fell into a pattern of firing, then resting while the pistol recharged. It was a comfortable, leisurely rhythm that raised one's spirits. Jason continued to experiment with the gun, trying to figure out how to make the shot go where he wanted it to. He also continued to shift his weight as the mouse key chain underneath his leg continued to cause him issues. Parch watched silently, checking the time occasionally.

After several more missed shots, Parch spoke up. "You're leaning too much to one side. Are you sitting on a rock or something?"

Jason's eyes grew wide. He said nothing, and instead looked up and away from Parch. But as the awkward silence persisted, he grew increasingly nervous. As Parch waited for a response, that silence eventually became too much to bear. In a sudden burst of movement, Jason snatched the mouse key chain from beneath his leg and placed it on his far side, out of sight of Parch.

"That's just my key chain," Jason sputtered, then hurriedly raised the gun and pulled the trigger. But the runes were still recharging from his last shot, and the gun didn't fire.

Parch looked at Jason curiously, with his brow furrowed and eyes squinting. "Your key chain?" Parch asked. "Isn't that what you pulled out back when we were on the sand dune too?"

Again, Jason hesitated. But he eventually nodded sheepishly.

"Why?" Parch asked. "What's so special about it?"

Dropping his head, Jason begrudgingly reached over and grabbed the key chain on his side. He looked down at it in his hand. "It's just something my wife got me." Jason held up the small metal figure of a mouse and showed it to Parch. "It's a grasshopper mouse," he said.

As he held the mouse carving in his hand, Jason's heart waivered. He smiled as he thought back to that day. Back then everything had been so perfect; his life with Lily had been so hopeful and full of joy.

"Years ago, we went to the zoo," Jason said, only just able to keep his voice steady. "We had just gotten married, and it was a fun little trip. We saw all the big animals — the giraffes, the elephants, the tigers — all of them. But then we walked through the small animal enclosures and came to the grasshopper mouse exhibit. I'd never heard of them before, but they're incredible little creatures. They're so small and weak, you'd think they'd be piddling, timid things, but you'd be wrong. We got there right at feeding time, and the zookeeper dropped a live scorpion inside the enclosure. I thought the mouse was done for; I thought it would run away. But it didn't run away, it charged right in, fought the scorpion, won, and ate it. It was the most amazing thing I'd ever seen."

"As I was watching it, I said to Lily 'That mouse has the heart of a lion. It's unstoppable. It could do anything.' But it was strange. When I looked over at her, she wasn't even looking at the mouse. She was looking at me. She had been watching me the whole time I was watching the mouse. She had her head tilted to the side, with this little smile on her face. She was looking at me like she had just found out a secret. When I asked her what her look meant, she leaned in and kissed me and said, 'Nothing.'"

"Later on, we went to get ice cream. While I was waiting in line, she snuck away to the gift shop and bought this." Jason looked down at the trinket. "When she gave it to me, she looked at me and said, 'I think *you* can do anything.'"

Tears welled in Jason's eyes. He closed the trinket in his hand, hiding it. "But she was wrong," he said. Suddenly the blissful memories of the past vanished, and the crushing reality of the present state of his relationship with his wife all came back at once, bringing with it nothing but feelings of frustration, regret, and failure. He looked away and set the trinket down. "I can't do anything," he said.

The waves of despair crashed harder and harder on Jason's heart as he sat there dwelling on how different things were now. Now whenever Lily looked at him there was no hope or delight. Now there was only an unspoken disappointment in her eyes, no matter how hard she tried to hide it. Jason felt like he had failed a million times in a million different ways, and his wife was worn out from waiting for him. He leaned back and stared up into the sky. "She's going to leave me," he declared, choking back his feelings.

It took several minutes before Jason was able to speak again, but once he had partially regained himself, he continued. "It's my fault," he said. "I've ruined everything. I'm the one who made us move into that terrible house."

Jason sighed, then took a deep breath. "Several weeks ago, before we moved," he said, "we were living in a little apartment in the city. It was nice, but our lease was coming up and the landlord was selling the building, so we had to find a new place to live. About that same time, I ran into an old friend from college one afternoon. We got lunch to catch up, and it turned out he was doing very well for himself. He'd started his own financial company after graduating, and things had gone so well that he was now looking to start aggressively expanding. He offered me a job right there, director of the new 'Business Development department', which I'd be building from scratch. It paid almost double what I make now. He said he'd be happy to throw me into the deep end. I told him I'd have to think about it."

Raising the pistol, Jason halfheartedly took another shot at the root tumor. He missed wildly.

"When I mentioned it to Lily . . ." He slouched over, pulling his arms in, and shrinking into himself. "I never should have said anything, but when I told her, she was more excited than I'd ever seen. She said she had been praying for something like this. I didn't know it, but she had already been looking for a new place to live. She'd found a house and had fallen in love with it. It was big and expensive. It had all these extra rooms that we didn't need. No way I could afford it with my current job, but with this new one, we might have been able to make it work." Jason shifted uncomfortably. He hung his head and stared down into the clouds below. "I shouldn't have told her. I shouldn't have let her get her hopes up. I never said I was going to take the job."

"That job . . . it just wouldn't have worked out. It was crazy for my friend to even offer it to me. I took a few business classes in school, and he thinks I can build a whole new department? I wouldn't even know where to begin. I'd have to be in charge of people, too. And the stress. I wish I was the kind of person that could just step into the fray like that, sail into those uncharted waters, but the truth of it is, I can't. I would've failed miserably and gotten fired. And then where would we be? But when I tried to explain that to Lily, she lost it. She cried for hours, and since then, all we ever do is fight."

Staring down at the wood attachments on the gun, Jason watched as the runes filled in with blue light. Tears formed in his eyes as his thoughts continued to spiral. "There's something wrong with me," Jason whispered. "I'm missing something. I'm not enough. I can't be the man she needs me to be."

Jason slouched even more. The hideous truth was out, and all hope abandoned. Despite the protests from his heart, there was a peace to giving up — on the mission, on his marriage, on everything. He set the pistol down beside him and stared despondently out into the ever-churning clouds.

Parch glanced at Jason with concern but said nothing. He then closed his eyes, crossed his arms, and sat quietly. When he opened his eyes again, he looked at Jason directly. "Stop hunching your shoulders," Parch said flatly.

Confused, Jason looked at him.

"When you're shooting," Parch continued, "you're bracing too much for the recoil. You're tensing up and going in scared. You're worrying about every little thing. It's throwing off your aim. You need to relax. Just stand up straight, and shoot."

"Oh," Jason said, completely perplexed. Was Parch not going to say anything about Jason's story? Or maybe he *was* saying something? Jason wasn't sure. He suddenly felt embarrassed that he'd revealed so much. He quickly decided to return to shooting and pretend like he hadn't said anything.

"Here, stand up," Parch said, as he stood up himself. "Let's try something."

Jason stood up, and Parch took position behind him, looking over his shoulder. Parch took a moment to adjust Jason's stance. Jason was hunched over, but Parch forced him to stand up straight and tall with his chest out. Jason's head drooped; Parch made him hold it up high. Jason was askew from the target; Parch squared him up so he faced it directly. Once Jason was completely in line, Parch signaled his approval with a slap on the back.

"There," Parch said. "Try that out. Remember to relax. You can do this."

Despite still being disquieted, Jason pushed all his thoughts aside and, for the moment, focused only on shooting. He breathed deeply and closed his eyes. Parch was right; Jason could feel how tense and wound up his body was. His shoulders and jaw were taut, as if waiting for an attack. Jason forced himself to relax, and the tension slowly dissipated. He now felt calmer and more focused. In this relaxed state, Jason raised the gun toward the target, exhaled, then fired.

The round ripped through the sky and smashed into the top right edge of the root tumor. The force of the bullet shattered a section of wood and sent splinters flying through the air.

Parch roared in celebration, throwing his fists in the air. Jason blinked in disbelief, unable to take his eyes off the hit.

"There ya go! Now adjust a little down and to the left," Parch instructed. "But just a little."

Encouraged and growing excited, Jason eyed the oozing black bit of the root tumor: his bull's-eye. For the first time, he started to believe he could hit it. Jason closed his eyes and remembered all the pieces he had learned. He organized all this information in his mind and formed it into a routine.

He started by relaxing. He let all the tension out of his body, specifically his shoulders, and stood up straight. Next, he adjusted his hands on the pistol, reestablishing the proper grip. Then he drew in a deep breath and raised the pistol. He sighted the tumor and aimed at the black ooze, adjusting slightly down and to the left to compensate. Finally, he exhaled and, when he felt at his most steady, he fired.

The round smashed into the root tumor, but Jason had adjusted a little too much. He hit below and to the left of the oozing orifice's center. Still, it had been very close. Jason proved the first hit wasn't a fluke.

"Close!" Parch shouted. "So close!" Excitedly, he reached out to slap Jason on the back, but held back at the last moment. Instead of a celebratory back slap, Parch backed up, giving Jason space to shoot. Pacing nervously behind his companion, Parch held his hands up to his mouth. "Adjust a hair back." he said, in a much more calm and restrained tone.

Despite trying to stay relaxed, Jason, too, was exhilarated. Shooting was feeling more and more natural, and the progress was intoxicating. But before he got too excited, Jason stopped himself and closed his eyes. He had to stay calm. He couldn't celebrate yet. Focusing on his breathing again, Jason concentrated and collected himself.

Seeing this, Parch also went quiet. His eyes darted between Jason and the target, and he continued to pace quietly, his movements filled with nervous energy.

Just like before, Jason thought. He relaxed his body and stood up straight. He adjusted his grip. He opened his eyes and took a deep breath. Everything was easy; everything felt natural. Jason looked out at his target across the open sky. It was far away, but he knew exactly what he needed to do. He aimed and, after a calm, focused exhale, he fired.

The bullet pierced the middle of the black ooze, and the whole root tumor lurched backward. It remained mostly intact, but the black ooze splattered everywhere, and daylight shown out of the hole that Jason had punched straight through the center.

Parch let loose with a primal roar. Jason roared, too, but his was mixed with laughter.

"What a shot!" Parch shouted. "You're a natural! What do you mean you can't do anything?! You just hit a shot that no beginner should be able to hit!"

With a wide grin, Jason relished his victory. It was a little thing, ultimately, but he had thought it impossible only moments before. The success stirred something in him.

After the laughter and cheers died down, the two sat back on the edge, staring out at the conquered target. There was a hopeful air now, a cheerful feeling. The situation didn't seem quite so dire.

"I can't believe I hit it," Jason exclaimed, replaying the moment over and over in his mind. "I guess I should be more confident. Lily is always telling me that."

"No, no," Parch said, waving his hand in disagreement. "Confidence is an empty illusion."

Taken aback by the statement, Jason looked at Parch. "What do you mean?"

"Well, confidence is a feeling," Parch said. "It comes and goes as it pleases; you can't rely on it. When you have it, you don't need it, and when you need it, you don't have it."

Parch sat up and cleared his throat. "'Confidence is useless, Parch,'" he said in a gruff, forced tone, clearly meant as an imitation. "That's what the guy who taught me this job always used to say," he said, briefly switching back to his normal voice before once again resuming the imitation. "'Confidence is useless! Courage and nerve, now that's what you need. Courage and nerve! Courage to get you started, and nerve to see you through. If you can find those two friends, they'll be with you to the very end.'"

Dropping the imitation, Parch resumed his normal voice, and sat back. "When things get tough, I remember that, and then I head into whatever storm fate has for me."

Confused, Jason sat there wrestling with what Parch had said. "But why do it at all?" Jason asked finally. "Why go into the storm? Why take the risk? You could die in here!"

"Because people need me to," Parch replied, "and when I think about those who are counting on me, I just go in and do whatever it takes, no matter how horrible it is, or how scared I am, or how long the odds are. I do it because . . . because I like people, I guess."

Parch stood up and dusted off his hands. "Plus," he said with a big smile, "you just gotta take some risks in life. Otherwise, it all gets boring." Glancing down at his watch, he made a surprised face. "We better get going. Don't want to run out of time." He held out his hand to help Jason up.

But Jason didn't take Parch's hand immediately. He sat there for a moment, hesitating. He'd been serious before about not wanting to go on, but maybe things were different now. Maybe he could go just a little further, for just a little while longer.

After several seconds, Jason reached out and grabbed Parch's hand. Parch pulled him up. Then, with a slap on Jason's shoulder, Parch turned and walked back toward the root line.

Left standing there by himself, Jason bent down and picked up his key chain from the ground where he'd left it. With the trinket in his hand, he looked over the edge into the clouds below. But after watching the swirling mass of white for several seconds, he slipped the key chain back into his pocket, then he followed Parch toward the roots.

CHAPTER 11

Jason and Parch took considerable time crossing the next section. The recent excitement had shown just how delicate the decaying roots could be. Parch cautiously tested and probed the root line's strength before the next crossing, pulling and shaking as hard as he could. The roots moved little, so they climbed on top and crawled across at a snail's pace. The section held, and Jason breathed a sigh of relief when he set foot onto the next pillar.

The section after that went much the same, only slightly faster. And the one after that, faster still. Their trust in the roots soon grew, and they began making considerable progress, quickly nearing their destination: the enormous gray tree.

The closer they got, the steeper the root bridges became — not completely a vertical climb, but steep enough to be forced onto their hands and knees. They quickly gained elevation, working their way up toward the level of the Mortem Cor plant.

As they got closer, it was impossible to not appreciate the enormous size of the tree. The trunk looked thirty meters wide at its narrowest. Its branches spread far and wide above them in a huge canopy. The rock pillar it all rested on was the biggest so far and was at least one hundred meters in diameter.

As they stopped on one of the pillars for a momentary break, Jason wondered at the sight. Parch was intent on finding the second source that connected to Jason's house, and maybe this was it. Maybe this would be the end of the journey.

Jason surveyed the vast web of roots extending out from the Mortem Cor plant. It was truly impressive. Seeing the root lines run out for miles on top of the stone pillars made Jason wonder just how old this plant was. Then the realization struck him that each root line must go off to a bridge, and those bridges must lead somewhere. He desperately hoped one would lead them home.

"That's our next root line," Parch said, handing Jason a canteen of water and pointing to a root line on the other side of the tree. "But where it leads, I can't be sure. At least, not until we check out what's up there." Parch motioned toward the tree.

Jason furrowed his brow. "If you don't know where it leads, how do you know it's the one we have to take?"

"The root lines might look like jumbled messes, but there are patterns to them," Parch said. "Patterns to how the root strands weave together, to the root line's colors, to how the root line twists and curves through the Ignotus, patterns to all of it. These patterns show up in the black stains that mark the bridges in the human world. That root line over there has the same pattern that's on your living room wall. Well, part of the pattern, anyway. These root lines have been tricky today — lots of conflicting signs mixed together. Never seen it before, and I have no idea what to make of it. But I'm sure we'll get answers if we keep following them."

Jason looked out at a root line and tried to find the patterns Parch spoke of, but no matter how hard he squinted, he couldn't tell one line of roots from another; they all looked the same to him. But Parch seemed sure, so Jason didn't question him. After a long drink, Jason handed back the canteen and their short break ended. Quickly, the two men were on the move again.

After several more tense but ultimately uneventful root crossings, they finally arrived at the last section. The next root bridge climbed the last twenty meters up and connected with the giant rock pillar the Mortem Cor plant rested on. Jason felt uneasy. Just like with the last one, his anxiety had only grown as they moved closer to the terrible tree in front of them. Now they were here. If Parch was right, they'd soon have answers to what was going on, and Jason fervently hoped it was good news. He hoped this was the end. As he followed Parch crawling up the roots, Jason's mind filled with worst-case scenarios. What if this wasn't the second source? What if they couldn't even find the second source? What if the Mortem Cor plant was already hurting Lily? What if something went wrong with the torch and they couldn't escape?

The question's continued to build in Jason's mind until, in an effort to distract himself from the fear, he started nervously asking Parch questions. "What are we looking for, anyway?" he asked.

Parch continued crawling, but called back in his normal, friendly tone, "I've got to take a look at the plant's heart. Its heart is its essence, and it's where all the roots grow from. I'll be able to tell what's going on when I see it. With any luck, this is our second source. If it is, we can just burn the whole thing to ashes and button out, then seal the second bridge from the human side. After that, all there is left to do is grab a couple beers to celebrate a job well done."

Jason liked that plan very much, and hearing Parch's assured voice put him at ease. "So, if we use that button on the torch, we're instantly back to that box in my house, right? No more Ignotus, just right back to the human world?" Jason asked.

"Yeah, the torch will put us right next to the box in your entryway," Parch replied.

"What's it like when it happens? Does it feel weird?" Jason inquired.

"No," Parch answered. "You don't even feel it. It pulls you out in an instant; blink and you'll miss it. The only thing you notice is the smell. Inside the torch there's a special mix of stuff that gets pushed into the flame when you press the button. When it burns, it smells like . . . it's hard to describe really. Like pine needles and rosemary mixed with rubbing alcohol, and other things, too. The smell sticks in your nose for days. But when you've been doing this job a long time, you actually start to like it. Smells like safety; smells like a job well done."

Parch went on talking as they made their way up the roots, keeping the same pleasant, reassuring tone. "We're doing this real old school," he said. "I haven't seen a heart in a while. When you're learning the job, they teach you to always find and check the heart to look for irregularities, but after a while, you get good enough to just read the roots. You can't tell everything from them, but they usually tell you enough. Of course," Parch said, "the Mortem Cor plants aren't normally this big. They're normally smaller and have maybe one or two root lines at most, so it's typically a lot easier."

Jason looked up and saw they were now only five meters away from the edge of the pillar. In a few moments, they'd arrive. In a few moments, for good or bad, Parch would have answers to his questions. Jason paused for a moment on the roots. He took a deep breath and steadied himself. *Please be the second source*, he thought over and over.

While Jason was ruminating on the future, Parch, who was bored by the gentle climb, continued talking. "We're lucky, though," he said. "We have torches, guns, and other gear that makes everything easier. Back in the old days, and I mean the really old days, they didn't have any weapons except knives. Well, they were swords back then — huge swords. But that's all they had. Fighting Malus with nothing but steel and grit. It's crazy to think about. They still have some of the swords, but they keep them in glass cases now like a museum or something."

Parch's ramblings were starting to have an effect on Jason. For a brief moment, he forgot about his worries and listened intently while he climbed.

"And the bridges!" Parch exclaimed. "They had these huge kilns where they would burn a bunch of weird stuff to get the fire just right so they could see the bridge, then used actual torches to carry the fire in. No buttoning out for them. This job is hard enough with all the gear — I don't know how they did it without it. Though, I guess they did have stuff like the chain"— Parch nodded toward the chain, which was still wrapped around Jason's chest —"so I'm sure that helped a lot."

Jason looked up, dumbfounded. "*Who* do you work for?" he asked.

Parch looked back and laughed. "Doesn't matter," he said. At long last, Parch reached up, grabbed the pillar's edge, and pulled himself over the top.

Jason's fears all rushed back to his mind at once. They had arrived. He took a moment to brace himself, then climbed over top as well. Once he was up, he took in the sight.

The ancient tree towered over them. It stood, looking massive and terrible. Even in its decrepit and diminished state, it was imposing and made even the large pillar feel small. Jason craned his neck to look up at the thousands of branches spreading out above them. The tree was so tall that the top branches were lost in the misty clouds. Jason's eyes followed the Mortem Cor plant all the way down, until he was staring directly ahead. Infront of him, atop this stone pillar, was a massive heap of tangled roots.

Just like the previous Mortem Cor plant, this present Mortem Cor plant's massive trunk didn't run down to the surface upon which the plant resided, namely the top of the stone pillar. Instead, the trunk rose out of an enormous pile of tangled roots that was created by all the root lines — coming from all directions — converging into a single giant mess. The tangle was thirty meters tall and had a considerably wider diameter than the trunk. At its base, the tangle of roots was loose and spread out, with significant space between the roots as they began to weave together. But as the tangle rose higher it grew smaller and more compact, until all the roots eventually combined and formed the tree's trunk.

Parch stared up at the tree. "This thing is ancient," he said. "Probably old enough to be from those sword-and-kiln days." Parch's chipper tone dropped and his eyes narrowed. "I bet it's hurt a lot of people. The heart will be at the center of this mess." He walked over to the tangle of roots. Parch tried to peer through them, but it was impossible to see inside very far. He pulled out his knife and touched the edge to one of the roots. He raised his arm back as if to hack at the roots, like cutting into a dense jungle, but then stopped and lowered the knife without swinging. Turning to Jason, he said, "This plant is falling apart too much as it is, let's try and make it to the heart without cutting anything."

Jason agreed but was more concerned with something else. To Jason, the tangle looked like a giant nest. It was impossible to tell what horrors could be lurking in the shadows. He couldn't stop himself from imagining all sorts of terrible creatures. To make matters worse, there wasn't much space between the roots. Should something attack them in that dark, claustrophobic space, they wouldn't be able to get out. "Is it safe?" Jason asked. "Does anything live in there?"

Parch looked at the tangled web of roots, then back at Jason. He stuck out his hand. The chain, which was still around Jason's chest, jumped to Parch. It coiled around his arm and back. When it was securely in place, Parch held it out toward the tangle. Both men watched in anticipation, but nothing happened. The chain stayed motionless, calmly wrapped around Parch.

"Looks good," Parch said with a shrug. But he drew his pistol anyway. "No harm in being safe, though," he said.

Despite the apparent good news from the chain, Jason's fears were not assuaged. The tangle was about the least inviting place he could imagine, but when he saw Parch already searching for the best way in, he soon realized that unless he wanted to wait outside by himself, he'd have to follow.

Parch found a promising spot, and carefully looked it over. He'd found an area where the spaces in between the roots were wider and larger than elsewhere — large enough that a man might be able to squeeze through. But there was only one way to know for sure. He pulled the torch off his shoulder and held it carefully so as not to set the tree alight with the bright green flame. Then, after taking a deep breath, he pressed himself into the tangle and vanished.

Jason hesitated. He looked around, as if in search of any option other than following Parch. But soon, with clenched teethed and frayed nerves, Jason cursed, then gritted his teeth and pushed into the tangle as well.

Once inside the tangle of roots, the light from the outside quickly dwindled. Soon the only weapon against the darkness was the torch's green flame and the narrow beams of their flashlights. The shadows were deep and pervasive. Dark crevasses filled the spaces between the random twists and turns of the roots. As they continued in deeper, the roots grew closer together, the spaces tighter. Eventually, the men were crouching, crawling, and squeezing through to make progress.

It started to get very quiet. Jason could no longer hear the wind from outside; all he heard was his own breathing and effort as he continued to work his way through. The dry bark scraped against his hands and shoulders and hips as he moved. Several times Jason's clothing got snagged on a root, and he had to wrench it free, often ripping it in the process. They didn't have far to go — only fifteen meters worth of roots to squeeze between — to reach the center of the tangle. But even that short distance was exhausting because of the maneuvering required to get through.

To make matters worse, the air reeked of the same dull smell of rotten meat that the Mortem Cor plants always stank of. In the tight space of the root tangle, there was no way to escape it.

In the darkness, Jason's mind began playing tricks on him. Every shadow had eyes looking out, and every dark void that he was forced to stick his hand through, he imagined some nasty creature waiting to bite it off. But each time his hand came back intact, and each time he shone his light at the shadows, there was nothing. After struggling for nearly ten minutes, Jason caught up with Parch, who was waiting for him at the edge of a large opening.

"We're here," Parch said.

Jason peered in curiously. They had arrived at a hollow circular chamber that was five meters in diameter and five meters tall. The roots that made up the ceiling formed a dome-like structure, so that they rounded and ended up forming the walls before running down to the rock of the stone pillar that made up the floor. The mighty roots feeding into the tangle all shrank, collected, and spun together at various points as they approached the chamber. Once spun together, the roots continued to shrink so much they ended up becoming the diameter of a pencil. Then they dropped down and ran along the stone floor into the chamber, coming from all directions, zigzagging randomly before finally converging at a single point in the center. At this central point, where all the thin roots combined, they rose from the floor up to a raised black misshapen orb about the size of a fist.

This suspended black orb, which was the centerpiece of the whole chamber and clearly the heart, rose a meter off the ground. It was the vile, putrid nucleus of the tree, and from where all the roots originated. A slimy dark ooze seeped out and covered it, making it look alive and even more foul.

Its smell was like the roots, only much more concentrated. It smelled like death and decay; it smelled like someone vomited on top of roadkill. Jason gagged and tried to cover his mouth and nose, but there was no keeping the repulsive stench out of his nostrils. And it wasn't just the smell, something about the heart was making Jason sick. It was unsettling being close to this thing, and every instinct told him to leave.

"Never seen anything like this before," Parch said, entering the room despite the smell. "Usually, they're the size of a pea, and buried in the wood. But this one made a whole room for itself in here."

Jason was quickly growing tired of hearing Parch say he'd "never seen anything like this before." He followed Parch into the chamber, unsure of his surroundings. After quickly glancing around the space, Jason stood still, watching and waiting to see what Parch would do next.

Parch looked at everything. He began walking around the room, careful not to step on any of the roots that ran along the floor. He worked methodically, taking in the whole chamber. He started by walking around the entire perimeter of the chamber, then moved in, walking in concentric circles as he worked his way toward the center. Several of the root lines caught his attention as he moved through the chamber; he crouched down to inspect them, observing their entire length as they ran to the heart. After circling around the chamber three times, slowly getting closer to the center, he finally arrived at the heart. Leaning in close, he stared with furrowed brow, cupping his chin in his hand.

Jason was left to watch and wonder. Nothing in this chamber made any sense to him. He had no idea what anything was, nor what it all meant. The roots looked like roots, and the oozing black orb revealed nothing to him. All he could do was wait patiently for Parch. The anticipation was tight in Jason's chest, and he felt like he was in a doctor's office waiting for a prognosis.

Parch continued staring at the heart for a little while longer, but eventually he stood up and turned toward Jason. "Okay, I've got good news and bad news," he began. "Bad news first: this isn't our second source."

Jason exhaled sharply through clenched teeth. He squeezed his fists so hard, his knuckles turned white. He turned his back to Parch and the heart as he tried to collect himself.

"But the second source isn't far," Parch continued, with a hopeful tone. "That root line I pointed out earlier will lead us to it. It's weird. I don't know why, but this plant has many connections to other Mortem Cor plants in other Ignotus, just like the one that brought us here. It's very strange. It's like a big . . . network." Parch stared at the heart for a moment, lost in thought. "The good news is the second connection to your house, the one in the living room, isn't done yet. The bridge has been open since before I got here, but the roots are still immature, still growing. So, not yet a threat. But that's another strange thing; those roots trying to get into your house are very . . . strange. I can't tell everything from here, but it looks like they're tidy, and I don't know what it means." Parch looked at several of the roots around the chamber. "And that connection isn't the only one that's like that either; a lot of this tree's root lines are the same. Actually, the next one we're going through looks like it. Everything's normal until the root lines enter the Abyss, and then they suddenly start to . . . arrange themselves. I need to see it up close." Parch went quiet again. Lost in thought, he returned to staring at the heart, focused and serious.

"What does it all mean?" Jason asked, after it was clear that no further explanation was coming. He had listened politely as Parch had rambled on, but none of it made any sense. All he cared about was the second source, but Parch kept talking about root lines and the Abyss, and Jason had no idea why that even mattered. He just wanted to know when their journey would be over.

"I'm not sure, but —" Parch was interrupted by the chain, which started shaking in a frenzy of excitement. It rattled loudly and crawled all over Parch.

Jason's eyes went wide, and he gasped in sudden realization. He leapt away from the dark chamber walls and toward the center, where Parch had already drawn his gun and was sweeping the dark spaces all around them. Jason looked around too, quickly recognizing they were trapped. There was no quick way out of this chamber. *What's in here with us*? Jason thought, as he clumsily pulled his own gun out of the holster.

Seconds felt like hours as the two men waited to see what would come. Jason huddled low to the ground, jumping at every shifting shadow. Parch, conversely, remained steady and focused, constantly looking around the chamber. After a moment, Parch dropped a hand from his pistol and grabbed the torch from his shoulder, holding it close to, but not touching, the Mortem Cor plant's heart.

The tense silence was finally broken by a strange, loud noise. Something between a hiss and a rattle echoed through the tangle and into the chamber. Parch and Jason frantically searched for the source, but it was coming from all directions. And it was getting louder.

Both men scanned the dark holes in the chamber's walls. Whatever was approaching could come through anywhere. The strange noise was now so loud, it filled their ears. Parch pulled Jason up. Standing back-to-back, they watched and waited.

But just as suddenly as it started, the noise stopped. After a brief moment of quiet, it was replaced with a voice that was eerily similar to the hissing rattle. "Vermin in my master's orchard," it said.

The voice was sinister and spoke with a strange lack of cadence. Whatever was speaking, it obviously wasn't human. The situation was made even worse because of the tangle, which diffused the voice and made it so the two men couldn't even tell what direction it was coming from. Parch and Jason shared a nervous look.

"Vermin in my master's orchard!" the voice repeated, but this time in a furious, unhinged scream.

"Who are you?" Parch shouted back.

The reply came not in the form of words, but instead in the form of a large pincered claw that shot out of the dark tangle and tried to catch Parch in its sharp grasp. Parch narrowly avoided it by diving out of the way, throwing himself and Jason to the ground in the process. The claw was huge — nearly the size of a man's torso — and the monstrous, segmented, insect-like arm to which it was attached was long and powerful. The appendage pulled back into the dark tangle as quickly as it had appeared. Parch responded in kind by firing into the darkness from which the claw had come. The sound of the blast filled the chamber, and the round flew through one of the gaps in the chamber walls, disappearing into the tangle. The creature screamed defensively with another of its hissing rattles.

Jason got to his feet and faced the side of the chamber the claw had attacked from. Now pointed in the right direction, Jason realized there was a noise he hadn't heard before: skittering and scratching. It sounded like insect legs moving around on the hard wood of the tangle, only they must have been extremely large insect legs, judging by the sound. Jason also noticed that the roots in that direction were shaking and shifting, as if being forced out of the way by something moving around in them. It was clear something large was hiding in the shadows of the tangle. Jason began to worry the creature would burst through into the chamber, but it didn't. Instead, it remained hidden among the roots, perhaps reluctant to present a clear target for Parch's pistol. Jason squinted, trying to see the thing, but the darkness was too deep — too prevalent — to see anything.

"Who are you?" Parch called again.

"Merely a servant to my master," the voice answered. Then another loud, aggressive rattle filled the chamber. "You tried to burn my master's tree in the desert," the voice screamed. "But the tree lives. You fools merely pruned it — a valuable service. If another tree had interfered with my master's designs, my master would have been displeased."

"The desert?" Parch said, confused. "From the last Ignotus? How did you follow us from there? And how are you able to speak?" he shouted.

"I go where my master wishes," the creature said, "and in return, my master blesses me with the tree's fruit made with your sweet blood. But for every flower I eat, unlike the mindless brutes, I grow wiser. I serve my master better than they, and that is why my master will take me with him on the day of the great feast."

The fear had set in, and Jason was already sweating. He cowered low to the ground. This new creature was significantly more terrifying than any previous one. Hearing it speak was profoundly unnerving. This creature had intelligence along with its malevolence. Suddenly Jason was overwhelmed with the feeling that this monster had planned everything, like it was all a trap to lure them in here, and now they were caught. *I'm going to die down here!* Jason thought frantically.

As if it could sense Jason's distress, the creature's claw once again burst forth from the darkness. It raced toward Jason, who was frozen in fear. He was only saved by Parch, who tackled him out of the way, causing both men to narrowly avoid being caught.

"I can taste your fear, weakling!" the creature screamed. There was a frenzy in its voice now. Like a shark that had the scent of blood, it was becoming more aggressive. "You are right to be afraid. You were right to run from us in the desert. You are nothing to my master. With the blood of the woman, my master will begin the day of the feast, and none of you will escape!"

"Woman?" Jason responded, still sprawled on the ground. "Lily? What . . . what do you want with my wife?!" Jason shouted, his voice faltering halfway through.

The creature's voice changed and took on a more mocking, boastful tone. "I have watched her through the trees," it said. "She has the sweetest blood. My master was pleased when I found her. I will deliver her myself, and I will be greatly rewarded."

"I won't let you hurt her!" Jason screamed.

Parch glanced at Jason with concern as he spoke to the monster. "What do you mean 'sweetest blood'?" he shouted.

"No longer will the trees take their portion," the creature said, ignoring Parch's question. The frenzy was building in its voice again, and it went on speaking, lost in its own furious tirade. "My master will drink it all, and, strengthened by the sweetest blood, he will begin the feast!

"You fools cannot stop my master. He has killed all those who were impudent enough to trespass into his orchard. But my master need not be troubled over you. My swarm will kill you here, and I will be rewarded when I bring my master your broken bodies." The creature ended with the loudest and most aggressive hiss-rattle yet. And as it did, Parch's chain once again went wild with forewarning. Suddenly, the sound of scratching and scraping was all around them. Malus were crawling through the tangle. These Malus were giant insects, the size of dogs, and they were crawling into the chamber from every angle. They were of all kinds — spiders, centipedes, cockroaches — but no matter the variety, they all had oversized, razor-sharp teeth protruding from their large mandibles.

Parch had seen and heard enough. He pressed the flame of the torch into the plant's heart, which ignited like it was doused in gasoline. The green flame immediately enveloped the heart, and then spread through the roots to the rest of the tangle. The chamber, and everywhere else, was instantly turned into a green inferno.

The fire was harmless to the two men but proved deadly to the Malus. They were engulfed by the green flame and reduced to writhing on the ground as they burned.

Jason's heart rejoiced both at the turn of events and at how protected he was within the fire. He felt nothing but a pleasant warmth from the flames, like sunshine on a cool day. Hearing the rush of the flames as they spread was like the sound of absolute victory. But this feeling of triumph was immediately replaced with fear when one of the large load-bearing roots in the chamber's walls, now weakened by the raging flames, shattered under the great weight of the tree above. The tangle groaned terribly as the weight shifted, and the root ceiling lost several centimeters of height as it did, before coming to an eventual, precarious, temporary rest.

Both men held their breath during this sequence of events, half expecting the tree to come crashing down on top of them. But once the tree's shifting stopped, a single look between them was all the communication they needed. They both hurried out of the chamber and into the tangle, desperate to get out from under the tree.

The men squeezed and shimmied through the roots as quickly as they could and found themselves in another spacious and open section of the tangle. On the far side, they saw a clear path out of the tangle in the form of a tunnel. They both broke into a sprint toward the exit. Along the way, they saw hundreds of the Malus insects writhing in the flames, falling from above them, or having already succumbed and lying still. The dancing green flames, which by now had spread throughout the tangle, made it difficult to see; but there wasn't far to go.

Once inside the tunnel, they covered ground quickly. They were soon approaching the mouth and were able to see daylight. But just as they were about to exit the tangle, Parch stopped quickly and grabbed Jason before either of them could leave the safety of the flames. It didn't take long for Jason to see why.

Just beyond the flames was an enormous beast, alert and waiting off to the side of the mouth of the tunnel. Standing three meters tall, the beast had the body of a giant lion and bat-like wings that spread maybe fifteen meters wide from tip to tip. Its head and face were vaguely feline, except for the mouth, which was far wider, and filled with rows of razor-sharp teeth like that of a shark. When it saw the men, it let out a terrible screech and charged. But it dared not enter the flames. Frustrated and frenzied, it paced near the edge of the burning tangle, waiting for the men to come out. It waited with its muscles tense and ready, along with its claws out and its teeth showing.

Parch cursed. He drew his gun, but the beast dove to the side of the tunnel, using the exterior of the curving tangle to hide beyond sight. The beast was no doubt setting a trap to coax them out and then pounce on them. Parch moved to the edge of the flames, trying to peer around the tangle, looking for the beast. But he couldn't see anything.

Cursing again, he looked around desperately. The tunnel had brought them to the same side of the tree that their exit root line was on, but unfortunately that was of little help. Even if they could get past the huge beast waiting for them outside the tunnel, the root line was covered in the same insects that had attempted to swarm them in the tangle. And to make matters worse, they had chewed through the root bridges before the fire had reached them. In fact, those same insects were on every root line in sight. A large root next to Parch snapped as the green flame consumed it. "We don't have time for this," Parch said.

Jason's eyes shifted around nervously as more roots began to fail all around them. The tree's weight shifted again, and the tunnel lost several more centimeters. The tangle continued to hold, but it wouldn't for long. This tree was coming down.

"What do we do?" Jason shouted over the roar of the flames.

"We have to get to that bridge!" Parch shouted back, pointing at a stone pillar off in the distance.

"How?" Jason responded.

Parch's brow furrowed in concentration, he leaned out and looked up at the tree towering over them. He looked at the web of branches. Then he looked out to the thousands of pillars in the sky, and finally back to the bridge. He turned to Jason with a eureka moment on his face. "Cut the roots!" Parch roared as he drew his knife.

Shocked and confused, Jason watched as Parch started cutting through every root around them. Jason didn't think it was the smartest thing to cut the roots that were holding up the tree, but Parch's ferocity as he attacked every root nearby left no room for second guessing. Jason drew his own knife and started cutting as well. The blade slid through the roots with little resistance, and the runes glowed brightly.

The two men made quick work of the already weakened tangle, and as a result, the supporting structure on their current side of the tree started to collapse. The massive weight began to shift again, causing a tremendous creaking and groaning. The tree started to lean, pressing the roots above them down lower and lower, until each man was forced to crouch.

"To the other side!" Parch yelled over the turmoil, and the two men began moving back into and through the tangle.

With roots buckling, snapping, and shattering around them, they made their way back through the tangle. By the time they'd made it to the heart chamber, they were crawling as the weight above continued to press down, nearly crushing them. The smokeless, green fire that engulfed everything made it difficult to see, but at the same time it had weakened the roots so much that Jason didn't even need to cut them; he could break a path through with a single hand. The two men barely squeezed through the heart chamber in time, nearly being smashed to oblivion with the rest of the roots. They ran across the chamber to reach the other side of the tangle.

The situation on this other side was the opposite. Here, instead of being crushed, the tangle was being stretched and ripped upward. The groaning wood was growing louder, and there was even more snapping, tearing, and shearing. It was like an orchestra building to a crescendo. Only a few seconds remained before the tree would break free and topple over.

It was clear their time was up. Parch bear-hugged one of the thicker roots. "Grab on!" he roared to Jason.

Jason wrapped his arms and legs around one of the roots just in time. The tree began to fall, ripping the roots up as it did. Parch and Jason were dragged upward with incredible force. Jason felt his stomach drop through his naval. Terrified, he clung desperately to the root, wishing for it all to be over.

Parch, on the other hand, roared with laughter, despite the terrifying chaos of the moment. "Tiiiiiiimber!" he screamed with irreverent mirth.

The mighty Mortem Cor plant, which had stood proudly for so long, fell. The great web of roots that spread out from the tangle, half of them now on fire, was torn asunder by the immense force. The older, more fragile root lines snapped free immediately. Conversely, the newer and stronger root lines were ripped from their pillars like taut steel cables and flung in all directions. The mayhem echoed throughout the sky for miles.

The tree toppled over, making a huge arc. But as it fell, its great network of branches started to fall into, as well as catch onto, its own root network, which also included the rock pillars. Because of the enormous momentum and weight, the first few branches that caught were instantly shattered to pieces. Yet as the tree fell even farther, more branches — thicker branches with the strength to hold the tree up (at least, temporarily) — began to catch, as well. As the tree's trunk reached a nearly horizontal position, these forces won out, bringing the tree to a sudden halt, and stopping it from falling into the endless clouds below.

Much of the violence caused by the tree slamming to a stop against the stone pillars was contained to its crown and branches. But even the diminished force from the impact that travelled down the trunk and into the roots was nearly enough to shake off Jason. With his eyes shut and his arms and legs clenched in a death grip around the root, Jason was barely able to hang on as the immense forces thrashed him around. But hang on he did. After the brief but extreme upheaval, Jason and Parch were left suspended in the sky.

The Mortem Cor plant came to a dubious stop, and Jason opened his eyes and looked out at the cataclysm that was its upheaval. Hundreds of meters of burning trunk and branches were caught precariously in the sky. The entire web of roots was in disarray, with some root lines burning, some severed completely, and others that had ripped down the stone pillars they were attached to. The monstrous tree lay nearly flat, caught upon the stone pillars and the remains of its own web of roots, but it wouldn't be for long. The fire was rapidly consuming every bit of the plant that it touched, including the roots Jason now clung to. Soon the pieces holding it up would burn through, and all would fall between the pillars down into the sky below.

"Come on," Parch said to Jason as he started climbing through what was left of the root tangle toward the now horizontal trunk.

Jason was having difficulty keeping up with Parch. Everything was chaos; everything was overwhelming. Jason's chest felt tight, and his arms and legs felt weak. His hands shook and fought him as he tried to reach up to climb. He had to force himself to breathe. But there was no other choice. He blocked out everything and pressed upward, fighting his body the entire way.

When Jason reached the point where all the roots melded together and formed the trunk, Parch, who was already there, pulled him up and onto the horizontal surface. Jason set foot on the trunk and immediately bent over, bracing his hands on his knees for support. He sucked down air, like it was his last breath, as he tried to recover. But there was good news: Parch's insane plan had worked.

When they had cut the roots in the tangle below, they had destabilized the entire Mortem Cor plant. With so much weight only supported on one side, the massive weight above had shifted and leaned over to the weaker side, eventually falling over. Parch had been strategic in knowing exactly where to cut the roots, lining it up so the tree would fall closely toward the bridge they needed to exit. They now had a convenient, if only temporary, path to the bridge, which was located on a stone pillar a few hundred meters away. They would have to hurry, though, or it would all be for nothing. After a final breath, Jason followed Parch, sprinting down the trunk toward the bridge.

The two men made quick progress running down the length of the trunk. The green flames leapt up all around them. They would need to run along the trunk for about four hundred meters, and then, because the tree hadn't fallen precisely onto their exit bridge, they'd have to veer down one of the tree's branches. The branch would take them directly above the bridge, but they would still be nearly twenty meters above it. They'd have to figure something out once they got there.

As he ran, Jason noticed something moving parallel with them. He squinted and quickly recognized that it was the beast from outside of the tangle before. Using its huge bat wings and its agile strength, the beast was following alongside them, jumping and flying from pillar to pillar.

Its eyes never left the two men; its intense focus was disturbing. Although it still didn't dare enter the flames, the beast followed them as closely as possible, seemingly looking for any opportunity to attack.

"Parch!" Jason called out, his eyes darting between the creature and Parch. "That thing from before — it's following us."

Parch glanced over quickly, but then returned his focus to the bridge off in the distance. "It can't get us here in the fire, and we'll be in the flames all the way to the bridge," Parch said. "It'll never get a chance."

With only fifty meters to go before they reached the branch that would take them to the bridge, Jason's hopes were growing. They were almost out. But as they had been running, the fire had been doing its work. One of the larger branches holding up the tree had reached its limit. The weight of the tree, combined with the devouring fire, became too much. With an ear-shattering snap, the load-bearing branch broke free, causing a cascading effect as the immense weight shifted. Many more branches snapped the same way, and the tree fell out from under the two men's feet. Both the men and the tree were suddenly in free fall.

Jason's heart skipped, and his breath caught in his throat. He tried to scream as he fell, but every muscle in his body went tense, and no air escaped his lungs. His mind went blank with terror.

Fortunately for him and Parch, another of the tree's larger branches crashed into a rock pillar, and the tree caught again. They had fallen nearly ten meters, and as it abruptly stopped so too did Parch and Jason. The two men slammed down onto the tree, but thankfully the fire-softened wood cushioned their fall. Jason and Parch both sunk nearly a meter deep into the trunk before they were stopped, but that didn't mean it wasn't painful. Jason was left confused, disoriented, and groaning.

The shock of the fall made it crystal clear just how temporary this path would be. As Jason came to his senses he was hit with another terrible revelation: the tree was still moving. The massive tree had slammed to a near stop but was now gradually sliding off the rock pillars that kept it from falling any further. And to make matters worse, the sound of snapping branches was increasing. The fire had completely enveloped every part of the fallen Mortem Cor plant at this point; where it had once been gray and lifeless, it now had leaves of green flame that filled its whole canopy. These leaves of fire were quickly eating through the branches. There wasn't much time left.

Jason quickly forgot his pain, climbed out of the hole he'd created when he hit the trunk, and took off with Parch at a mad dash toward the bridge. The tree's constant movements under their feet made it difficult for them to maintain their balance, and they stumbled as if running across the deck of a ship at sea. But the adrenaline pumping through Jason's veins pushed out all distractions, and he sprinted on recklessly behind his companion.

As they turned on to the branch, the bridge came into view. They were only twenty meters from where they would have to jump off, and, because the tree had fallen, the branch was now only five meters above the bridge. Furthermore, the tree was still slipping, and the branch was losing height every second. It would soon fall below the top of the pillar the bridge was on, and there'd be no way to get back up.

The bridge itself was unique. It was much bigger than anything prior; the portal took up the entire surface of the top of the stone pillar it was on. There were also a large number of roots neatly feeding into it all along the perimeter of the portal mouth.

But Jason didn't concern himself with any of the irregularities as he ran. His only aim was sprinting to the safety of the Abyss; so, if this bridge was bigger and easier to jump into, all the better.

Jason was a few meters behind Parch as they approached the jump point. The tree was barely three meters above the bridge, and the branch was now so close that it was an easy jump. Jason watched Parch leap off the Mortem Cor plant without breaking stride, then vanish through the bridge and into the safety of the Abyss.

In the few seconds it took for Jason to reach the jump point, things changed dramatically. As he approached the jumping-off point, the tree unexpectedly dropped another meter. The sudden fall knocked Jason's legs out from under him and sent him sprawling and sliding toward the side of the branch. Panicked, Jason threw his hands down onto the Mortem Cor plant and sunk his fingers into the fire-weakened wood. His hands dragged through the wood for nearly half a meter before it was enough to stop his momentum and prevent him from sliding off.

As Jason clung to the branch along its curvature, nearly off the edge, things were getting worse by the second. With precious little time left, Jason summoned every remaining ounce of strength he had. He crawled back up the branch. Then he stood upon his shaking legs, knowing it was now or never. Desperation and pure survival instinct pushed everything else out of his mind, and his focus narrowed to only the jump. An ear-piercing screech sounded somewhere behind him, but Jason didn't look back and instead only moved all the faster. With all his strength he ran and leapt off into the open sky.

CHAPTER 12

Jason screamed as he fell. He'd flung himself into the air, and now could only hope he hadn't traded one deadly fall for another.

The bridge mouth was massive, nearly twenty meters in diameter, and Jason felt as if he was jumping into a giant pool of darkness as he left the gray world of the Ignotus. No more clouds or light now, just darkness and an empty void. Jason passed into the Abyss and his eyes frantically searched below him, looking for anything he could grab on to.

Jason, remembering the first time he was in the Abyss, expected this experience to be similar. But instead of finding a tangled mess of branches, he was met with something very different. In here, the roots were uniform, regular, and orderly, as if purposely configured. Starting from the Ignotus side, the roots ringed the edge of the bridge. They packed together tightly along the bridge's perimeter and fed into the Abyss. As the roots passed through, they held their shape and spacing, and formed a kind of tunnel running through the Abyss. The roots ran together and made the walls, ceiling, and the flat floor, and by doing so created a large, spacious passageway twenty meters tall and wide. The tunnel ran at a forty-five degree angle, sloping downward from the bridge mouth.

With no branches to grab on to, Jason fell hard onto the downward slope. He tried to land on his feet, but the angle was too steep and his momentum too great; his feet landed, and his body kept going, sending him head over heels in a violent, uncontrolled tumble down the decline. He rolled and spun, unable to stop, causing himself to become completely disoriented. His arms, legs, and shoulders smashed into the roots over and over again. He was only saved as the angle of the slope grew shallower, until it eventually flattened out. After sliding to a halt, he lay still, confused and in pain. He tried to stand, but quickly fell back down and stayed there.

While Jason was collecting himself from the fall, Parch had already risen. The two men had fallen only a few meters away from each other. Unlike Jason, Parch hadn't tumbled, but instead had landed on his backside and was able to slide feet first down the decline in a safer, more controlled manner. After grimacing at seeing Jason's painful tumble, Parch looked around in astonishment at the strange root structure. But his attention was pulled away when an ear-piercing screech suddenly echoed through the tunnel, followed by the chain shaking violently at his hip.

The winged feline beast from before had followed them down through the bridge and was now charging at full stride toward the two men. It deftly handled the slope as its powerful legs and wings propelled it forward at incredible speed. With eyes full of bloodlust and its giant mouth open in anticipation, it rushed at them.

The beast was so fast, Parch couldn't react. In the time it took for it to close the gap and lunge toward him, Parch could only gasp in wide-eyed horror. The terrible creature pounced and reached out with its razor-sharp claws. But Parch was saved by the chain. In an instant, it shot from his side and entangled the monster's front legs. Ensnared and thrown off balance, the beast slammed into Parch, clumsily crashing to the ground and sending Parch flying.

A few meters away, Jason was pulled out of his stupor by the danger he was now in. He watched as the beast fought and scratched at the chain binding its front legs. He was so close that he could smell the creature's horrible stench. He felt the vibrations in the roots as it thrashed about in fury. But Jason didn't move, didn't breathe. Paralyzed with fear, he hoped he wouldn't be noticed as he tried to make himself as small as possible.

But it did no good. As the beast rolled around in a feral rage, struggling to free itself, its eyes fell upon him. The beast's attention immediately concentrated on Jason, and its eyes narrowed. Forgetting its bound paws, it maneuvered onto its stomach and launched itself at Jason with its powerful back legs.

Jason tried to evade, but it was no use; the monster easily pounced on him. He was smashed to the ground by the enormous force and held down by the Malus's bound paws. Like a cat playing with a mouse, it paused to watch Jason feebly squirm. Jason tried to scream, but the creature pressed down on his chest, forcing all the air out of his lungs. Helpless and gasping, all he could do was stare up at the creature's gaping maw as it descended toward him. But just as Jason was about to be ripped apart, a bright light flashed, and the beast's face exploded in white flames.

Parch lowered his pistol as the monster's limp body slumped over. Breathing hard and still shaken from the beast's impact, he had barely been able to get the shot off to save Jason. With a groan, he collapsed to the ground and lay there silently.

Wrestling beneath the beast's paws, Jason struggled under its now dead weight. Each paw was the size of a manhole cover, and its fifteen-centimeter claws protruded from soft brown fur. Jason couldn't even lift them off himself. Instead he had to wriggle out from underneath. Once free, he crawled away from its dead body as fast as he could.

Still frantic from the adrenaline dump due to nearly being killed, he twitchily wiped chunks of the dead monster's flesh off himself. Sticky, black ooze filled with bits of bone, hair, and flesh had splattered all over Jason when the monster's face exploded. The goo was warm and smelled like raw sewage. He hysterically spit and wiped his face, trying to keep it from going into his mouth, as he crawled farther and farther away. Once he was half a dozen meters away from the carcass, his energy faded, and he too collapsed onto the ground.

As Jason lay there, his body began to feel the toll from all he'd gone through. Deep pains tormented him, and a profound tiredness was beginning to set in. Somber and quiet, he didn't move for some time. But after a while, a question filled his mind. Despite his tiredness, Jason spoke up: "I thought the Malus couldn't come in here. Where were those . . . things? Those . . . whatever they're called — why didn't they tear that creature to shreds?" he asked.

Parch sat up with some effort. "Void fingers," he corrected. "And I've been wondering the exact same thing." Parch pulled the torch off his shoulder and held it so its light shined on the roots beneath him. He peered down, until his face was only a few centimeters away.

"These roots — they're packed together so tightly, it's like they're sealed shut." Parch traced his finger over the wood, then scanned all the way to the next bridge a hundred meters down the tunnel. "All the roots in here are the same. They're smooth and consistent with no weak spots or holes. It's like the roots have been directed to grow like this."

Glancing over his shoulder, Parch saw the Malus's body remained undisturbed, and his eyes lit up with an idea. He drew his knife and drove it into the roots. The blade cut through effortlessly as Parch carved out a rough circle. The middle fell out, dropping into the Abyss, and then thin black whisps, the void fingers, gradually emerged from the hole. They entered the tunnel slowly at first, drifting in randomly, but soon started to move deliberately toward the Malus's body. And once the fingers reached the carcass, once they bit into its flesh, hundreds more followed, rushing through the hole and viciously attacking the Malus's remains. It took only seconds for the fingers to completely annihilate the Malus's body, leaving nothing left.

Parch's eyes narrowed as he watched the whole series of events. "This root . . . tunnel," he said, "it's somehow keeping the void fingers out. I don't know how, but it's obvious the Malus are protected so long as this tunnel is completely sealed."

Parch cupped his chin in his hand and stared off blankly. "This must be how that Malus," Parch continued, "the one that talked to us, followed us from the desert. It must have come through one of these, which means there are more than just this one. The Malus can pass through the Abyss into other Ignotus with these tunnels." Parch stood up and started pacing. His brow furrowed, and he threw up a hand as he shook his head. "But why? What's going on here?"

Jason was becoming increasingly nervous. He still didn't understand how these Ignotus worked, but whatever was going on had clearly unsettled Parch. It was obvious the situation was dangerous, but not being able to fully grasp it made it that much more terrifying. The worst part was being reminded of the talking Malus: with its hidden, calculated hostility and strange threats. Jason spat out a question, trying to distract himself and quell his growing fear. "But I thought the roots grew randomly, like when we came through the first time from my basement," he said. "Did this grow naturally?"

Pulled out of his thoughts by the question, Parch replied, "No. Mortem Cor plants connecting to other Mortem Cor plants like this, forming these tunnels — this doesn't happen naturally. This 'network,' or as that Malus called it, this 'orchard,' is unprecedented. Even the size of these bridges is strange; I've never seen one that big. There's no way I'll be able to seal it. I don't know what's going on here, but it's not good." He looked at Jason, and his tone turned somber. "Although it explains one thing," he said. "That Malus said we're not the first ones to find this . . ." Parch's face grew dark. "We've been losing guys recently," he said. "Obviously, this can be a dangerous job, so of course we lose people occasionally, but this is different. Before, we might lose one guy a year, but now, in the last six months, we've lost fifteen. Not newbies, either. Every one of them was solid, experienced — the kind you could count on."

Parch kept pacing, his mind working while he talked. "We've been trying to figure out what's been going on for months. When someone fails to check in after a job, a strike team is sent to investigate. The missing guy will have sealed the bridge behind him — standard procedure to protect those on the human side in case anything goes wrong. But if the Mortem Cor plant is still alive, it will naturally reopen the bridge, and the team can go in and begin their sweeps. But recently, none of the bridges have reopened. As usual, Higher is complacent. The people in charge are asleep at the wheel. They brush it off and explain it away by saying it's nothing but a coincidence, assuming the guys died after killing the plant. But that doesn't make any sense. Normally, there's only one source, and after you torch it, you use the button on the torch to pull yourself out immediately. There's no reason to wait around.

"But now that I've seen this," Parch motioned toward the root tunnel around them, "and after hearing what that talking Malus said . . ." Parch let his sentence trail off into silence. He stopped pacing, folded his arms, and went still. Several tense seconds ticked by, then he turned and looked squarely at Jason. "Something is controlling this," Parch said finally. "Controlling these Mortem Cor plants, directing them to form these tunnels. Every one of those guys who went missing stumbled into this mess, just like we did, and they were killed for it." Parch's eyes narrowed in anger, and he looked back at the tunnel walls. "Then, whatever killed them stopped the bridges from reopening, so no one could find out what happened. This is all connected. Something is at the center of all of this, controlling everything."

Jason was growing profoundly unsettled as Parch spoke. He already felt powerless and weak as it was. But now, hearing that people had already been killed in here by this thing, it was starting to push Jason to the breaking point. "That talking Malus kept mentioning its master. That has to be who's behind this, right?" Jason asked.

Parch broke from staring at the root tunnel walls long enough to nod at Jason. He then put his hands on top of his head, interlocking his fingers, leaned back, and stared up at the tunnel ceiling twenty meters above. "There's something else we're missing," he said. "There has to be a reason for all this." Parch went silent and continued to stare off into nothingness as his mind worked.

For Jason, even the short silence was unbearable. "But what is this 'master'?" he asked.

"I don't know," Parch replied, "but to be able to control and direct Mortem Cor plants like this, especially ones so large, it has to be a Malus of immense power." He bent down and ran his hand along the smooth root floor. "The old guys . . ." he began, "the old timers that hang around headquarters sometimes tell these stories from long ago to scare the new guys. Nobody believes them, but they'll talk about ancient horrors, terrible creatures the size of mountains, thousands of years old, lurking in some hidden Ignotus. They call them Titans. If you're unlucky enough to find one, it means certain death. They're made of nothing but hatred and malevolence. They're ever hungry, ever seeking life energy, wanting nothing but to kill and devour . . . or worse . . ."

Parch's eyes suddenly went wide with revelation. "The day of the feast," he said to himself, remembering what the talking Malus had said. "The trees will no longer take their portion . . . it all fits." Parch looked at Jason in shock. "It's making one of these tunnels into your house."

"What?" Jason said. The panic in Parch's eyes spread to Jason and multiplied. Any shred of resolve Jason had left was instantly shattered.

But Parch wasn't done. He continued to talk his way through the situation in a frenzy of understanding, both his words and his thoughts flowing freely. "That's why the roots looked so weird in that heart chamber!" he said. "Whatever this thing is, it wants to use that second source's connection to your living room to break through to the human side and . . . feast." Furrowing his brow in confusion, Parch paused for a moment. "But wait, that bridge is small. It's barely big enough for you or me to fit through. No Malus of any serious size could get through." But just as Parch finished stating the problem, his eyes lit up with an answer. "The sweetest blood! Of course! That's why they're after Lily!" he exclaimed. "That's why the talking Malus chose your house!"

"Lily?" Jason cried even louder. "I don't understand. What does my wife have to do with this?"

Parch was so swept up in the moment of revelation that he continued on without addressing Jason's question. "Looks like this thing — this master — is sick of living off the scraps of life energy it gets from the plants. It wants to go straight to the source. I suspect the master will send one of its smaller minions through into the human world to grab Lily and drag her back. After it has her, after it consumes that much concentrated life energy, it'll be able to use the plant to tear that bridge open as wide as it likes. And once it does that — once it can enter the human world . . ." Parch's face turned somber and dark as he trailed off. But he quickly shook his head. "We won't let that happen. We have to get in there, through that next bridge, and burn that second source before things go any further." Parch looked down at his watch.

"We have two hours of torch left. Just enough time to save the world. Come on!" he shouted and turned toward the next bridge.

Beside himself, Jason hadn't taken the new information well; especially the news that Lily was in danger. His mind was overwhelmed, and his emotions were boiling over. This confusion turned to anger as he watched Parch walk off toward the bridge. "Stop!" Jason screamed. With his head still swimming, and nearly at a loss for words, he could only stammer, "What are you talking about? I don't understand any of this!"

Parch stopped, turned back, and stared in silence. Jason tried to collect himself, but his thoughts were scattered, and his mind filled with questions. Eventually, though, Jason's deepest concern was the first question he needed answered. "Lily is in danger? I thought she was safe. Why are they after her?" he asked.

"Well, because she's . . ." Parch started to say but stopped suddenly. Now, in a silent state of high alert, Parch stared at the other man, his eyes trying to read Jason, trying to discern something.

The awkward, sudden change in Parch's behavior drove Jason into a state of high alert as well. "She's what?" Jason demanded, locking eyes with Parch.

Parch's eyes grew wide. "You don't know, do you . . . ?" he whispered involuntarily. But he quickly snapped out of his stupor. "Nothing — it's nothing," Parch said, putting his hands up.

"Tell me! Why are they after her?" Jason shouted.

Parch broke eye contact and looked away. He covered his mouth with his hand as his eyes darted around frantically. He chewed his lip as he thought, but then finally turned back and looked at Jason with kind eyes. "Has Lily been acting weird lately?" Parch asked in his softest tone.

The subtlety was lost on Jason, however, and Parch's evasive speech only angered him more. "Why are they after my wife? Tell me why these things want her!" Jason cried, stepping toward Parch with his hands up in clenched fists.

Backed into a figurative corner, Parch sighed, then cursed as he looked off to the side. He then looked back at Jason. "Okay, but everything is going to be fine — just remember that. Back there, that creature mentioned 'sweetest blood,'" he said. "I think he was referring to concentrated life energy. Adults like you and I have life energy, but only the regular kind. Concentrated life energy only occurs in children and"— Parch took a deep breath and braced himself —"pregnant women."

Jason scoffed. "But Lily's not—" The words caught in Jason's throat and his eyes grew wide. He instantly understood all the clues Lily had dropped. The big house, wanting to be close to a hospital, 'care about *US*'. It was all so obvious now! As his heart flooded with emotion, his strength failed him. He stumbled and sat down on the roots, overwhelmed by it all.

Parch rushed to Jason's side. "Easy, easy," Parch said as he knelt down, putting a comforting hand on Jason's shoulder. "Calm down. Everything is going to be okay."

How could I have been so blind, Jason thought as his face fell into his hands. He grimaced and cursed as his mind grappled with everything. To find out like this, in this place, so far from Lily, was too much for him to bear. "Why didn't she just tell me?" he said. But despite the storm of emotions raging inside, there was one thing that was crystal clear. Jason turned to Parch abruptly. "I have to leave. I have to go to her; she needs me," he said.

"Easy. Relax, it's all going to be fine. You and I are going to fix everything, together," Parch said.

But Parch's consolations only incited Jason to lash out. "You said she'd be safe!" he shouted, glaring at Parch.

"She is — she is still safe! Those roots aren't finished, so they can't get to her yet," Parch said.

"How long?" Jason demanded. "How long until those roots finish?"

"Well, it's impossible to say," Parch said.

Jason had had enough. "No!" he shouted. "I'm done with this. I have to go to her right now! We need to use that button on the torch!" He looked hard at Parch. "Pull us out right now!" Jason demanded.

Parch's stared back at Jason in silence.

Feeling the implicit judgement, Jason rebutted, "This isn't like before! This is different! I need to protect my wife!"

Parch's eyes softened. "We will, but running isn't the answer. If that thing gets into the human world, no one will be safe. We need to keep it trapped where it is.

If we can just destroy that plant in the next Ignotus —" Parch pointed to the next bridge at the other end of the root tunnel.

"What?" Jason interrupted. He stood up and Parch rose with him. "We can't go in there!" Jason cried. "To do what? Die like all those other guys who tried the exact same thing? You said it yourself, this 'master,' this Titan, is incredibly dangerous. And if the next Ignotus is where it's building that tunnel into my house from, then it has to be in there. If we go in there, it'll kill us like it's killed all the rest. We're going to end up dead like all the others. And then who's going to protect Lily?"

"We can beat this thing!" Parch said, his voice forced and much too emphatic. "You and me, together. We can stop this Titan and save everyone; I know we can!"

"No, you don't!" Jason yelled, seeing through Parch's empty bravado. "You don't know anything," he said, pointing his finger in Parch's face. "You've been wrong about everything. You said this would be easy. You said it was a sure thing. But the truth is, you don't know what you're doing, and you don't know what's going on. Ever since we stepped foot in here, things have gone from bad to worse. We've almost died I don't know how many times, and it's only been sheer luck that's kept us alive. You have no idea what's through that bridge, except that it's terrible, and it's killed everyone that's come across it. And if we go through that bridge, it'll kill us, too!"

"We don't have to fight that thing, the Mortem Cor plant is the priority," Parch countered.

"My wife and child are my *only* priority!" Jason replied. "Can you tell me one hundred percent, absolutely, for sure that we'll make it out of there alive?"

Parch glowered in frustration. "Nothing in life is certain."

"See?" Jason said. "You can't. You don't know what's through that bridge. Well, let me clear it up for you: if we charge in there, it's certain death. We'll die horribly and accomplish nothing. And I'm one hundred percent sure of that!"

Parch rolled his eyes and threw his hands up in exasperation. But then he took a deep breath, recovered, and turned back to Jason. "You're right," Parch said. "I don't know for sure if we can beat this, and I don't know for sure if we'll make it out. But just the same, you don't know for sure if it's hopeless, either. The only thing we know for sure is there are countless lives at stake here. Countless people, just like you and Lily, who are going to be killed, and you and I are the only ones who have a chance to save them. If this thing breaks through into the human world, it would be cataclysmic; the death and destruction would be unimaginable. Whatever it plans to do in our world, no one could stop it. The military would be useless because conventional weapons don't work on Malus, and my people don't have guns big enough to fight it! Our only chance is to keep it trapped in the Ignotus, and you and I are the only ones who can do that. There's no one else here; it's up to us. We have to take this risk, because we are the only ones who can. People are counting on us, and we owe it to them to try and stop this."

But Jason was unmoved. "I don't owe anyone anything," he said coldly, "and I'm not going in there." He stared hard at Parch. "Give me the torch," he demanded. "I'm using that button, and then I'm taking Lily and running as far away from this thing as possible."

Parch stared back, unyielding. "Running won't save you or Lily."

"Give me the torch!" Jason shouted, extending his hand.

"You want the torch?" Parch took the torch off his shoulder and held it in his hand. "Fine, I'll give it to you, but only if you answer this question: Why did you come into the Ignotus with me in the first place?"

"What?" Jason asked confused.

"Why did you come in here?" Parch repeated, louder than before.

"Because you said this would be easy!" Jason replied.

"No! Why did you really come in here?" Parch was shouting now, emphasizing every word.

"I don't know!" Jason roared back, and locked eyes with Parch in a battle of wills.

Jason was trying not to show it, but inside, he was in turmoil. For some reason Jason couldn't explain, the question made him feel naked and exposed, like all his secrets had been laid bare. And the shock of those feelings welling up from deep inside had knocked him out of his rhythm, sending his mind into overdrive. *Why* did *I come in here?* he wondered.

As the silent struggle between the two men dragged on, Jason's inner turmoil grew. *Is this really what I want?* he thought. *Is this really who I am?* He began to feel ashamed and humiliated. The more he thought about the situation and what he was demanding to do, it began to feel like there was a hole in his chest, like his insides were scrambled, like his stomach had dropped down on to the floor. He couldn't explain it, but he started to hate himself. Jason's will to challenge Parch for the torch faded. His eyes dropped to the floor, and he was silent.

Parch watched as Jason's eyes drifted to the ground. Without a word, he returned the torch to his shoulder, then turned and walked off to the next bridge.

CHAPTER 13

The next bridge was a hundred meters farther down the tunnel, and as Jason approached it, he knew this next Ignotus would be different. The bridge mouth was equally as large as the one they had just come through, but this one had an indistinct cacophony of noise coming from it. It was like a dull, low-pitched roar or howl that oscillated louder and quieter. Jason shined his flashlight in to try and see the source of the sound, but the darkness of the Ignotus quickly swallowed the beam the small flashlight produced.

Jason stood a few meters back from the bridge mouth, watching as Parch advanced into the Ignotus. He didn't like it, but Jason, once again, had little choice but to follow.

Before he did, though, Jason took a moment to try and steady himself. Questions filled his mind — deeply confusing questions about himself. He tried to calm down, but his inner turmoil didn't diminish. The storm raging in his heart hadn't yet been solved, and it was clear there would be no easy answers. But he couldn't solve it now; so, for the moment, he would just have to push through. The bridge into this next Ignotus was oriented like a large irregular doorway. After taking a deep breath, he walked through the bridge and into the darkness.

Jason's face was hit with a blast of cold, damp air and the smell of fresh water. Droplets of water dripped around and on him. He felt the smooth roots beneath his feet change to crunching gravel and wet sand. The closeness of the Abyss receded and was replaced with a feeling of spaciousness.

Shining his flashlight around, Jason saw he was in a gigantic rock cavern. It was so big, it dwarfed even the large bridge mouth. The stone that made up the cave was dark and jagged and glistened in the light. Nothing in this place was dry; water dripped off everything. The cavern ceiling rose maybe fifty meters above him, and the cave was even wider than it was tall. The cavern itself, however, was not very deep. Even while standing in the very back, where the bridge was located, Jason could see the exit thirty meters ahead. And as he looked out the massive mouth of the cave, he saw the source of the noise.

There was a fearsome storm raging outside. Rain was pouring down so hard it was like a wall of water in front of the cave. Lightning flashed, and the accompanying thunder boomed so loud, Jason could feel it through the ground. Squalls whipped the rain around every which way, and howled as they gusted through the cavern. The rain crashing into the ground created a pervasive mist that filled the cave. It stuck to Jason's clothes, slowly dampening them. The clamor of the storm spilled into the cave and echoed off its high walls.

Seeing Parch standing at the mouth of the cave, Jason walked up next to him. The enormous opening of the cave gave a wide view, and Jason looked out into this new Ignotus.

The two men stood on an island of rock in the middle of a tumultuous black sea. The island jutted out of the water like the tip of a narrow mountain. The storm above filled the sky with fierce billows of pitch-black clouds, roiling in the strong winds. Near constant lightning flashed above, and each flash helped reveal the dark world. The rain was torrential, covering everything. Any low points were filled with standing water; everything else was covered in perpetual runoff that flowed down into the sea. The cave seemed to be the only relatively dry spot.

Both the mouth of the cave and the ground they stood on were about ten meters above the tempestuous surface of the sea. The waters below them were the stuff of sailor's nightmares. Fierce waves, five meters high, crashed onto the rock of the island. Huge swells, double or triple that size, surged in the deeper water. The sea was angry. It seemed that even without the storm the waters would be this fierce and the waves this terrible. All together it was hard to imagine a more perilous body of water. Jason tried not to think of the horrors that no doubt lurked beneath the waves.

Parch leaned toward Jason and shouted over the storm, "I've got a good feeling about this one!" But Jason didn't laugh and instead looked back with a glare, so Parch returned to looking at where the roots led.

Fortunately for them, it appeared they wouldn't have to brave the terrifying seas. After the roots exited the cave, they ran down to a small, thin spit of rocks that rose only a couple meters above the water. The rocks formed a kind of land bridge, and the roots ran half submerged alongside it. This narrow rock bridge jutted out into the sea toward a much larger rock island that rose out of the water a couple kilometers away.

As Jason looked around, he noticed other smaller islands like the one they were on, all clustered around the large island that was in the center of them all. It made Jason think this was all part of a single feature, like an undersea mountain range, where only the highest peaks rose above the water, with the central peak — the one the roots led to — being the tallest and most massive. Jason wondered if the other smaller islands had bridges and root lines too, and if they all led to the large island.

Looking at the dark central island ahead of them, Jason felt uneasy. Something about the huge island was unsettling, even ominous. It was the most foreboding place he'd ever set eyes on. Jason couldn't take his eyes off it. Anxiety lodged in his throat, and the hairs on the back of his neck rose. It felt like all his fears were substantiated — they were heading straight toward certain death, just like he'd said only minutes before. He looked to see Parch's reaction to it all, but, when he turned, motion drew his eyes. It was the chain wrapped around Parch's arm. Jason hadn't heard it because of the clamor of the storm, but it was rattling like mad! He grabbed Parch's shoulder violently. "The chain!" he shouted.

But instead of diving for cover, Parch kept staring out at the distant island. "It's . . ." Parch began, "It's been doing that since I stepped in here. I don't think it's reacting to any specific Malus around us. I think it's this place that's upsetting it."

The fear in Jason's eyes was unmistakable. "What?" he cried. "What does that mean? Is it trying to tell us something?"

Parch's lips pressed tightly closed and his eyes narrowed. He swallowed hard. "I'm not sure," he said. "It's never been this distressed before." He stared out at the island. Under his breath he whispered, "Courage and nerve." He then turned to Jason, his eyes sharp and fierce. "Let's go see what fate has in store for us," he said with a smile.

Jason cursed and shook his head. Everything inside him screamed at him to flee, but their argument in the bridge had proved Parch wouldn't be dissuaded. So, Jason resigned himself to this terrible endeavor.

The two men stepped out into the storm and were immediately soaked to the bone. Jason followed as Parch led the way, moving slowly and carefully. The way down to the shore was made of uneven rock, with large boulders scattered around. The wet stone was slick as ice, and the edges were hard and sharp. The terrain was dangerously rugged. It would be all too easy to twist an ankle, break a leg, or worse: slip and tumble down into the waves below.

Their cautious, deliberate pace, however, staved off these disasters.

They arrived at the rock bridge, and Jason was daunted by the sight. As terrifying as the waves had looked from the mouth of the cave, they were even more intimidating at eye-level. Jason looked down the rock bridge extending out in front of him. It was only barely above the surface of the water, and the waves constantly crashed over it. Often, the waves overwhelmed the strip of rocks and swamped the whole width before the water eventually ran back into the sea.

How can we possibly cross this? Jason thought as he watched the waves crash on the rocks, deluging their intended path. "Do you think there's anything in the water?" Jason shouted.

Instead of answering, Parch merely pressed forward resolutely, his jaw set and his eyes looking toward the large island ahead.

The rocks that made up the land bridge were fixed and immovable; the battering of the waves had washed away anything that wasn't. This meant that despite the rocks being slippery, they could be trusted as stable anchor points. Parch got low to the ground and started to crawl, making sure to place his hands and feet in recesses in the rock. As the first wave crashed over him, he held fast. The water broke over his back and drenched him, but he defied the waves and remained on the bridge as the water ran back into the sea. "Treat it like you're climbing" he shouted back to Jason as he pressed on.

Jason watched anxiously, but after seeing Parch withstand that first wave so well, he was inspired with confidence. *Maybe we can do this*. Regardless, Parch left no time for hesitation and was already moving farther out. Jason shook his head in frustration, but then gritted his teeth and followed, crawling out onto the rocks. The second he did, a small wave hit and splashed his face. It cleared his mind and helped him focus on the task at hand.

The two had made decent progress before the first truly big wave hit them. Jason's arm was extended mid-reach out toward a rock ahead of him, when Parch suddenly screamed, "Brace!"

In an instant, Jason wrapped one of his arms around a thick chunk of rock protruding up from the ground. He extended his other arm out and pushed hard against the side of a boulder, creating a firm, stable tension in his body. He sunk his knee into a depression in the rock and laid out his other leg as flat as possible. Then he waited.

The force of the mass of rushing water was fierce when it hit. The water slammed into Jason, trying to drag him off and into the sea. It knocked out his breath, but his grip held. After the water receded, Jason was left gasping for air.

Parch roared with laughter. "That was a good one," he shouted. "You still with me back there?"

"Y-yeah," Jason shouted back.

As they continued on, Jason started to figure out the waves. The key to it all was sound. As the waves neared the bridge, they made a rushing sound that swelled up until they impacted the rocks. With some concentration, it was possible to block out the roar of the storm and just focus on listening to the waves. Consequently, Jason knew when a wave was about to hit, even without having to look to see it, and could brace accordingly.

Predicting the waves helped, but even still, resisting their relentless battering was exhausting. There were no breaks — the two men were either scrambling forward in between waves or being hit by them. It was a stressful, wearying rhythm.

Jason was quickly getting tired. The giant mountain loomed in front of them, but it didn't feel like they were getting any closer. He looked behind him, and was shocked to see that, despite not feeling they had made any progress forward, they had moved quite a distance away from their original island. There was no choice but to push through and keep going, no matter how tired he felt.

As they passed the halfway point, Jason noticed a strange vibration that happened every few seconds. It was a deep and powerful tremor, like an earthquake, that traveled through the rocks and into his whole body. But it clearly wasn't an earthquake because it was regular and predictable. It also didn't match with either the waves or the thunder. Boom . . . Boom . . . Boom . . . it went.

At first, Jason tried to ignore it. He tried to explain it away, hoping it was something caused by the storm. But the vibrations continued. They were distinct and undeniable, and each one caused his heart to tremble. "Do you feel that?" he called out over the storm. He looked forward, and, to his horror, saw the chain flailing wildly about Parch, desperately trying to signal to them both.

Parch didn't stop, however, and kept crawling forward. "We have to keep moving!" he screamed, the fear clearly evident in his voice. "We have to get off these rocks!"

Through his clenched teeth, Jason whined involuntarily. Something bad was happening, but there was nothing he could do about it. They were exposed and vulnerable out on these rocks; so no matter what the vibrations were, no matter what the chain sensed, no matter what was going on, the only solution was to press on as fast as possible.

Jason was about to scramble forward after withstanding another wave, when a deafeningly loud noise battered the two men. It was a low-pitched, guttural sound that reverberated through the water and echoed off the rocks. The sound was so loud, Jason felt his bones vibrate and his teeth rattle. He clasped his hands over his ears. But it was no use, there was no keeping out the terrible noise, or the ear-splitting pain it caused. He clenched and contracted into himself in pain. The few seconds it lasted seemed an eternity, but finally the noise subsided.

As Jason lay on the rocks, astonished and trying to recover, his mind was frantically trying to make sense of what had just happened. He alternated between staring at Parch in wide-eyed horror, and peering out from the rocks, trying to find the source of the horrible sound. But there were no answers to be found. The waves, the storm, the islands, everything looked the same as before. Parch shouted something to Jason, and while Jason's hearing was still too dull to tell what Parch was saying, he understood all the same. The two set off at a reckless pace; they had to get away from the water as fast as possible.

Driven by terror and panic, they scrambled forward on the rock bridge. They were no longer crouching low and bracing for each wave. Now, caution was sacrificed for haste. They were desperate to get off the rocks and away from the water. Between waves, it was a mad dash toward the large island. When a wave was about to hit, they hastily bear-hugged the biggest rock they could find, each time only barely preventing themselves from being swept off into the sea.

With their reckless pace, they were quickly approaching the island. There were only a couple hundred meters to go, and Jason was starting to think they might just make it. That's when he saw a massive upheaval near a smaller island, something like five-hundred meters off to their left. A colossal black shadow burst forth from the waves, rising higher and higher. Using the small island for support, the monstrous Titan pulled itself out of the water, its unimaginable weight shattering the rock island as it did.

In shock and terror, Jason stared dumbstruck at the gigantic figure as it rose out of the water. *What new horror is it now?* The creature was obscured by darkness and storm, but what couldn't be veiled was its size. It was over a thousand meters tall, even taller than the large, central island. As it reached its full height it came to a stop, no doubt standing atop some undersea part of the mountain range.

Instinctively, both men tried to hide. Jason sunk down into a shallow crevice behind a rock, desperately hoping he hadn't been seen. Even with his adrenaline-dulled senses, he could still both hear and smell the Malus Titan as he hid. It made a strange, low-pitched gurgling noise that was as loud as the creature was huge. It also gave off a strong stench of sulphur and blood that reeked even from hundreds of meters away. But the most unsettling thing wasn't the smell or sounds, it was the frightening feeling that it induced; Jason was suddenly overcome with an oppressive sense of inevitable, impending doom, as if it would all be over, as if it were hopeless to continue.

Frozen where he was, Jason couldn't think; he couldn't move. He looked to Parch for strength. But when he turned, he was surprised to see Parch peering out from behind the rocks. Appalled, he quickly got Parch's attention. "No," Jason mouthed, as he shook his head.

Parch put up his hand in a reassuring gesture, then slowly, cautiously, peered back out from his rock cover, intent on seeing what they were up against. After a moment, Jason couldn't help himself and did the same, his whole body shaking with fear.

The Malus Titan stood reveling in the storm. It towered above them (and everything else, for that matter). Jason squinted hard, trying to separate the gargantuan black shadow from the dark sky it stood against. This proved a challenging task. The conditions made it hard to see anything, but there was something else that made it difficult. The creature seemed to blend with the darkness around it. The edges blurred together, and there was no clear boundary, like the creature was part of the darkness, or maybe it was the other way around.

With a morbid curiosity, Jason continued to stare, transfixed by the sight. The creature was fascinating, in a horrific, terrible way.

In a sudden burst of movement, the Titan shook, then tensed and let out another clamorous low-pitched roar. No longer muffled by the water, this one was even louder. Jason slammed his hands over his ears in another vain attempt to lessen the sound. It didn't help, but, thankfully, this roar subsided much quicker than the last. Jason uncovered his ears, which were ringing like crazy in the absence of the roar. His hands shook as his numb fingers found the sharp end of a rock in front of him.

The Malus Titan turned back toward open water and dove into the sea. Completely devoid of any grace or dexterity, the lumbering beast slammed into the water. When it did, the impact was so great, waves as tall as buildings rose in every direction. Jason's eyes grew wide as he saw the water rushing toward them. They only had seconds before it would hit.

"Grab on!" Parch screamed.

Jason panicked as he looked around for something sturdy to brace himself on. With only moments until the wave hit, none of the boulders looked like good choices. He wavered back and forth as the wave approached.

"Just pick one," Parch shouted.

Jason grabbed the closest rock and, placing it between him and the wall of water rushing toward him, wrapped his arms around it. But he immediately regretted his choice when he struggled to get a good grip, and there wasn't time to try another. Jason clenched down as hard as he could on the rock, and pulled in as close as he could.

The wave was forty meters tall when it hit. It subsumed everything, and the force of the water was overpowering. It flowed over and through the rocks, and both men were ripped off their holds in the overwhelming force. There was nothing they could do to prevent it; the wave was too strong.

Jason tried to scream, but his lungs filled with water instead. In the midst of the wave, and while being dragged into the sea, something caught his waist. Something was wrapped around his waist, and he was suddenly held fast. Confused and disoriented, he dangled in the current as the water flowed past him.

When the wave subsided, Jason was thrown down on the very edge of the rocks, nearly in the sea. He struggled on the ground, coughing up all the water he'd inhaled. He saw Parch nearby, gasping for air as well, and Jason was thankful his companion hadn't been swept away, either. Once he'd recovered, Jason felt his navel, curious to know what had saved him.

The chain! Before the wave had hit, it had wrapped around the waists of both men, and then cinched itself on a sturdy rock. Jason had been so preoccupied that he hadn't even noticed. The chain had been able to fasten itself around the rocks far more securely than the men had. Consequently, it had saved them from being swept away into the sea.

Parch and Jason both lay on the rocks, stunned and trying to collect themselves. Jason felt the chain uncoiled from him and return to Parch. "Thank you," he mumbled. Parch too patted the chain as it returned to him. The two men shared a look of aghast exhaustion. It was all just too much. But they were soon splashed by another wave, reminding them they were still in a dangerous position. They got up and set out at a hurried pace, frantic to get off the rock bridge.

They quickly covered the remaining distance and made it safely to the island. Although, it was hard to consider this island safe. It was no less foreboding now than when Jason first saw it. But after seeing what lurked in the sea, Jason would have gone anywhere to get away from the water. So, despite his fears, he didn't complain as he scrambled onto solid ground.

As Parch made landfall, he looked up and quickly assessed the island. This huge land mass was far bigger than any of the dozens of islands surrounding it. It was a mountain that rose out of the water, with gentle slopes that slowly ascended at least three hundred meters to a flat plateau on top. The plateau ran for several kilometers and made the island much wider than it was tall. The slopes were covered in shattered pieces of smooth, dark volcanic glass, whose sharp edges glinted in the lightning. Rivers consisting of rainwater ran down the island's sides and into the sea.

But Parch didn't stay looking at the island for long. With his lips retracted over his clenched teeth and his hands shaking, he looked back out over the water, scanning the area where the creature had disappeared. He said nothing, but the veins in his neck bulged and his breathing was sharp and rapid.

Jason was far less stoic about his concerns, still gasping for air from the mad dash to the island. "Did you see that thing? Was that it? Was that what's trying to tunnel into my house?" Jason wheezed hysterically.

"Had to be," Parch responded with a tense but restrained voice. "That thing was huge. How deep is that water?" he wondered aloud.

The two men looked out at the stormy sea in a vain attempt to discern more. But the mysteries it held under its turbulent waves would not be revealed so easily.

As Jason stood there, he tried to control his shaking. The Titan was more profoundly disturbing than anything he'd seen so far. That thing was like death incarnate. They didn't stand a chance. Jason felt fear coursing through his entire body; it choked his thoughts and was like a weight pressing down on his chest. His breathing was ragged and irregular, and it wasn't just because of exertion. He looked at the torch burning on Parch's shoulder but said nothing.

"We have to get away from the water," Parch said finally. He looked at their root line that ran out of the water nearby. It led up the mountain.

Without another word, the two men started making their way up the island slope with Parch in the lead. The way was uneven, slick, and treacherous. The broken pieces of volcanic glass shifted under Jason's feet as he climbed. It was difficult going, but the thought of what he was fleeing from pushed him on.

The rocks grew larger the higher they went, and soon they were climbing over boulders as they followed the twisting roots. The roots interwove between the rocks, and in the low light, it was sometimes difficult to see where they went. But Parch was always able to find the way, even when the roots disappeared beneath the rocks. He'd look ahead for where the roots emerged again as they continued up the slope.

Jason felt strange as they climbed. He was still terrified, but in spite of it all, he continued on. This conviction, however, waivered every time he looked at the chain around Parch's arm. It was still shaking and was a constant reminder of the terrible danger present all around them.

As they ascended, Jason started scanning the skyline, hoping to see branches peaking over the edge of the plateau above them. But so far, there was no sign of the Mortem Cor plant. And the longer he went without sight of it, the more anxious he grew. He began to fear that the plant was on a different island, and they would have to make another dangerous crossing. But as they continued, something strange happened: the roots completely disappeared behind a large boulder ahead of them.

Parch went to investigate. He climbed the boulder, then peered down behind it, trying to find where the roots went. He then jumped down behind the boulder and disappeared from sight.

Jason heard Parch curse, so he climbed the boulder to see what Parch had found. Nestled in a pile of boulders was a cave that ran down into the mountain, and the roots led right into it.

Jason's heart sank. He grimaced and exhaled sharply through clenched teeth.

As Jason made his way down, Parch knelt at the edge of the cave mouth. The cave was about three meters in diameter and descended sharply into the depths of the mountain. He shined his flashlight into the cave, and could see a dozen meters in, but that hardly revealed much. He saw rock and then darkness. Anything could be further inside. Parch shuddered.

Jason knelt down next to Parch and peered into the cave. "Well, this looks awful," he said.

Parch smirked. "I keep hoping we'll catch a lucky break, but it's just one tribulation after another." Parch dropped his face into his hand and sighed.

"We can still use that button," Jason said sheepishly. "If that thing back there had seen us . . . if it knew we were here . . . I'm just saying we might not get another chance to leave."

Parch was quiet for a moment, keeping his face covered in his hand. He then inhaled deeply, turned to Jason, and smiled. "Let's not get ahead of ourselves here.

We don't know what's in this cave. It might be smooth sailing all the way to the Mortem Cor plant. We might be close to the end here." Parch turned back and looked into the cave. "I bet there's no one even home."

Jason looked down at the chain, which was still shaking violently, then looked back at Parch. "What if this island *is* that thing's home?"

Parch looked down at the ground. He placed his hand on top of the chain and spoke a strange language that caused it to go completely still and remain coiled placidly around his arm. He looked at Jason and said, "Let's just go a little farther and see where it goes."

There was a long, quiet moment before Jason responded. He looked hard at Parch, but eventually drew in a deep breath, steadied himself, exhaled, and nodded.

The two men rose, still staring into the black depths in front of them. Jason pretended to adjust his gear as he prepared himself mentally. But eventually, he drew his gun and followed Parch forward into the cave.

The cave was large and spacious. It looked to be three meters wide and just as tall, which left plenty of room for the two men to walk side by side unhindered. Inside, it was like a long narrow corridor. It was filled with jagged chunks of rock and ran farther and farther down into the mountain. While their descent was more or less consistent, the journey was sporadically interrupted by sudden sharp drops, which they were forced to climb down before continuing. The darkness receded in front of them as they moved forward, but also closed in behind them. There was an oppressive, uncomfortable feeling within the cave. Jason could almost feel the weight of the rock above pressing down on him.

Even in here, the men couldn't escape the water. Rain drained into the cave and formed a stream that trickled along the middle of the solid rock floor and ran down into the mountain. Everything in the cave was cold and damp. Water dripped down from small, five-centimeter stalactites above and ran down the cave walls.

The rock walls were salt-and-pepper colored, with whites and grays intermixed. The rock had a rough but not sharp texture, with crystals formed in the rock jutting every which way. Jason ran his hand along the wall and felt its strength, which was reassuring.

As the men continued to venture downward, the sound of rain and thunder quickly diminished. They were soon beset with an intimidating quiet. The sound of the stream of water and their gentle footsteps were the only sounds left to be heard. Parch and Jason searched every shadow for danger, sweeping their flashlights around constantly, guns at the ready.

Jason was getting antsy. Being underground made him feel hemmed in, despite there being plenty of space in the cave tunnel. He kept thinking he saw movement out of the corner of his eye, but when he looked, there was nothing. The darkness, the uncertainty, it was unbearable, and he hated it. He felt it in the pit of his stomach, and the tension in his shoulders. It felt like something was down here, and it was only a matter of time before they found it, or rather it found them. Jason's eyes constantly returned to the torch on Parch's shoulder, looking to confirm that their only escape was still there. *Sixty minutes left*, Jason thought to himself after checking his watch. He hoped they would have the opportunity to escape before this terrible place killed them or time ran out.

Eventually, the two men came to a deviation in the cave. Another tunnel intersected with theirs, creating a four-way junction. After pausing to listen for a moment, and hearing only the sound of flowing water, Parch proceeded cautiously into the middle of the intersection. He shined his flashlight down each of the three new tunnels and saw nothing but rock and water. Everything appeared to be safe.

This new intersecting tunnel brought with it its own small river that flowed through the junction and down the tunnel on the opposite side. It was only ankle deep, but it was much bigger than the trickle that flowed down their original tunnel, which joined the larger stream like a tributary.

"This one must go to the surface too," Parch said, shining his flashlight up the intersecting tunnel. After a few moments of staring down the side tunnels, Parch and Jason continued on, following the roots.

The tunnel now started to twist and turn, making it impossible to keep any sense of direction. It was also growing steeper. Jason began to suspect they had descended farther inside the tunnels than they had ascended outside when they climbed up to the cave entrance, meaning they were probably below sea level by now. And as the tunnel went lower and lower, it began running into more tunnels. Like a labyrinth, new tunnels branched off, crossed one another, and twisted around. There was no way to keep it all straight, and both men ended up disoriented, without any idea where they were. They still had the roots to follow, so they weren't lost yet, but this new aspect of the caves added to the disquieting feeling of the place.

Many of the tunnels they passed contained their own small rivers that flowed down into the depths. And the more streams Jason and Parch passed, the more they could hear the sound of rushing water echoing through the caves. All this water draining into the tunnels had to be combining somewhere, forming an increasingly powerful current of water.

After traversing a particularly sharp three-meter dropoff, the tunnel fed into a large, open cavern. The men halted at the cavern's edge, listening for any movement. Jason could hear the sound of rushing water in the chamber, but he wasn't concerned about that. Instead, he was listening for a hint of what ever terrible danger could be ahead.

As Jason sat and listened, his unease only grew. He began to feel like they shouldn't be here. He was convinced there was something terrible in these caves — another "servant" of the Titan outside — and if they continued to venture down, they would eventually find it, or rather *it* would find *them*. But most unsettling of all, he started to feel Parch shared his concerns. Jason had noticed a slight hesitation in Parch's stride and a nervousness in his watchful glances as they made their way down. It seemed even Parch was scared down here. Jason began to wonder if Parch would linger at the entrance of the large cavern, but just as quickly as he thought that, Parch stood up and stepped boldly into the new domain. Jason felt he should have expected as much. He stood and followed him in.

This new chamber was large and irregular. Its ceiling had to be over thirty meters high, and it was wide enough that the light from Jason's flashlight didn't reach the far side. The ground was a wide, uneven, sloping surface that descended away from them into the darkness. The root line ran into the chamber from the tunnel, then down the slope, and disappeared into that same darkness. But the most obvious thing about the chamber was the noise: the sound of cascading water filled the otherwise silent space. It was as if you were standing next to a waterfall. Searching for the source of the ambient noise, Jason scanned the perimeter. He saw dozens of other tunnels that fed into the chamber. He kept looking, and finally found the source of the noise twenty meters ahead.

Down the slope in front of him and off to the side, torrents of water gushed out of one of the tunnels. It was like a gigantic pipe had burst; the volume of water pouring out was incredible. This was clearly the result of all the rainwater combining in the cave system. The water spilled out from the tunnel, and then ran off somewhere down the slope. The powerful flow looked strong enough to sweep away anything that passed into it, Jason thought.

Jason stood there, appreciating the mighty flow as Parch looked all around the cavern. Neither said anything, but Jason silently wondered how this new hazard would affect their progress. They followed the root line a short distance down the slope, and Jason was disheartened with what he saw: the roots ran directly through the water and into a tunnel on the other side.

They both sized up this new obstacle, and it was clear upon further investigation that instead of the roots taking the brunt of the current's force, much of the water rushed into a gully that ran under and perpendicular to the roots. The gully looked to be about eight meters wide, but not deep enough to handle all the water. As a result, water pooled on one side of the roots, spilled over the top, then fell down the other side and rejoined the violent current. It was like the roots were a bridge over a mountain stream that had swelled to dangerous levels due to spring runoff.

All things considered, while falling into the underground river would likely be deadly, the roots — presuming they held — appeared to be a safe way across. In fact, it seemed they were the *only* safe way to cross.

Parch stepped forward and kicked the roots in a superficial test of their strength. They superficially held strong. He gave Jason a shrug, then pulled himself on top of the root line.

Jason grimaced, lowering his head. His nerves were strained, but he closed his eyes and remained silent.

He took several deep breaths, making peace with his circumstances. And after pushing everything out of his mind, he pulled himself onto the root line behind Parch.

Jason could feel the strength of the water through the root line. The vibrations from the onslaught of rapids spread through the roots into his hands. He swallowed and gripped the roots all the tighter.

"I'll go first," Parch said quietly. "Wait here for me to cross."

Jason nodded.

Parch crawled out over the river, the cold water running over his hands. The surface rapids were deceitfully playful and light, and there was a constant spray of mist sprinkling his face. He stayed low and balanced, moving swiftly but deliberately as he crept across the roots. There wasn't far to go, and as he passed the halfway point, everything was going well. The force from the current had a stabilizing effect on the roots, holding them consistently taut and reliable. When he was near enough, Parch scrambled the last bit of the crossing, and put his feet triumphantly on solid ground.

After breathing a sigh of relief, Parch looked around this new side of the river. He shined his flashlight around and saw several cave tunnel openings nearby that were similar to the one they had entered this cavern from. But Parch didn't see any movement or danger. He turned back toward Jason and gave a thumbs-up, and then, after checking his watch and making a face at how much time they had left, followed the thumbs-up with an insistent beckoning gesture with arm extended, palm up, drawing it toward himself. They had to hurry.

Parch's insistence on speed, however, only served to annoy Jason. Even though Parch had made the crossing look trivial, Jason found it impossible to overlook the danger. He couldn't help but imagine himself slipping on the wet roots, falling into the river, then being carried away and lost forever. On top of it all, he was tired and unsure of himself. He resolved to take as long as he needed to cross safely.

With that, Jason ventured out over the water, moving at a slow and cautious pace. The wet roots were cold to the touch, and the water made them slippery despite their rough texture. Before every movement, he took a deep breath, steadied himself, and checked his grip. He would then move a small distance forward before repeating the process. There had already been enough excitement crossing previous root spans; Jason wanted to make sure this crossing was nice and boring.

Seeing Jason's glacial pace, Parch folded his arms and checked his watch again. He rocked back and forth on his heals as time ticked away. After half a minute, he cupped his hands around his mouth and shouted over the sound of the water: "Hurry up, we gotta keep moving!"

Irritated, Jason looked up, but before he could respond, his eyes picked up movement in the darkness. Panic struck him like a bolt of lightning as he peered into the shadowy tunnel behind Parch, trying to discern what he thought he had just seen.

Reacting to the look in Jason's eyes, Parch snapped to high alert. He turned around, only to be met with a deep and terrifying bellow that resounded through the caves.

To both men's horror, a nightmarish Malus emerged from the tunnel. It had the body of a giant hippo with thick, dark skin that blended into the rock around it. Its head was that of a crocodile, and its neck was covered in fur like a lion's mane. It was thick and muscular, standing over two meters tall and looking like it weighed several tons. It took one look at Parch and charged him, letting out another deep bellow.

The creature moved so fast that Parch's only chance was to dive over the roots for cover. In so doing, he just barely escaped the creature's jaws. The beast, on the other hand, clumsily slammed into the roots with such force that the whole root line lurched. Jason was thrown like a rider being bucked off a bull.

Screaming and flailing about in a frenzy, Jason fell into the river, still reaching for the roots that he'd been thrown off of. The cold water hit his back first, knocking all sense from his mind. He was instantly confused and disoriented, and he tumbled through the currents as the powerful river pulled him downstream. Instinctually, he struggled to find the surface, thrashing about wildly, but he didn't know which way was up. By chance, his head broke the surface of the water, and he involuntarily drew in a breath full of air. This breath restored a bit of clarity to his mind, and his first clear thought was the realization he was being swept out of the large cavern and down into the depths of the tunnels.

CHAPTER 14

Jason was swept down into the tunnels and into total darkness. He thrashed about frantically as he was dragged along, but it was all in vain. He was at the mercy of the water. The powerful rapids constantly tried to pull him under. He had to fight desperately to keep his head above the surface, gasping for air every chance he could. Several times, Jason was slammed into the hard rock walls without warning and could feel the scrapes on his face and body.

Abruptly, the river washed him down a long straight section of the tunnels where the water was calmer, giving him a moment of respite. The river was still flowing swiftly, but for the moment, there weren't any twists or turns. In the relative peace, Jason was able to collect himself enough to focus on the light from his chest rig flashlight, which was still on. He used the glimmer of light it provided to locate the tunnel wall and swim toward it. In desperation, he clawed at the rock, trying to stop himself from being pulled further along. But his hands couldn't find enough purchase, and the river ripped him off with ease. It was a devastating confirmation of the hopelessness of his situation. All he could do was stay afloat, breathe, and keep his feet pointed downstream.

The river forked, with a new smaller tunnel branching off and taking a small portion of the water with it. Jason was swept along with the prevailing flow, and as he continued to be carried downstream, he noticed a crashing sound that was growing louder. The water started to feel different, too. It was getting choppier, and there was suddenly more mist in the air. Jason shined his flashlight ahead, trying to see what he was heading into, but it was too late. He realized only once he was falling what the sound had been: a waterfall.

Jason fell three meters, then landed in a pool at the bottom of the waterfall. He tumbled about in the swirling pool, until the swift-moving water eventually pulled him back into the river's current. In the darkness, his hands tried to find the surface, but instead found solid ground. Jason had drifted close to a sloping bank along the riverside, and once he realized it, he latched on and fought to pull himself up. In triumph, he burst out of the water and dragged himself ashore.

After coughing hard for several seconds, Jason was able to clear his lungs of all the water he'd inhaled. He collapsed on the ground, gasping for air. He was dizzy, confused, and had no idea where he was. His whole body ached from the collisions he'd received on the way down. It hurt to breathe, but he still gulped down as much air as his lungs could take. He lay there on the bank, recovering and thankful to be alive.

Once he'd partially regained himself, Jason's concern shifted to his surroundings. Was he safe? Were there more Malus nearby? He shined his flashlight around, and saw he was in another large cavity of this underground cave system. The space was twenty meters wide, ten meters tall, and ran for another twenty meters. With the exception of the small bank Jason had landed on, the river took up all of the cave floor. It poured out of a large opening in the wall on one end, ran the length of the chamber, then exited through a new tunnel on the opposite end.

The rough, hard cavern walls dripped with condensation. It was cold and damp in the cave, and the sound of the water reverberated off the stone. The smell of water filled the space, crisp and clean like the rain that the river was formed from. Despite being large and open, it felt like a tomb, buried deep underground.

Jason scanned the whole area, and to his relief, he appeared to be alone. Nevertheless, he reached for the safety of his pistol, but all his hand found was an empty holster. A jolt of panic shot through him, and he checked the shallow water around the bank, hoping his gun was close. But he found only water; his pistol was lost to the river.

In a fearful frenzy, Jason began searching for a way to get back to Parch. He looked at the waterfall, hoping to find a way to climb back up. But even just a quick glance made it obvious that was impossible; the river was too powerful, and the rock too steep. *Maybe there's another way out*, Jason thought. This idea ended in disappointment too, as there were no other entrances or exits to the chamber beyond the ones the river flowed through.

Fear gave way to despair as Jason realized the full gravity of his situation. He was trapped — trapped in this awful, terrible place without any hope of escape. He ground his teeth and winced as he collapsed to the ground once more. *It's over*, he thought. *I'm already dead.* The oppressive tension of hopelessness seized his body, and his face contorted into a grimace, which he covered with his hand. "I never should have come here," he growled through clenched teeth. "How could I have been so stupid?"

In the midst of Jason's agony, something caught his attention. There was a noise just barely perceptible over the roar of the waterfall. As Jason listened, he realized it was a voice. A human voice was shouting! He turned his head just in time to see Parch tumble over the waterfall. Immediately scrambling to his feet, Jason screamed out, "Parch!" and moved to the edge of the shore.

"Ja-Jason!" Parch screamed back as he floundered in the water. He had been particularly unlucky when going over the falls, and instead of ending up near the shore like Jason, Parch was now in the middle of the river — the fastest flowing part.

"Parch!" Jason screamed again. He knelt down at the edge of the bank and leaned out with his hand extended. It would be close, but Jason saw he might be able to reach Parch and pull him onto the shore as the current swept him along. But Parch was being carried downstream quickly, and there wasn't much time. "Here!" Jason shouted.

Parch saw Jason and started swimming toward him. He fought hard to cover the distance, moving laterally across the rushing water. There would be only one chance at this. If he missed Jason's hand, there'd be no way back.

As the two men neared each other, Jason reached out farther, and Parch swam harder. Parch and Jason drew even, and Parch threw his hand out as far as he could. The edges of Parch's fingertips grazed Jason's, but in the end, there was no chance. Parch wasn't close enough.

Jason's breath caught in his throat as he realized what was happening. In shock, he watched as Parch passed by, pulled farther and farther downstream. Terror filled Parch's eyes as he stared back at Jason. "Help!" he screamed. And then he was gone, vanishing into the darkness of the tunnel.

With his arm still outstretched, Jason remained still, frozen in shock. He stared at the darkness that Parch had just disappeared into. His mind replayed the last few seconds in a loop over and over again, trying to process it all, but failing. The look in Parch's eyes, the sound of his cry for help, and now, nothing but the mute sound of the water.

Jason didn't know what to do, and his mind ground to a halt. He was completely overwhelmed by the situation. All he could do was slam his fist into the shallow water in frustration. But then, in the midst of the crisis, one more surprise came floating down the river.

Green light hit the corner of Jason's eye, and he snapped to attention when he realized what it was: the torch! It came tumbling down the waterfall, bobbing aimlessly in the rapids. In an instant, it became Jason's sole concern. He watched in fearful suspense as the lightweight, buoyant torch was tossed around erratically in the currents. And, luckily, it was moving toward the shore.

Jason shot to his feet and dashed to where he guessed the torch would pass, then crawled out into the shallow water as far as he dared. He felt the river's pull, deceptively gentle in these shallows, on his legs and body as he reached his hand out over the running water. Jason leaned out so far, he was on the cusp of losing his balance, but he absolutely had to get that torch; there was no other choice.

Jason watched as it approached, and when the moment arrived, he stretched as far as he could . . . and he touched it! His fingertips just barely halted the torch's progress, and then, with dexterity and determination, he coaxed the torch in using his fingers. "Got it!" he shouted as his hand wrapped around the torch and he pulled it in.

In an instant, Jason went from the depths of despair to the peak of joy. He was saved! With the torch in hand, he could now escape this horrible place. He clutched his prize and crawled up the bank. Finally, things were going his way. After sitting down as far back from the river as he could get, he held the torch out triumphantly and admired it. But he paused, glancing down the tunnel where Parch had just disappeared.

He shook his head, and returned his attention to the torch, but now his beaming smile had vanished, and his mood darkened. Turning the torch on end, he found the cap on the bottom, and with a little force began unscrewing it. He smiled and breathed a sigh of relief as he stared at the button that would get him home. *Just hit the button and hold on; the torch will pull you out*, Parch had said. Parch . . . . Suddenly, all Jason could think about was the look of fear on Parch's face as he was swept into the darkness. The image was burned into his mind, and Parch's cry for help still rang in Jason's ears.

Jason sat still, but he was being torn apart inside. It felt like everything within him was in flux. He wanted to look at the tunnel again, but he wouldn't let himself; he couldn't. If he did, it was impossible to know what would happen. He tried to relax. He tried to listen to the running water. He breathed deeply, but nothing worked. There was a war going on inside him.

Questions flooded his mind. Was Parch alive? Could he have just been swept down into another chamber like this one? *No, no there's no way*, Jason concluded. *He's dead. I'm sure of it. And there's nothing I or anyone else can do about it.* But that answer came far too quick and was too insistent; something deep inside Jason, something important, remained unconvinced. They had already been swept down this far into the tunnel and had both survived. Was it really right to assume Parch was dead? Even still, his thumb moved ever closer to the button.

Even if he wasn't dead, Jason continued, *how could I ever find him in this place? It's a maze down here. I could run into another creature, and then what would I do? No gun, just a knife, trying to fight those things? I'd be killed instantly.*

Jason sat silently, listening to the water and trying to think, when abruptly, the image of the creature from outside, the Titan, appeared in his mind. His blood ran cold as he remembered how enormous and horrible it was, standing there in the rain, roaring into the sky. It created such fear in Jason — such dread — that even in the caves, surrounded by incalculable tons of rock, he still felt that terrible Titan could get to him. It felt like, at any minute, the rock above him would be torn open, and Jason would be face-to-face with death.

As Jason's thoughts continued to spiral down, he started to feel sick with despair. It blinded him and pierced him, but he offered no resistance against it. *I need to just go — right now*, he thought. *I need to get back to Lily; she's in danger . . . and pregnant!* Just thinking about it made his heart race and his whole body go numb. To find out here, like this, was awful. Why hadn't she told him? He stared off into the darkness, trying to process it all, but thinking only made things worse. He felt helpless. *I can't do this*, he thought. *I never should have come in here.*

A drop of water, from a hanging stalactite, dripped into his face. His teeth clenched in frustration. Sweat was forming on Jason's palms from gripping the torch. *Just hit the button*, he kept thinking over and over. Jason held the torch in front of his face, staring at it intently. He placed his thumb over the button. *Push it*, he thought with increasing urgency. *Push it now.* Every muscle in Jason's body tensed, and all of his attention concentrated on the button, but he didn't press it. *It's always going to be like this. I'm always going to be like this. It's who I am! I'm going to hit that button sooner or later, so stop wasting time and do it!* Jason's entire being strained against itself, tears streamed down his face, but his thumb didn't move. With teeth clenched hard in frustration, he sat still, not moving a muscle, trapped in indecision, until the moment passed.

And once it passed, it was replaced by one of unexpected tranquility. Like moving into the eye of the storm, Jason experienced a brief moment of sublime calm. For an instant, his mind was temporarily unburdened from the crushing weight of his situation, and, in that reprieve, he remembered something. He reached into his pocket and pulled out his grasshopper mouse key chain. He stared at it. *Courage and nerve*, he remembered.

Suddenly, his way forward was clear. He turned and looked once again at the tunnel. "I know why I came in here," he whispered.

The task before him still seemed dangerous and impossible, and he had no idea what he was going to do; but he knew one thing for sure: right now, he had to fight. Lily and his child wouldn't be safe until all this was stopped. So, he took a deep breath, sighed, then screwed the cap back on the bottom of the torch. He felt good. Despite the horrible circumstances, he felt better than he had in a very long time. *I must be crazy*. He stared at the torch and saw the flame flicker for an instant. Alarmed at this sign of weakness, Jason checked his watch: forty-five minutes — not much time left.

He clipped the torch onto his gear and stood up straight. He was filled with a strange mix of fear and hope; a nervous, jittery excitement. All his movements were light and easy, almost like a weight had been lifted. Trying to keep calm, he busied himself with checking the rest of his gear. He gripped the handle of his still-sheathed knife and made peace with the fact it was all he had to defend himself. Lastly, he pulled out his keys, and reattached his mouse key chain to them. Then he took his first step toward the dark tunnel where Parch had disappeared.

Jason walked down as far as the bank would take him. But even standing at the farthest point, there were still several meters of river separating him from the tunnel. He had to find a way to continue forward, and the idea of getting back in the water wasn't particularly appealing. Searching the area, he saw that the rock ledge which formed the bank didn't end entirely, but instead dropped down and continued on, submerged in less than half a meter of water. It looked crossable, running along the cavern wall all the way to the tunnel mouth. Jason shined his flashlight along the length of this new path and saw the water was moving slower here due to the shallowness and closeness to the wall. The more he scrutinized, the better this way forward seemed. Jason decided that, seeing as there weren't any other options, he'd give it a try.

After several deep breaths, Jason stepped down off the bank like a small puppy walking downstairs for the first time. His leg submerged up to the knee in the gently swirling eddy before he found solid ground. With his first foot secure, his confidence grew, and he stepped down with the other as well. The cool, shifting water tugged gently at his legs, but not enough to unsteady him. Jason smiled. *This is going to work.*

Now feeling bold and sure, Jason set off. But with his very first step his foot landed on a large loose rock hidden in the dark water. The rock slid, his ankle buckled, and he was thrown off balance, causing him to lurch forward uncontrollably. Providence and luck were the only things that kept him from toppling into the deeper, rushing waters beside him. Once he'd steadied himself, he stood, stunned. "Courage and nerve," he said to himself when he could breathe again. With redoubled care, Jason pressed on toward the tunnel.

As he approached the tunnel mouth, he realized it wasn't actually a tunnel at all. Instead, it appeared to be only a small chamber. This begged the question: where was all the water going? But as Jason got closer, the answer became clear. He could hear the roar of another waterfall.

Jason reached the chamber's entrance and saw that the sunken rock ledge he was on met up with another, higher, unsubmerged ledge that extended into the new chamber. There was just barely enough room for Jason to pull himself up. He climbed with excessive care. Once settled, he took a moment to take in his precarious new surroundings.

In front of him was a straight drop into black oblivion. This new floorless chamber was really just a big hole, three meters across, and with a ceiling high enough for Jason to stand up in, which he was too scared to do. The ground simply stopped at the chamber's entrance, and the water cascaded in white torrents over the edge and down into the Abyss. The sound of the waterfall was deafening in this small space, its cacophony reverberating off the rocks and drowning everything else out. The only horizontal surface of note in the chamber happened to be the ledge Jason crouched on. It was about a meter wide by a little over a meter long, but Jason felt it wasn't nearly enough. Even all the way back against the rock wall, the edge was terrifyingly close. To make matters worse, the mist from the waterfall made everything wet and slick, and Jason felt like he could slip off at any moment.

Jason cursed. But despite his fears, he persisted. While staying as low as he could, he shifted onto his knees and slowly peered over the edge. Immediately, he was hit with a sense of vertigo as he looked down into the hole. His mind was flooded with thoughts of falling. But Jason shook his head; he had to stay focused. He shined his flashlight down into the hole, hoping it would reveal some clue as to Parch's fate. The flashlight helped little, however, because the darkness was too deep, and the white torrents of water nearly filled the entire space, obscuring everything below. "Parch!" Jason called out as loud as he dared, still worried about hidden Malus. "Parch, can you hear me?" But it was pointless. The water was just too loud; nothing could be heard over it.

Jason continued to stare down into the Abyss, but the hole kept its secrets. It was impossible to see through the darkness and water, and equally impossible to know what was down there or what had happened to Parch. Trapped in this uncertainty, Jason quickly assumed the worst. *Maybe Parch really is dead.* Jason stepped back off the edge and leaned against the rock wall. Closing his eyes, he tried to calm himself and think.

Despite his best efforts, it was difficult for Jason to suppress the flood of negative thoughts filling his head, and he was growing increasingly frustrated at the situation. It had been such a struggle to leave that riverbank, such a struggle to make the choice to go after Parch, but now his journey seemed like it would end before it even truly began. And, worst of all, the result would be the same as if he'd never left the bank in the first place; he would be forced to leave without Parch, and without stopping the terrible machinations going on here.

But the more Jason remembered his decision, the more his resolve grew. That struggle he'd had with himself only minutes before would not be in vain. He made this choice for a reason, and he was determined to stay the course. Recommitted, he opened his eyes. *If there is some way I can help Parch and stop all this, I'm going to find it.*

Refocused, he went for another look. He scanned the dark hole again, intent on finding something he previously missed. He squinted and peered, trying to discover some hidden secret, some veiled clue, some piece of information that would help him. But, just as before, there was nothing. He shifted around the ledge. He angled his flashlight different ways. He tried everything and anything he could think of; all without success. Then, finally, after several moments, his persistence was rewarded: he saw something.

He hadn't noticed it before, because it was so dark, but there was something off about the water as it fell past a certain point. Several meters down, at the very limit of his vision, the movement of the water seemed to abruptly change. It looked like the water was hitting something . . . maybe. Jason couldn't exactly tell what was going on because of how obscured it was by the darkness and water. If something *was* happening, it was difficult to see what it was.

Jason leaned over the edge and squinted, trying to get a closer look. After he focused all his attention for a few moments he felt confident it wasn't just some trick of his eyes — there actually *was* something different going on down there. But he still wasn't sure what it was. Jason leaned over just a little farther. Was the water hitting a rock jutting out from the wall? Was it the base of the waterfall? Or was it something else? If he could only get a bit closer, he might be able to tell for sure. He leaned just a little more . . . and without warning, Jason's hand, the one bracing him, slipped off the wet rock, and he tumbled over the edge.

Jason would have screamed, but the fall was so sudden his entire body tensed, squeezing all the air out of his lungs in a grunt. He flailed helplessly, tumbling down the hole into the torrents of falling water. Fortunately, Jason only fell half a dozen meters before slamming into the pool of water below. What he had seen from the ledge *was* in fact the base of the waterfall.

He hit the water hard and was immediately driven down into the pool by the force of the falling water on top of him. Jason fought for his life as the crushing, battering strength of the falls pushed him deeper and deeper under. He thrashed about, clawing at the water, when suddenly his back struck solid rock, and he realized he had been pushed all the way to the bottom. Recognizing he could use this, Jason turned over, grabbed the solid ground, and pulled himself out from under the crushing downward pressure. Once he was free, he kicked upward off the bottom and broke the surface not a moment too soon; his oxygen-starved lungs gulped down air.

This time, Jason was filled with rage instead of fear. He was back in the river again, and it made him furious at everything, most of all himself. Slamming his fists down on the surface in a frivolous attempt to attack the water, he roared curses at the river, the Malus, and the whole situation. As he came to his senses, he checked that the torch was still secured to his shoulder strap, and it was. So, too, was his knife. With his gear still in his possession, there was nothing to be done; he was at the mercy of the currents once again. All he could do now was stay afloat, keep his feet pointed downstream, and wait to see where all this water ended up.

The river made swift downward progress, coursing deeper and deeper into the subterranean depths. As it did,

Jason's tunnel began to intersect with new tunnels that had their own rivers. The rivers merged and separated as the tunnels combined and split. The whole cave system was like a gigantic honeycomb, with water draining in from every direction. It was so labyrinthian that it was impossible to keep any sense of direction.

Jason's second time in the river was just as violent, hazardous, and unpleasant as the first. But the longer he fought the rapids, the better he became at it. He started to develop a feel for the water, how the river changed directions, and how to avoid the rocks and walls. As a result, he was less susceptible to the river's violent severities. It still wasn't easy, but Jason was able to protect himself from serious injury.

Finally, Jason arrived at one last small waterfall, where he was abruptly ejected from the tunnel into a large open area. He briefly fell through the air, then landed in a pool just deep enough to break his short fall. In the pool, the force of the water quickly dissipated, and there was no longer a dominant direction of flow, so Jason had no trouble swimming to the surface. He moved away from the falls and off to the side, where he found solid ground, and after pulling himself up, he collapsed onto the rocky shore to recover.

Lying on the shore, Jason laughed out loud. He was sore and tired, but at the same time, he felt invigorated. He'd done it; he'd survived the river! He relished the moment, and how strong he felt. But as his thoughts came back to him, he remembered where he was, and shifted to high alert. He sat up and scanned the area for danger.

Wherever he was now, it was so big that it was hard to believe he was still underground. It was impossible to even guess at the true size of this new cave because the vast, empty darkness of the cavern's interior seemed to go on forever; both sound and light faded as they travelled into the dead space. This black nothingness stretched out in every direction except to Jason's rear, where a giant wall of rock, the one from which he was just spat out via the tunnel, rose up and extended to either side. The utter enormity of the place made Jason feel small, powerless, and extremely vulnerable.

Looking around, Jason saw that the ground was level but rough and uneven. All along the cavern floor there were shallow depressions and small heaps of rock everywhere. The water pouring in filled the low spots and turned the cavern floor into a knee-deep sea, filled with countless rock mounds poking out of the water. It reminded Jason of a rocky shoreline.

Jason gazed down into the clear, tranquil water. He could easily see the rocky bottom with the light from his flashlight. It gave him some relief that the water was so pristine; it allowed him to see that nothing was swimming around in it, at least not around him.

As he continued to investigate his surroundings, Jason noticed the water wasn't just coming from the one waterfall; there were more falls pouring into the chamber farther down in either direction along the immense wall. Jason suspected there were as many ways into this vast cavern as there were tunnels above. But even all that water flowing in had no chance to fill a cavern so large.

After scanning the area as best he could and not seeing any Malus, Jason supposed he was safe for the moment. His mind then began to wonder how he could ever find Parch down here. On the trip down, the tunnel had split dozens of times; Parch could have gone down any of those different routes and ended up anywhere.

Jason stood up, slowly and quietly. "Parch?" he called out in the loudest tone he would risk, just barely audible over the sound of the water. There came no reply, except the constant churning of the waterfall beside him. "Parch?" he repeated slightly louder, but again no response. He realized he'd have to try something else, so he began walking around the pool, thoroughly checking the rocky banks around the waterfall. He supposed if Parch had come this way, maybe he had left some sign. But the search came up empty.

After only a few minutes, Jason was already becoming discouraged. The sheer size of the cavern, as well as the cave system above, made it seem absurd to think he could find Parch in the little time he had left. Jason sighed and sat down to think.

There were no obvious answers here. What Jason needed, and what he was hoping for, was a flash of genius, a clever idea that would solve his problems. But the longer he waited, the more he suspected one wasn't coming. Without any clues as to what had happened to Parch, all Jason could think to do was pick a direction and go bumbling around in the darkness until he ran out of time. Was that really the best course of action? So much depended on Jason getting this right, but the solution evaded him.

Trapped in indecision, Jason's mind started to wander. He stared into the darkness above, and wondered how deep he was below the surface. How much rock and seawater hung over his head right now? What would happen if it all came crashing down on him? Suddenly, he heard a noise; something was splashing in the water.

Jason's head snapped toward the direction of the sound. There was something near him, and whatever it was, it was moving. He hadn't heard the splashing before because of the noise from the waterfall; but now that he focused on it, the sound was clear. He cowered low to the ground and clumsily drew his knife.

A waist-high ridge of rock separated Jason from this new mystery, and curiosity ultimately won out over apprehension. He cautiously crawled forward and peered over the crest of the rock. On the other side, there was a shallow puddle hidden in the darkness, and on the banks of this puddle something flopped around, half submerged in the water. Whatever it was, it was slender and about a meter long. Jason's first thought was that it looked like a rope, except that it was moving. Was it a snake, maybe? Or an eel? He shined his flashlight over the crest and squinted, trying to figure out what it was . . .

The chain!

Instantly, Jason rushed over the rocks and down to the puddle. He bent down and stretched his arm out, and the chain shot up and coiled around him. Like reuniting with an old friend, Jason was overjoyed, but this joy quickly turned to shock when he noticed how short the chain was, only a meter in length. Looking at it, it was clear the chain had broken somehow, and this was just a fragment. But despite its broken state, it was as lively as ever. It cinched around Jason's wrist with one end and stuck straight out toward the middle of the chamber with the other.

Jason realized what it was trying to tell him immediately. "You know where to go, don't you?" Jason asked. The chain tugged on his wrist in response. "But what are you pointing at?" Jason wondered aloud. "Parch? The Mortem Cor plant? The rest of your links? Or maybe something else?" To this the chain didn't react at all and remained sticking straight out.

Looking toward where the chain was pointing, Jason stared into the dark void in front of him. Fear and hope mixed together inside Jason. It was impossible to know what lay ahead, but for the first time, he started to believe he could do this. Jason set his jaw, then nodded. "All right, let's go find out what you're pointing at," he murmured, then surged forward.

Jason rushed headlong into the darkness. With the chain as his guide, he jumped from rock mound to rock mound, staying out of the water and running whenever the terrain allowed it. It was difficult to see ahead. His flashlight on his chest only illuminated a few meters ahead, and the light from the torch wasn't focused enough to help, so he had to stay vigilant and focused. The uneven ground was difficult to traverse, and even more so at speed, but still Jason raced forward. His apprehension had been replaced with boldness, and he wasn't going to waste another second, no matter what lay before him.

Making quick progress over the rough ground, Jason was startled when the chain suddenly changed directions and reached out off to his right. Jason came to a stop, then allowed the chain to lead him toward a dark pool of water nearby. A morbid thought crossed his mind, and he was suddenly worried he was about to stumble upon Parch's dead body.

Jason shined his flashlight down to where the chain was reaching, and to his great relief another chain fragment jumped up to meet his own. The two fragments reformed instantly on touch, and with this new addition the length of the chain more than doubled. Even more importantly, finding it inspired confidence in Jason that they were heading in the right direction. Now reunited with its kin, the chain returned to pointing in the same direction as it had previously, and Jason took off once more.

As he continued on, Jason came upon another chain fragment, then another, and another. Eventually, he recovered so many fragments that the chain wrapped around his entire arm, his back, and down his other arm. It was now long enough to help out in a fight. Jason wondered if the chain was whole now, or if there were still pieces left to find. His mind then quickly shifted to wondering how the chain had been broken up in the first place. And what had happened to Parch? His imagination quickly set about creating nightmare scenarios until Jason gritted his teeth, pushed the thoughts out of his mind, and focused on moving forward. He was committed to this, and he was going to see it through no matter where the chain led.

Soon, something new appeared in the darkness. It was an oddity in the terrain. A dozen meters in front of him, still partially hidden, there looked to be a waist-high wall running perpendicular to Jason's course. As he approached, however, Jason realized it wasn't a wall at all — it was a root line! In a gasp of sudden epiphany, Jason understood. "The Mortem Cor plant is in here! In this cavern!" he couldn't help but exclaim.

But the chain continued to point over the roots and off into the darkness, away from the direction the roots were heading. Hesitating, Jason's eyes shifted between the chain and the roots. What was the right choice? What would Parch want him to do? The chain tugged at his wrist. If only it could speak; if only it could tell him what it knew.

Jason checked his watch, and saw he only had twenty-five minutes left. There wasn't enough time or information to make a considered decision. He looked down at the chain, which still tugged gently but insistently on his wrist. "I hope you're right," Jason said with a pat on the chain's coils. Then he hopped over the roots and hurried toward whatever the chain was pointing at, hoping it was Parch.

Rushing forward, Jason skirted around pools and maneuvered over rock mounds. After only going a few dozen meters, however, a dark shadow came into view ahead of him. It was wide and bulky, over two meters tall, and it looked noticeably out of place. Jason saw it, slowed, and covered his flashlight and the torch. He didn't know what he was looking at, and he didn't want to take any chances. Creeping closer, he squinted, trying to peer through the darkness and figure out what it was, but the answer eluded him. When he was barely three meters away, his curiosity got the better of him. He uncovered his flashlight very slightly, pointing it at the shadow, and saw . . . teeth!

Jason panicked and ducked behind a small hill of rock. It was the creature from before! The one that had charged them in the caves above, and he'd just shined a flashlight right in its crocodile face!

Holding his breath, Jason remained frozen behind the rock mound. He wanted to reach for the torch, but he was too afraid to move, too afraid to make a sound. Every second seemed like an hour, and at any moment, Jason expected the creature to charge him and tear him to shreds.

But after thirty seconds of sheer terror and panic, nothing happened. The cave was silent and still — peaceful even. Most remarkable of all, Jason noticed the chain seemed totally unconcerned. It wasn't shaking or rattling, but instead continued to calmly coax Jason forward. Puzzled by the quiescence, Jason started to wonder what was going on. *No way that thing didn't see me. I shined my flashlight right at it!* Jason thought. But as the seconds ticked by, his fears slowly turned into curiosity, and eventually he peaked out from behind the rock.

Cautiously, he shined his flashlight once again toward the creature. And upon this second look, a wave of relief swept over him, because the Malus was clearly dead. Its wreck of a corpse was a gruesome sight. It lay on its side, torn in half at its midsection, with its rear half nowhere to be found. Its lifeless eyes were fixed open, and its huge maw hung slack and contorted. A slimy black ooze dripped out from all over its shattered carcass, and it smelled like an open sewer.

Jason marveled, transfixed by the sight. "What happened to this thing?" he whispered. Moving out from behind the rock mound, he walked up to it, looking over the corpse with morbid interest. This monster had caused him quite a bit of trouble, so Jason was glad he got to see it broken and defeated like this. He circled around it, fascinated with the carnage, and as he did, something else came into view. A few meters behind the creature's body, collapsed on the rocks, was Parch.

"Parch!" Jason called out. He rushed over and knelt down beside his fallen companion. The last bit of chain was wrapped around Parch's arm, and as Jason knelt, the final links connected to his own and completed it.

Parch, in contrast, could not be mended so easily. He lay on his back, rigid and stiff. His eyes were open, but glazed over, and they stared off into nothing. He was breathing, but it was forced and labored. He looked to be in extreme pain. His teeth were tightly clenched, and he didn't react to Jason's presence. Blood from his lower abdomen had soaked through his clothes and was pooling underneath him.

The sight sent Jason into a panic. "Parch! Can you hear me?" Jason asked, as he lightly shook him.

Parch's eyes moved, and he looked at Jason. Through clenched teeth, he forcefully exhaled, producing a sound that could only be described as a harsh grunt.

Jason had no idea what to do. "You're going to be okay," he said over and over, more to convince himself than anything. He felt completely helpless.

Parch exhaled hard again, another harsh grunt, and this time Jason realized he was trying to say something.

"What is it?" Jason asked, leaning closer.

Parch looked at Jason with unmistakable dread in his eyes. He took in another ragged breath, and with all his strength grunted, "Ruuuunnnnn!"

As he did, the chain on Jason's arm erupted in excitement, which was followed by a familiar sound: a hissing rattle that Jason had last heard in the previous Mortem Cor plant's heart chamber.

CHAPTER 15

Jason gasped in terror as he realized he'd walked into a trap. He looked up just in time to see a huge, segmented tail strike at him from out of the darkness. The deadly stinger on the end was aimed at his heart, but the chain darted up just in time and deflected it. The chain couldn't, however, deflect the force of the massive tail. It smashed into Jason and sent him tumbling to the ground. Jason's spiking adrenaline had him up in an instant, and he quickly fled, diving for cover behind some nearby rocks.

Wide-eyed and breathing hard, Jason cowered behind the rocks. The hissing rattle sounded in the dark again. He looked for the Malus, but it hid in the darkness well. Wherever Jason shined his flashlight, the Malus was just out of view. He couldn't see the creature, but he could hear it. He heard the clacking sound its legs made as it skittered around on the rocks. It was circling him.

"Pathetic vermin!" the creature screamed — the sound both familiar and unhinged. "I knew the weakling was hiding somewhere. It just needed to be lured out. Fool! You will obstruct my master's plans no longer! I will kill you now!"

The hissing rattle erupted again, and the creature emerged from the darkness, revealing itself to be a monstrous scorpion! It was over five meters long, not counting its lengthy tail, and its all-black body rose off the ground to Jason's head. In place of a mouth, there was an eyeless, skinless, human skull whose face stuck halfway out of its body like a hideous growth. Its deadly tail floated above it, venom dripping from its stinger. Its huge claws snapped eagerly at Jason as it rushed at him.

Jason fled before the creature, scrambling backward in a terrified panic. He flailed the chain about wildly as he ran, in a desperate attempt to keep the monster away. The chain, which didn't fear the Malus, deftly used Jason's flailing movements and turned them into accurate strikes at the scorpion, slowing its advance and stopping it from catching Jason.

Instinct led Jason to seek the rockier areas. He wanted to get near the rock mounds and put as much solid material between himself and his pursuer as possible. He was the smaller of the two, so he hoped to use the terrain to outmaneuver this gangly creature. But after diving behind some rock mounds, the Malus simply clambered over the rocks, snapping and striking at Jason as it did.

Once again, Jason ran for his life. The Malus scorpion was getting closer, and Jason needed to figure out something else fast. Shining his flashlight around, he spotted a large rock mound nearby. It was a mountain compared to the others — several meters tall and even wider still. More importantly for Jason, it had a large split down one side. This divide in the rock looked big enough for Jason to fit inside: a refuge he could hide in. With no other option, Jason sprinted toward it, with the creature in bloodthirsty pursuit.

As Jason neared the large rock mound, the scorpion was nearly upon him. Jason could hear the creature's legs thumping on the rocks behind him as it closed in. The creature rushed forward, pressing through chain strikes. It reached out its claw toward Jason. But, by a hair's breadth, Jason slipped in between the rocks just in time, and the creature's huge claw slammed into the mound before it could cut him in half.

The space was tight, but Jason pressed farther in, squeezing between the rocks and moving as deep into the divide as he could. Outside, the creature was furious. It attacked the rocks in a frenzy, smashing its claws and tail into the split, trying to find a weakness, trying to get at Jason. But the rock held strong, and the irregular angles and tight space prevented its massive claws and tail from reaching their target. Enraged, the creature screamed and hissed, continuing its pointless attack unabated.

Jason was hyperventilating. Crammed into the rock, he was safe for the moment, but his heart pounded in his chest, and he was dazed from the blood rushing to his head. He tried to pull himself back into the moment, but his thoughts were hopelessly scattered. *What do I do?* he asked himself over and over again. Without thinking, his hand went for the torch on his shoulder, gripped it, and squeezed hard.

The scorpion's frenzy was unrelenting. It continued to attack the rocks, probing and searching for a way at Jason. Each time its claw or tail impacted, its fury and frenzy grew. In its unhinged, hissing rattle voice it began screaming at Jason.

"Fleeing and hiding, just as before. Weakling! I saw many through the trees; there were many to choose from, but none were as weak as you! A pathetic vermin too craven to defend his own! Easy prey! I will slay you here, then I will deliver the sweet blood of mother and child to my master!"

And with that, Jason's mind cleared. His hand left the torch, and instead drew his knife. With clenched teeth bared in rage, his eyes narrowed. All his focus concentrated on the Malus scorpion. He sat up, shifting his posture in the crevasse to better engage this wretched creature, all while the chain rattled in excitement at Jason's shift in demeanor.

The Malus continued to strike at the crevasse with its tail, persistent in its search for a way at Jason. The bulky tail could fit a little way into the entrance, but then slammed into the awkward angles of the rock that Jason had slipped between. The tail couldn't get in, but Jason could still reach out. He gripped the knife and watched the tail stab at the entrance. It was fast, but there was a rhythm to it; there was a timing in which Jason could strike back, but it'd have to be perfect. Jason watched the tail strike several more times, then cocked his arm like the hammer of a gun. And when next the tail struck, Jason did as well. With perfect timing, he plunged his knife into the monster's flesh.

Screaming in pain, the scorpion jerked its tail out from the crevasse. As it did, Jason held the knife in place, and it tore through more of the monster's flesh on the withdrawal. The runes on the blade shone brightly through the black blood that now covered it, and to Jason it almost felt like the blade was pleased, even happy. The Malus, conversely, was not happy. It continued screaming while it lurched backward, retreating into the darkness, with blood streaming out of its wound.

With the Malus driven back, Jason finally had a chance to recover. He breathed deep, and his mind cleared. For the briefest of moments, all his fear, confusion, and panic melted away. He stared at the black blood covering his hands, and in that quiet moment, Jason knew that now was the time. This was it. He clenched his teeth harder and squeezed the knife's handle, steeling himself. Stoking the fires of violence and rage in his heart, Jason vowed either to kill that thing, or die trying.

With his heart pounding and adrenaline coursing in his veins, Jason crawled out of the crevasse and stood up in the open cavern. Without the protection of the rock, he felt unsure, nervous, and jittery. But bolstered by his commitment to his purpose, he ignored it all. No matter how he felt, no matter his weaknesses, he would meet his fate head on.

Jason looked and saw the scorpion skulking in the darkness at the edge of his vision. It had watched him crawl out of the rock and done nothing. Seeing it hesitate on account of its recent wound, Jason sneered. He stood tall and stared at the creature with his eyes full of aggression and challenge.

The creature stared back and rallied. "Insolent scum!" it screamed. "How dare you! You will suffer a thousand-fold for this!" The scorpion slowly advanced toward Jason. It emerged from the darkness and came into full view.

The creature was huge, and Jason's nerve waivered as it approached. But Jason held strong. He began to swing the chain, slamming it down onto the rocks in front of him as the creature got closer. With the chain's strength adding to his own, the chain hit hard enough to cause serious damage, even through the scorpion's thick carapace, forcing the scorpion to keep its distance.

But the scorpion still drew closer, stopping just out of range of Jason and the chain. The creature snaped its pincers at the chain with each strike against the rocks. It did not, however, attack with its injured tail.

Squaring off, the two traded superficial attacks, gauging each other for weaknesses. The scorpion continued to snap its pincers, and Jason swung the chain wildly. The stress built as they both waited for the other to act. Sweat dripped down Jason's face. After the scorpion feigned an attack, Jason hesitated and took a step back. This hint of weakness was all the scorpion needed; it screamed loudly and charged.

Jason's boldness wilted, and he fled once more from the scorpion. He ran, whipping the chain and maneuvering through the rock mounds once more. This strategy was proving ineffective this time. The scorpion ignored the lashings and began to anticipate Jason's moves, trying to cut him off and trap him. All the while, its claws were getting closer and closer. Jason realized he couldn't win this fight.

Amid it all, Parch hadn't moved. He was still lying incapacitated on the rocks, where Jason had found him. Now, however, his eyes were alert and responsive. As the noise from the battle sounded around him, his twitching increased. His fingers wiggled, his body strained, but it was useless; he remained trapped in the prison of paralysis. But as Jason's battle grew increasingly more desperate, suddenly Parch's eyes grew wide with realization. Parch sucked in as much air as he could, and then, through clenched teeth, screamed, "GUN! WATER!"

Jason heard Parch's words and understood immediately. *Parch's gun!* As he scrambled over rocks in his flight from the scorpion, he looked around. In an instant he saw a glowing pool of water a dozen meters away. *The runes!*

He raced toward the glowing pool. But despite Jason's speed, the scorpion was faster. It was nearly upon him. It reached its claw out toward Jason, but the chain lashed out and intercepted the creature's claw, wrapping around it, and cinching it shut. Instead of catching Jason and clipping him in half, the bound pincer slammed into Jason with terrible force, piercing his left shoulder and sending him flying.

Jason crashed down hard on the rocks and was left gasping for air. Meanwhile, the chain tangled around the scorpion, binding several of its legs and slowing its rush forward. This bought Jason a few seconds. He pulled himself up and ran frantically for the gun.

Despite being hindered, the scorpion pursued its fleeing prey. But then the chain reached out and cinched itself around a nearby boulder. The scorpion's pursuit came to a sudden halt when, like an animal caught in a snare, its bound claw and legs were jerked back violently by the chain as it caught on the rock. The scorpion hissed and fought ferociously against the chain. It pulled so hard, the chain finally broke into pieces and fell from the beast. But it had done its job. In those precious few moments the chain had bought him, Jason had made it to the glowing pool, reached in and snatched Parch's gun from the bottom. Jason and the scorpion turned at the same moment, facing each other just as Jason swung the gun around. In his panicked state, Jason fired wildly. The shot missed, but it was enough to send the scorpion fleeing into the darkness, as the roar of the gun boomed throughout the cavern.

Breathing hard, Jason sat up and aimed the gun in the direction the scorpion had disappeared. His heart pounded in his ears, but he listened intently and was just barely able to make out the thumping of the scorpion's steps. It sounded like the Malus was moving away from him. *The gun must have scared it off*, Jason thought. He looked down at the runes as they recharged. There was still some time to wait before he would have another shot, but thankfully the scorpion didn't know that.

"Fool!" the scorpion's voice echoed through the cavern. "This means nothing. You will not stop my master's plan. I will see to that myself!"

A tremor shook the cavern floor. It felt like an earthquake, and it made Jason's breath catch in his throat. It ripped away any feelings of relief or comfort he'd won from driving the scorpion back.

The scorpion hissed in a hideous, twisted version of laughter. "My master comes for you! You shall face the terror of his wrath!" the scorpion screamed, before the sound of his footsteps skittered off into the distance.

Silence followed the scorpion's terrifying threat. Jason braced himself, not knowing what to expect next. But after a few moments, it was clear that, whatever was coming, it wasn't here yet. Jason didn't waste a second; he stood and ran to Parch's side. They had to get out of here quickly.

As Jason knelt down beside him, Parch was conscious but still unable to move. His arms and legs were rigid. All over his body, Parch's skin was flush red and hot to the touch, and he was sweating profusely despite the cold, damp cavern. The veins in his neck bulged as his body fought to breathe. His eyes darted around aimlessly until, in a brief moment of clarity from the pain, he looked up at Jason and spat out two words: "Pack. Med-kit."

Jason was up immediately, looking around for Parch's backpack. He spotted it on the rocks a few meters away, ran to grab it, then returned to Parch's side and opened it up. Inside, the pack held a large variety of gear and was meticulously well organized. Everything was color-coded with its own specifically sized pocket that kept it separate and in place. Jason quickly identified the red cross of the med-kit and pulled it out. "Got it," he said as he held it up to Parch.

"Anti-venom . . . green." Parch forced the words out.

Jason opened the med-kit, and just like the backpack, it was carefully organized and color coded. Among various other medical supplies, Jason saw three auto-injectors: one red, one blue, and one green. He grabbed the green one, quickly read the directions on the side, prepared it, then pressed it into Parch's thigh.

The injector clicked, and the needle pierced through Parch's pants and into his flesh, releasing the medicine into his bloodstream. Within seconds, Parch's body began to relax. His breathing became less labored, and his body less rigid. Despite the bleeding, enough of the medicine made it into his system to counteract the venom. The pain lingered, but he regained control of his body. His first move was to bring his hand in front of his face, to prove he wasn't still paralyzed. His second move was to grab Jason's arm. "Thank you," he said. Jason smiled and nodded in response.

Next, Parch pulled up the bottom of his shirt and exposed the side of his abdomen where the scorpion's stinger had struck him. "How's it look?" he asked.

Jason stared down at the area, but it was hard to find the wound because of how much coagulated blood there was. It looked straight out of a horror movie, but Jason continued to inspect the area, and noticed there wasn't any fresh bleeding. "It looks bad," Jason stated, trying to stay calm, "but it's off to the side, and I don't think it's bleeding anymore. I'll wrap it up as best I can."

"Best news I've heard all day," Parch groaned. Jason pulled bandages out of the med-kit and began quickly dressing Parch's wound. "After we got separated," Parch said, "I jumped in the river after you. I ended up down here, and somehow that hippo thing"— he nodded toward the huge Malus corpse —"found me again. I missed my first shot, and it rushed me. I dodged, but I think it broke my arm in the mayhem." Parch rubbed his broken arm with his good one. "The Malus kept after me, and the chain saved my life a dozen times, and got ripped apart each time for its trouble."

"That's how I found you — with the chain," Jason interjected.

"Makes sense," Parch said. "Anyway, it chased me all the way here before my gun recharged. I hit it that time and thought I was in the clear, but that's when the scorpion snuck up on me." He looked down at where Jason was finishing the bandages. "It got me good."

Jason sat back and looked over his work. The dressing was an ugly sight, but he'd done the best he could. "All right," he said, "it'll have to do until we can get you to a hospital." He paused and looked hard at Parch. "Parch," Jason said, his nervousness returning, "we need to leave. That thing from outside, I think it's coming for us right now. It'll be here any second. We have to use the button now. Right now."

Parch looked back at Jason with eyes of unyielding resolve. "We have to get that Mortem Cor plant first," he said. Even in his weakened state, he was determined. "Did you see the roots in here?" Parch asked.

Jason nodded. "Yeah, I saw them. I think the plant is in this cavern."

"That's right," Parch replied, "and it's close. Really close. We can end this right now."

Seeing his companion's stubborn determination lit a fire inside Jason as well. It overpowered all of his fear and hesitation. He smiled. "Let's finish it, then."

Without warning, another tremor hit, and the whole cavern shook violently. The two men looked at each other; it was now or never.

Jason ran and retrieved the chain from where the scorpion had shaken it off. He returned to Parch and handed it over. It promptly formed a sling around Parch's broken arm, securing it. Both men silently ignored how violently the chain was shaking just before it tightened down.

Too weak from his injuries to stand on his own, Parch reached his arm around Jason's shoulder, and the two men rose together. As they stood, Parch inadvertently touched Jason's wound and Jason winced in pain. Parch immediately pulled his hand away, then looked at Jason's back.

"You're bleeding," Parch said, the worry evident in his voice. "Your shirt is ripped, and you have a pretty bad gash."

"The scorpion hit me with its claw," Jason replied. "It didn't hurt until you touched it," he added with a smirk. "Now let's hurry."

Parch looked at Jason with concern but said nothing. Instead, he shifted his arm to avoid putting pressure on Jason's wound and tried to walk as much as possible on his venom-weakened legs.

Leaving the backpack behind, the two injured men set off, moving as fast as they could. They backtracked toward the roots, heading in the direction Jason had come from. The uneven terrain was difficult to navigate quickly, even more so in their current state. Every stumble, every drop, every lurch caused both men to grimace, but they pressed on.

Parch spoke up as they hobbled along. "You know, for someone who said he could never fight a Malus, you did a pretty good job."

Jason smiled. "I wish I had killed it, though," he replied. "I missed it, and it got away."

"Yeah, try aiming next time," Parch quipped. He winced again as Jason stepped off another mound. "You still did good, though."

The roots appeared out of the darkness in front of them. For an instant, their spirits lifted, but the next moment they were hit with the most intense tremor yet.

Like a powerful earthquake, the shockwave knocked their legs out from under them and sent both men tumbling to the ground. Large chunks of rock broke off from the ceiling and came crashing down onto the cavern floor around them. But what was more terrifying even than the earthquake was what came after: a familiar roar sounded from outside. Despite being muffled by water and rock the roar was unmistakable. The Titan they saw on the land bridge had returned. Jason looked upward, and could only imagine the terrible creature in the sea above, assailing the rock and attempting to break in through the cavern's roof.

All thoughts of pain and temptations of lethargy vanished, and both men rose together in a desperate scramble to the roots. "Light it," Parch yelled as they arrived, so Jason grabbed the torch and set the flame to the root line.

Per usual, the fire spread quickly, shooting off in both directions down the root line. As the flames grew, the enormous cavern was illuminated, and it was even bigger than Jason had suspected. The ceiling was nearly a kilometer above their heads. Even with all the light from the burning root line, Jason could only see two sides of the cavern which made up a corner of the domain. All that he had seen and experienced down here, from when he was ejected out of the tunnel by the river up to now, had all happened in but a small portion of the cavern's vast expanse, and even with all the light Jason couldn't see the rest of it.

But this corner was all Jason needed to see; it was where the Mortem Cor plant resided. The burning root line led right to it, and it was less than a hundred meters away. Like the last two, this Mortem Cor plant was a mighty tree that loomed over them. This one was even bigger than the other two, but it had been hidden in the darkness when Jason passed by before. With the fire rushing toward it now, however, it was clear as day. The fire travelled up the roots, and just before the flames hit the main trunk, the root line tore away, and was flung aside. The tree's involuntary defense mechanism saved it, but the root line landed across others, which caught on fire and were flung away as well. Soon the green fire snaked off in all directions, catching on all the root lines it touched, and racing off into parts unknown, both deeper into the cavern as well as up into the tunnels. Only the Mortem Cor plant's main body was free from the green flames.

Together, Parch and Jason set off toward the trunk, but the two men hadn't gone far before they were hit with another calamity. Without warning, a thunderous crash tore through the cavern, followed by the sound of rock breaking, then rushing water. Jason knew exactly what was happening, but he couldn't help turning to look in horror. His fears were soon realized when he saw a massive column of water flooding into the cavern. Several hundred meters away, the Malus Titan had smashed a hole in the cavern ceiling, causing water to pour in from the sea above. Thankfully, despite the tremendous impact, the ceiling hadn't collapsed. But the hole was so large, and the volume of water rushing in so great, that the water level at the two men's feet immediately started to rise.

Parch pushed Jason forward. "Go!" he screamed. "Burn the plant! You have to destroy it!"

Jason hesitated, reluctant to leave Parch behind. But he realized Parch was right and took off running. Too weak to continue standing, Parch slumped down next to the roots, resigning himself to his fate.

As Jason ran, the water started crashing in small waves at his feet. In less than a minute, the water level had risen to his knees. He was now wading through increasingly tumultuous flows. It was clear he had to get out of the water, so he jumped on top of the still-burning roots and pressed on. The tree was close now. Despite the pain, despite the horror of the situation and the monstrosity that would soon be upon him, Jason's only thought was burning the wretched tree to the ground.

Finally, Jason arrived. He stood at the end of the root line, where it had torn off from the tangle, and glanced up at the enormous tree towering in front of him. The tree's trunk was massive and imposing. Its branches reached so high that even with all the light from the green flames, Jason couldn't see the top. At the tangled base, the tree had more root lines than the previous two trees combined. Its vast network of roots, half of which were now torn off and on fire, snaked away from the trunk in every direction, climbing up the cavern walls and disappearing into caves. Jason couldn't help but wonder where they all went. But he had no time to lose. Jason jumped off into the now waist-high water, and reached out, touching the flame to the root tangle base. The fire took to it just as ferociously as ever, and in seconds, the flames were shooting up the trunk. The Mortem Cor plant's fate was sealed. It would soon be reduced to ashes, but Jason didn't wait around to see it. There was no time for celebration. The moment Jason saw the flames catch, he turned and was off, making his way back toward Parch.

As Jason scrambled out of the water and back onto the roots, the final catastrophe arrived. The Titan roared, then Jason felt one final, devasting impact shake the area. The cavern's ceiling where the Titan was attacking buckled and collapsed completely. Several hundred meters away, the entire sea crashed down into the cavern in one giant surge, and a wall of water rushed toward Jason. But Jason didn't hesitate. He sprinted back down the roots, focusing only on getting back to Parch. *You have to be touching the torch when the button is pressed to get pulled out*, Jason remembered, and he wouldn't leave Parch behind. While he ran, he ripped the torch off his gear, and his adrenaline-numbed hands fumbled with the cap on the bottom. "Parch!" he roared over the cacophony.

In his broken state, Parch had climbed onto the roots to get out of the rising water. He was watching the rushing wall of water bear down upon him but turned at Jason's call and saw his companion running toward him. Weakly, Parch stood and forced himself forward toward Jason and the torch.

Jason had gotten the cap off, and now ran with his thumb over the button, ready to press it in an instant. He was getting closer to Parch, but the water was approaching faster. He wasn't going to make it. There was no time left. In one last-ditch effort, right before the water hit them, Jason dove toward Parch, torch extended out in front of him. And as the water crashed into the two men, Parch's hand closed around the torch, and Jason pressed the button.

CHAPTER 16

Jason's vision went completely white, and for a brief moment his entire body tingled like he was full of static electricity. He didn't so much as smell the fragrant pine needles, rosemary, and alcohol as much as it was forced up his nose and crammed in to fill his entire nasal cavity. Then, an instant later, he and Parch both appeared in Jason's entryway. They arrived midair, then fell onto the floor right in front of the metal box Parch had dragged in earlier. They were soaking wet, exhausted, injured, but most of all: alive.

Lying there on the ground, Jason still clung to the torch. He coughed and sputtered, trying to force the smells out of his mouth and nose, but no matter how hard he tried, the smells stuck. As he came to his senses, he looked at the floor beneath him and saw the scuffed, worn, wooden floorboards of his entry way, and then exploded with laughter. They'd done it! They'd survived!

Parch, too, erupted with laughter. He let go of the torch and rolled over onto his back. He moved slowly, and he winced the entire time, but laughed all the same. He checked his watch. "Look at that," he said. "Six hours of torch burn, and we finished with five and a half minutes to spare. Told you it would be easy."

"Longest twenty minutes of my life," Jason shot back, smiling. He too rolled onto his back, still reeling, still barely able to believe he was back home. While he recovered, Jason looked up at all the roots that the still-burning torch revealed. They crawled along the walls and ceiling, and blocked doors and windows. *No wonder we couldn't get out with all this*, he thought, thinking back to when he and Lily had tried to escape the house earlier in the night.

But as his mind settled and he came to his senses, Jason noticed something was wrong — it was quiet. Where was Lily? A muffled scream sounded from the living room, and Jason went from relieved happiness to full panic. He was up in an instant and running toward the scream.

In the living room, the torchlight revealed the dark stain on the wall for the bridge it was. Nearly a meter and a half in diameter, the bridge was a hideous blight. The Mortem Cor plant's roots extended outward from the bridge in all directions, covering the walls and ceilings even more than in the entryway. But Jason didn't care about any of this. The only thing Jason noticed was that Lily wasn't there.

There was another scream, and it came from inside the Abyss. Jason's heart sank as his worst fears were realized. The connection was complete! The Malus had her! And they were dragging her back through the Abyss, back to that horrible Titan.

Jason ran to the bridge. “Lily!” he screamed as he looked in. The Abyss was as dark as ever. To make matters worse, after a few meters his vision was completely blocked by branches. He grabbed the bridge’s edges and prepared to pull himself in, when Parch, who had stumbled into the room, grabbed his shoulder and stopped him.

Jason turned and looked fiercely at Parch. “I have to go after her!” he shouted.

“I know,” Parch replied. He clutched at his injury. “I wouldn’t be any help in there,” he said contritely.

Jason nodded, then turned back to the bridge. Once more tried to pull himself up, and once more Parch stopped him.

“And,” Parch continued, “I need the torch. It wouldn’t be any help to you anyway, we already used the button, and this bridge is too dangerous to leave open. I have to seal it before the torch dies, no matter what. There’s five minutes left. You have to be out by then, or you’ll be sealed in.”

Undeterred, Jason simply tossed the torch to Parch, then drew knife and gun, and charged through the bridge into the Abyss.

The root tunnel Jason entered was unlike any of the ones before it. It was sealed completely like the previous one, but this tunnel was rough, unfinished, and significantly larger. The floor was even with the bridge, and the ceiling rose over a hundred meters high, with the walls wider still. The tunnel floor sloped upward from the bridge for a length, then evened out. All along the inside of the tunnel, branches jutted up and out from the roots, creating a dense thicket of tree limbs that almost filled the interior. What made the tunnel even more odd, was that it was massive, yet was still forced to conform with the relatively tiny bridges on either end. The roots shrank down in size upon coming even with the bridge, all converging and passing through the tiny bridge before growing in size again once they entered Jason's house. This quirk in the tunnel created a small area, several meters deep, in front of the bridge that was clear of branches. It was here that Jason found himself.

As he looked around, Jason saw a small black creature that was loitering near the bridge entrance. This new Malus was roughly humanoid in shape, but small. It rose only to Jason's knee. It had a thick torso, and four muscular, oversized arms: two in the normal place for arms, and two in place of its legs. Its hands were as big as a man's and looked strong and powerful. It had smooth, pitch-black skin, no eyes, and a massive mouth that took up all of its head. As Jason entered, the creature was busy fidgeting and biting itself until it noticed Jason's presence and attacked, lunging at him with its open jaws.

Jason, shocked by the sudden assault, reflexively slashed his knife at the creature, and hit it squarely on the head. The knife cut deeply into the creature's flesh. The impact from the strike sent it reeling. The creature yelped in pain, then fled. It scrambled on all fours into the thicket of branches, nimbly navigating the dense wood.

For a moment, Jason stared at the Malus while it fled. But he quickly came to his senses and realized this was a distraction he couldn't afford. "Lily!" he screamed. This time he got a response.

"Jason!" Lily screamed back.

She was close! The Malus hadn't stolen her away . . . yet. With renewed hope, Jason peered into the thicket, searching for his wife. And there she was, twenty meters up the hill in front of him.

Farther ahead, Lily was being dragged away by a group of Malus like the one that had attacked Jason seconds earlier. The creatures, about ten of them by the look of it, were weaving through the thicket and pulling Lily along with them. Lily kicked and fought the Malus, trying everything she could to stop from being dragged farther. But it was no use; there were too many of them.

"Jason!" Lily screamed again.

"I'm coming!" Jason screamed back. With a rage and ferocity he'd never known, he slashed at the branches in front of him, hacking his way through the thicket in a violent frenzy. Despite the Malus' quick and nimble movements through the branches, Jason gained on them through sheer force of will. He would not allow anything to stop him — not the branches, nor his tiredness, nor the pain, nor his own blood-soaked injuries.

Before he knew it, Jason was over halfway up the hill. He stopped for a moment to locate Lily and the Malus again. They were nearly at the top. At the pace he was going, he could catch them. Encouraged, Jason was about to resume his fight forward, when a familiar hissing rattle echoed through the branches. With eyes full of hatred and fury, Jason looked up and saw the Malus scorpion standing atop the crest of the hill.

The scorpion waited as its minions, the smaller Malus creatures, dragged Lily the last few meters. When they arrived, every muscle in Jason's body clenched as he watched the scorpion greedily snatch Lily up in one of its claws. It hissed triumphantly as it held her up, while Lily screamed in terror.

Driven mad with hate, Jason tried to point his pistol at the scorpion. But with all the branches in the way, he couldn't get a clear shot. By the time he found an angle, the scorpion had vanished from the hill, and Lily along with it.

"Nooooo!" Jason roared. With a nearly inhuman effort, Jason resumed his fight forward through the branches. Nothing mattered anymore; nothing except saving his wife. Every second he couldn't see her — every moment she wasn't safe — was unacceptable, was agony. Blood dripped off his clothes and arms as he pressed on. He would not let this happen; he would not let the Malus take her!

In less than a minute, but what felt like an eternity, Jason reached the top of the hill. Once there, it was easy to see which way the Malus had gone because the scorpion had cut its own path through the branches from the Ignotus side of the tunnel.

Looking down this cleared path the scorpion had made, Jason saw that the bridge into the Ignotus was fifty meters away. The bridge was about four meters wide, and Jason could see through it the rain and flashes of lightning of the terrible Ignotus he had just escaped. He also saw the scorpion retreating to that terrible place, clutching his wife.

In the short time Jason had lost sight of it, the scorpion, along with its group of minions, had covered most of the remaining distance back to their bridge. They were nearly there, nearly gone for good, and Lily with them. But the scorpion had overlooked something: the path it cut now gave Jason a clear line of sight.

Jason saw his opportunity and knew this would be his last chance. Like a predator, his senses sharpened, and his mind cleared. All the pain and exhaustion left his body, and a calm focus swept over him as he raised his gun. He relaxed and stood up straight and tall. His hands formed around the pistol perfectly. He took a deep breath and raised the pistol, aiming down the sights. He aimed for the scorpion's body, drifting as far as he could away from Lily who was still in its claws. It would be close, but Jason had no other option, he had to take this shot. Jason exhaled. And with the scorpion only a few meters from the bridge back to the Ignotus, Jason fired.

The white, streaking bullet rocketed through the tunnel at blazing speed, pierced the scorpion's rear abdomen, tore through its body, and finally burst out of its face. The shot hit with such force that large parts of the scorpion's flesh were vaporized in an instant. Huge chunks flew in all directions as what remained of its smoking corpse collapsed to the ground. Lily fell with it, still stuck in the creature's mostly intact claws. The sight of their dead champion sent the smaller Malus fleeing in terror. They surrendered their captive and ran through the bridge, disappearing into the Ignotus.

Jason roared in triumph and ran toward Lily, covering the distance in what seemed like only a few strides. When he arrived, he stepped atop the scorpion's smoldering carcass, and reached his hand out toward his wife.

Lily took Jason's hand, and the two pulled her free from the creature's posthumous grasp, then stepped off the remains. Eyes wide in terrified confusion, Lily reached for her husband and fell into his welcoming arms. Sobbing, she buried herself in Jason's chest. Jason squeezed her, his heart soaring with relief. He had come so close to losing her forever, but now everything was all right. They were together again.

As Lily calmed down, Jason released her and looked down at her intensely. "We have to leave right now!" he said.

Jason's words proved prophetic, because just then, something covered the bridge leading to the Ignotus. The movement drew Jason's attention. For a moment, he wasn't sure what he saw, but when he realized what it was, he flinched and took a step back. In the Ignotus, looking through the bridge, was a massive eye.

As if peering through a keyhole, the Titan's huge eye made the bridge seem tiny. The gigantic creature looked into the Abyss, his eyeball searching around the tunnel. It spotted Jason and Lily, and fixated on them with its terrible gaze.

Jason stared back. It was like staring at death itself. He felt small, powerless, and filled with more fear than he'd ever felt in his life. But instead of fleeing, his hand went to his pistol. Jason drew and fired, but nothing happened. *The runes!* Jason realized. He looked down, and saw the gun was still recharging. When he looked up, the eye was gone, and the roar that followed shook the roots he and Lily stood on.

Without hesitation, Jason and Lily took off running, with Jason leading the way. They ran as fast as they could back down the tunnel, making quick progress along the scorpion's path. Only seconds after the Titan's roar, every manner of nightmarish creature imaginable started crawling through the bridge. Soon, a wall of teeth and claws and Malus were pursuing them.

As he ran, Jason's gun finished recharging. He pointed it back at the mass of Malus and fired. The round brutalized one of the creatures in the lead and several in line behind it, but it did nothing to dissuade the rest. The waves of Malus trampled over any of their number that fell and continued their headlong race toward their prey. It was clear there was no stopping them; speed was Jason and Lily's only hope now.

The two reached the crest of the hill and dashed down the other side. Jason led them back down the path he had cut only moments before. His path was much rougher and narrower than the scorpion's, so they had to fight the thicket the entire way, and it slowed them down. By the time they neared the bottom, the Malus had crested the hill behind them, and were flooding into the thicket.

But Jason wasn't looking back; he was looking forward through the last few branches, trying to see the bridge, hoping it wasn't closed. He saw Parch's face, looking into the Abyss from the living room, and his spirits soared. The bridge wasn't closed yet! They could still make it!

Parch saw Jason, as well. "Ten seconds!" Parch screamed, "Hurry!" Parch had cleared the bridge mouth of roots, and now green flame danced all along the bridge circumference, all except the final few centimeters. He now held the torch in his hand and was watching the seconds tick down on his watch. Parch started counting down, yelling the time remaining into the Abyss. "Seven!"

Jason fought hard against the thicket, slashing and hacking at every branch in his way. He and Lily were almost there.

"Five!" Parch yelled.

Jason broke through into the open area in front of the bridge. He pulled himself out of the thicket, then reached back in and grabbed Lily, pulling her free as well. The yelps and growls of the Malus echoed through the branches; they were very close now.

"Three!" Parch screamed.

Jason and Lily were free of the thicket and sprinting toward the bridge.

"Two . . . one!" And with the last flames of the torch, Parch completed the circle of fire along the circumference of the bridge mouth, and the torch burned out.

Jason and Lily were only meters away from the bridge as Parch finished the seal. But the bridge wasn't closed yet, merely *closing*. The nearly meter-and-a-half gateway was shrinking, but there were still a few precious seconds left.

In a full sprint, Jason and Lily covered the remaining distance to the bridge. It was growing smaller by the second, and the Malus were nearly upon them. Jason pushed Lily forward. "Go!" he roared. She crawled through the bridge, and Parch grabbed her hands on the other side, pulling her to safety. Then, in the last remaining moments, with the bridge closing and the Malus almost in arm's reach, Jason dove through the bridge himself, barely squeezing through before it shut, once and for all.

CHAPTER 17

The first light of dawn streamed into Jason's living room through the large window. He and Lily were lying on the floor, still breathing hard and trying to recover from their flight through the Abyss. Parch sat nearby, leaning against the couch for support.

Outside, the sunrise bathed everything in a golden light, its warmth drying the rain from the night before. The peaceful woods surrounding Jason's house were slowly coming alive as the day broke and the night receded. Birds chirped happily outside, deer could be seen meandering at the tree line, and squirrels bounded across the roof. It was a triumphant, beautiful morning.

As Jason lay there, his smile was as bright as the sun. He hugged Lily and kissed the top of her head. He then turned to Parch. "That scorpion won't be causing any more trouble," he said.

"Glad to hear it," Parch said with a slight nod. With some effort and wincing, he rose and walked to his box in the entryway, waving off Lily's offer to help him. Parch opened the box, pulled out a handheld radio, then returned to where he had been sitting. After a moment to compose himself, he held the radio up to speak. "This is Agent Parch," he said after keying the radio, "requesting immediate medivac from my last known entry location. Two patients. First patient critical: deep puncture wound to abdomen, broken arm, blood loss, and significant lacerations. Second patient urgent," Parch looked over at Jason, evaluating his injuries. "Blood loss, deep lacerations to upper back, and possible broken bones." Parch unkeyed the radio, and the response was quick.

"Medivac en route. ETA twenty minutes," the voice chirped.

Even with all his injuries, Jason was in a joyous state. He felt alive. He felt like a new man. He felt like he could do anything. The world was brighter than it ever had been before, and everywhere there was hope and happiness. Despite his wounds, he had so much energy, vitality, and strength. Jason breathed deeply, relishing it all. He then looked at Lily, and saw she was in a much different state.

The moment Jason made eye contact, Lily's emotions boiled over. "What is going on?!" she wailed, her voice shaking as she stared wide-eyed at Jason. "Are we safe? Is it over? What were those things?"

Jason hugged his trembling wife again. "It's a long story. But yes; we're safe. It's over."

Lily wiggled out of Jason's embrace and stared up at him again with fear and confusion still in her eyes. She gripped Jason's arm tightly. "Where did you go?!" she asked emphatically. "You were gone for so long. You said you'd be back in twenty minutes, but then you didn't come back, and I called down into the basement for forever, and no one answered. So I went down there, and I was so scared, and you both were gone, and I didn't know what to do. I came back to the couch, and I tried to call someone for help, but we don't have any reception out here. So all I could do was sit and wait for morning, and I was alone, and I kept crying, and then all these things grabbed me in the dark, and I couldn't see what they were, and they pulled me into the wall, and I kept screaming!"

Jason was overwhelmed with concern as he listened to Lily's outpouring of emotion. He took her hand in his and gave it a gentle squeeze. "I'll explain everything," he said as he sat up. "But I'm going to need a glass of water first."

Jason braced himself against the wall and fought to get up, eager for a chance to move around. Seeing his difficulty, Lily came alongside him and under his arm. She helped him stand, then the two set off to the kitchen for some water.

As the couple moved into the kitchen, Jason heard Parch key the radio again.

"Agent Parch for Command," Parch said.

"Go for Command," the voice responded.

"Requesting immediate suspension of entry clearance for all agents until further notice," Parch said gravely. "I've found what's killing us in there, and the situation is worse than anyone imagined. There's a Malus unlike anything I've ever seen. It's ancient, powerful, and massive. It's somehow created a kind of network between the Mortem Cor plants. It can move around in there, between the

Ignotus . . . it even . . ." Parch paused and looked at the wall where that final bridge had been. "Sir, it even tried to come through into the human world, and it almost succeeded."

There was silence for several seconds, then the voice from the radio spoke again. "We'll send people to you. Once medical is done with you, you'll be debriefed ASAP. We need to know everything."

"Understood," Parch acknowledged. "One last thing: there are multiple entry points in the house. This location appears to be a hot spot. I can't say for sure what significance it has to the Malus' Mortem Cor plant network, if any. Maybe it's a coincidence, maybe it's not," Parch said.

"We're dispatching Financial as well."

"Roger," Parch replied. He set the radio down and leaned back against the couch.

Jason entered his kitchen like a prize fighter returning to the locker room after winning the fight of his life. He was exhausted but exhilarated. He felt so alive.

He and Lily walked to the counter and Jason leaned against it. He was about to reach for a glass from the cupboard, but Lily beat him to it. She filled the glass while Jason shifted uncomfortably, trying to find a way to rest without putting pressure on any of his several sore spots. Finally, he got into a position where his pain was minimized, and Lily handed him a full glass of water.

While Jason drank it down, Lily looked over his disheveled state with soft eyes. She circled to Jason's side, and when she saw the large wound on Jason's back, she gasped and covered her mouth with her hand. She gently peeled back the torn shirt to reveal the extent of the injury, and accidentally touched his gash. Jason winced and Lily drew her hand away in response. She looked at the bit of her husband's blood on her fingers, then moved closer and placed her hand on Jason's cheek and drew his head to her chest, hugging him intimately.

"What did those terrible things do to my husband?" she whispered.

For a moment, all the pain left Jason's body. Then, when his wife released the embrace, he straightened up and couldn't help but stared down into his wife's eyes, completely entranced.

Lily smiled and stared back, but after a moment she tilted her head and her mouth opened slightly. She squinted at Jason with a twinkle in her eye. "Something happened in there, didn't it?" she asked. She reached up and brushed a tuft of his hair. "You're different somehow, I can tell," she said with a coy smile.

Jason smirked proudly and kissed her. "I'll tell you all about it," he said, and the two headed back to the living room.

Parch was still leaning against the couch when Jason and Lily got back. The two sat down, Jason with some effort, on two folding chairs nearby. Jason removed his chest harness and held it in front of him. He pulled the pistol halfway out of his holster and looked over it one last time.

"I guess you'll be wanting this back," Jason said. He holstered the pistol then handed the whole chest rigging back to Parch, feeling a mix of relief as well as a tinge of sadness. His adventure was over.

After taking the harness, Parch detached the sheathed knife, then tossed it back to Jason. "That's yours now," he said. "You've earned it. You're the one who saved the day; you deserve to remember."

Jason looked at Parch, puzzled. *Remember? How could I ever forget tonight?* he wondered.

Parch didn't give him a chance to ask. "But," Parch continued, "don't tell anybody I gave it to you." Parch winked and Jason stuffed the knife into his back pocket.

"Now I believe the lady wanted to hear the story," Parch said.

Lily sat up. "Yes!" she said eagerly.

Parch looked over at Jason. "Well, go on, then," he said, raising an open hand toward Jason.

"All right," Jason said. He turned his chair toward Lily, who was staring at him with rapt attention, and began telling the tale. He was a bit scattered, and he didn't always have explanations to the frequent questions Lily asked, especially about the Ignotus or the Malus, but his wife was enthralled, anyway.

Less than halfway through the story, two vehicles came racing down the dirt road to Jason's house. The first was a small truck like Parch's, followed by a white van. Neither vehicle had any markings on them, there were no sirens, and there was nothing distinguishing about them in any way. They both stopped in front of Jason's house. Out of the van jumped three men in EMT garb, carrying several packs of medical equipment. Two men, in similar clothing to Parch, exited the truck.

All five men came through the front door and into Jason's house. The medical team rushed to their respective patients, with one medic going to Jason and the other two going to Parch. The two men not part of the medical team, those dressed like Parch, loitered in the entryway. After a quick nod to Parch, which Parch returned, the two men began talking quietly.

The medic that was treating Jason looked to be in his early twenties, with sharp features, pale skin flush with color, and short black hair. The medic started with a quick assessment, and, after looking him over, assured Jason that there weren't any life-threatening injuries. Jason was pleased to hear that, and while the medic began dressing Jason's wounds, Jason looked at the two men in the entryway.

As Jason watched, the two men in the entryway both pulled out opaque vials with eye dropper caps. Each man unscrewed his own bottle, and then, while looking up at the ceiling, squeezed a single drop of whatever liquid was in the vials into each of their eyes. When they did, there was a sound like pouring water onto an overheated pan, and gray-and-white smoke streamed from their eyes, but neither man reacted nor gave an indication of pain. The smoke continued flowing from their eyes, obscuring their faces, as both men capped the vials and then returned them to their pockets.

Lily, who was watching, as well, leaned over to Jason. "What is that? What are they doing?" she whispered.

After Jason shrugged, the medic who was treating him spoke up. "They're just clearing the house. Making sure everything is safe and nothing was missed."

Jason and Lily shared a look of curiosity, then watched as the two men with smoke still flowing from their eyes split up and began searching the house. The men looked all around each room, diligently scanning each area. Despite the smoke, which Jason thought would make it difficult to see, both men moved as if they could see perfectly, reaching for doorknobs and stepping around obstacles unerringly. As they passed into other rooms, Jason could still hear their footsteps as they moved around the house.

"Who *are* these people?" Lily asked.

"I don't know, and Parch wouldn't tell me," Jason replied.

At this the medic chuckled. He finished up with the dressing and stood up. "Change the bandages in a few days and keep an eye on it. But I think it'll heal up fine," he said. He then walked over and joined the other two medics who were attending to Parch.

The other two medics had their hands full. It was obvious Parch needed a hospital, so after ensuring Parch was stable, they immediately began preparing him for transport. The third medic joined them and, working together with practiced precision, they moved Parch onto a stretcher, started an IV, and stabilized his broken arm.

While the medics worked on Parch, the two men in military attire returned to the entryway, eyes still flowing with smoke. When Jason and Lily looked over, one of them spoke. "We didn't find anything. Everything in here is safe," he said in a gruff no-nonsense tone that left no room for debate or questions. "Someone will contact you."

Then, without another word, the two men grabbed the metal box from Jason's entryway, hauled it outside and back into Parch's truck. They then departed, with one man driving the truck they came in, and the other driving Parch's.

Jason was relieved to hear the house was safe, but at the same time everything was happening so fast he was at a loss. He was too tired to object, however, so he just went along with it all.

A moment later, the medics finished their work and prepared to move Parch. With a man on either end of the stretcher and the third at Parch's side, they lifted Parch together, and then all moved out to the van.

Seeing Parch being rushed away caused a swell of emotion in Jason. He and Lily rose and followed the medics out the front door, and watched from the steps as Parch was loaded into the back of the van. Jason looked to Lily, who let go of his arm in response, then he walked down the steps and over to the van's open rear doors.

The inside of the van was equipped like an ambulance and Parch was being strapped down in it. The sight cut Jason to the heart. Parch had gotten his injuries saving him and his wife. No matter what Parch had said earlier, Jason knew the truth, and who the real hero was. As the medical team finished their duties and were getting ready to leave, Parch looked up and saw Jason.

"Thank you," Jason said.

Parch smiled and gave a thumbs-up. And with that, the last medic jumped in and closed the doors.

The van took off, barreling down the dirt road and disappearing into the trees, leaving Jason and Lily alone in the bright morning sun. Jason walked back and joined his wife sitting on the steps. They sat in silence for several minutes, each trying to process the night they had just lived through. Lily returned to holding her husband's arm, and Jason took his wife's hand in his. They were starting to enjoy the moment when another car appeared through the trees, driving up toward the house.

"What now?" Lily muttered, exasperated.

This new car was different than the van with the medical team. This one was a black sedan, and it was in no rush at all. The car slowly pulled up in front of the house and came to a stop. A thin man in an immaculate suit exited the car and began walking toward the couple. He looked to be in his forties, unassuming, a little pale, with brown hair and blue eyes. He smiled and held up his hand in a polite wave. "Mr. and Mrs. Mures, I presume," he said as he got closer.

This new stranger shook Jason's hand. "My name is Henry," he said. He looked Jason over, his eyes widening at all the bandages. "What happened?" he asked. "Did Parch take you in there with him or something?" When

Jason nodded, Henry frowned. "Agents aren't supposed to do that," he said, then shrugged. "Oh well, it makes my job easier. I can skip a lot of explanations. I'll get straight to the point. I work for the same organization as agent Parch. We have reason to believe what happened in your house tonight could happen again. There are places where these sorts of things occur more frequently, and your house appears to be one of them. So, we think it's in everyone's best interest if we buy the house from you . . . for double what you paid."

Jason and Lily both gasped. The couple looked at each other with open-mouthed smiles, and Jason felt his wife squeeze his arm.

"Oh, thank goodness!" Lily exclaimed. "I can't imagine spending another night here!"

Jason shifted around with excitement, completely speechless.

Henry smiled back. "I'll take care of everything and expedite the whole process. The paperwork will be done by tomorrow morning, and the money should be in your account twenty-four hours following signatures."

Jason's excitement was only growing the more Henry spoke, and he could feel Lily's excited energy as well. After discussing a few more details, Henry brought the conversation to an end by saying that he had a lot of work to get to and he had to be going. They all said their goodbyes, and Henry headed back to his car.

Jason was left feeling a little beside himself. He hadn't even recovered from the nightmare he'd just lived through, and now they were jumping into selling their house. It was all so much, and so quick. But Lily was happy — very happy, in fact — so Jason decided not to worry.

As Jason watched Henry walking away, he thought of one last question. "Hey, Henry?" he shouted. "Is this all a secret? All this Malus stuff?"

Standing at his car door, Henry looked back and chuckled. "Well, we'd prefer you didn't talk about it to anyone," he shouted back, "but it doesn't matter too much. With this stuff, after a week, you won't be able to remember any of it. It's just how it works. You'll forget everything, and it'll all be like a dream." Then, after one last wave, Henry got into his car and drove off down the dirt road.

Jason and Lily were left alone, sitting on their front steps on a beautiful summer morning, wondering how what Henry said could possibly be true. How could they forget such a traumatic night? It sounded strange, but at the same time, it felt correct. It was hard to describe, but their memories from last night felt fragile and temporary.

"Do you think we'll forget?" Lily asked, leaning on Jason.

Jason thought of the knife in his back pocket. "I hope not," he replied. He recalled what Parch had said, but still didn't understand what it meant. This, however, was a question for another time because there was something else he'd remembered.

With a big smile, Jason got up and walked over to his car to retrieve the chocolates that were still there. As he brought them back, he was delighted to see Lily's face light up with her beautiful smile.

"My chocolates!" Lily exclaimed.

Jason returned to his place next to his wife, and they both started in on the chocolates. After a few bites, Lily grabbed her husband's arm again and returned to leaning on him. Despite the horrible night they had just both been through, the morning sun had a soothing, calming effect that overpowered their lingering distress.

But Jason had one more surprise. He squeezed her hand, then kissed her on top of her head. "I'm going to take that new job," he said. "We'll need the extra money for when the baby comes."

Lily looked back at her husband, dumbstruck. "You knew? I haven't told anyone!"

Jason just smiled in response.

The two embraced once more. Lily exhaled with relief. "I'm sorry I kept it a secret," she said. "I didn't know how to tell you. I didn't know how you'd react. I've been so awful lately; I was just so scared."

"I'm scared too," Jason said, "but we'll figure it out." He reached down and put his hand on Lily's stomach, and Lily placed her hand on top of his.

Dear Mr. Jason Mures,

It has come to our attention that a piece of our property was left with you. Because of this, we assume you know who this letter is from and also remember the events that occurred two weeks ago that led to you receiving the item. The agent who left the item with you was not authorized to do so nor was he authorized to bring you along while performing his duties. However, due to the assistance you provided, our organization has decided not to request the item back PROVIDED you agree to abide by our secrecy and non-disclosure guidelines (see other side).

Granting that you agree to adhere to these guidelines, your involvement in the events will be logged under our Recruitment Program. While you would not have met our Initial Recruitment and Assessment Criteria, your actions in the field demonstrate your worthiness for the program, so, in your specific case, those requirements will be waved. If you wish to continue in the recruitment process, please call #XXX-XXX-XXXX, and, when prompted, enter your Recruitment ID: ***************. Your designated call sign is: Gutter Mouse. If, instead, you do not wish to continue with recruitment, please memorize our secrecy and non-disclosure guidelines, then burn this letter.

Regardless of your decision, we would like to formally thank you for the help you provided. We are also happy to inform you that the agent you worked with is expected to make a full recovery from his injuries. He sends his best wishes.

Sincerely,

P.S. Congratulations on the beautiful new house. Much better than the last one.

www.ingramcontent.com/pod-product-compliance
Lightning Source LLC
LaVergne TN
LVHW100515110826
845146LV00002B/644

* 9 7 9 8 9 9 0 7 0 3 0 0 1 *